JAMES PATTERSON

"Patterson's books might as well come with movie tickets as a bonus feature." —*New York Times*

"Patterson's novels are sleek entertainment machines, the Porsches of commercial fiction, expertly engineered and lightning fast." —*Publishers Weekly*

"The prolific Patterson seems unstoppable." —*USA Today*

"James Patterson knows how to sell thrills and suspense in clean, unwavering prose." —*People*

"It's no mystery why James Patterson is the world's most popular thriller writer: his uncanny skill in creating living, breathing characters we truly feel for and seamless, lightning-fast plots. I do this for a living, and he still manages to keep me guessing from the first to last page." —Jeffery Deaver, *New York Times* bestselling author of *The Burial Hour*

"Every once in a while a writer comes along and fundamentally changes the way people read. He or she is so bright, innovative, so industrious that what they envision and create becomes the measure by which all others are judged. Now…with his mission still unfolding, James Patterson is the gold standard by which all others are judged."

—Steve Berry, *New York Times* bestselling author of the Cotton Malone series

"Patterson has mastered the art of writing page-turning bestsellers." —*Chicago Sun-Times*

"James Patterson writes his thrillers as if he were building roller coasters. He grounds the stories with a bare-bones plot, then builds them over the top and tries to throw readers for a loop a few times along the way." —Associated Press

"A must-read author…a master of the craft."
—*Providence Sunday Journal*

"The page-turningest author in the game right now."
—*San Francisco Chronicle*

"The man is a master of his genre. We fans all have one wish for him: Write even faster."
—Larry King, *USA Today*

THE STORE

For a complete list of books, visit
JamesPatterson.com.

THE STORE

JAMES PATTERSON
AND RICHARD DiLALLO

GRAND CENTRAL
PUBLISHING

NEW YORK   BOSTON

Copyright © 2017 by James Patterson
The End copyright © 2017 by James Patterson

Hachette Book Group supports the right to free expression and the value of copyright. The purpose of copyright is to encourage writers and artists to produce the creative works that enrich our culture.

The scanning, uploading, and distribution of this book without permission is a theft of the author's intellectual property. If you would like permission to use material from the book (other than for review purposes), please contact permissions@hbgusa.com. Thank you for your support of the author's rights.

Grand Central Publishing
Hachette Book Group
1290 Avenue of the Americas, New York, NY 10104
grandcentralpublishing.com
twitter.com/grandcentralpub

Originally published in hardcover and ebook by Little, Brown and Company in August 2017
First oversize mass market edition: June 2019

Grand Central Publishing is a division of Hachette Book Group, Inc. The Grand Central Publishing name and logo is a trademark of Hachette Book Group, Inc.

The publisher is not responsible for websites (or their content) that are not owned by the publisher.

The Hachette Speakers Bureau provides a wide range of authors for speaking events. To find out more, go to hachettespeakersbureau.com or call (866) 376-6591.

ISBNs: 978-1-5387-4550-2 (oversize mass market), 978-0-316-39554-0 (ebook)

Printed in the United States of America

OPM

10 9 8 7 6 5 4 3 2 1

For my sister Maryellen — who's always had my back since the 1950s. Love you.

THE STORE

PROLOGUE

ONE

I CAN'T stop running. Not now. Not ever.

I think the police are following me. Unless they're not.

That's the crazy part. I'm just not sure.

Maybe somebody recognized me...

My picture's been all over. I bet someone called the NYPD and said, "There's a crazy guy, about forty-five years old, stumbling around SoHo. On Prince Street. Wild-man eyes. You'd better get him before he hurts himself."

They always say that—"before he hurts himself." Like they care.

That crazy guy is me. And if *I* had seen me, I would have called the cops, too. My dirty-blond hair really *is* dirty and sweaty from running. The rest of me? I feel like hell and look worse. Torn jeans (not hip, just torn), dirty army-green T-shirt, dirty classic red-and-white Nikes. "Dirty" is the theme. But it doesn't really matter.

All that matters right now is the box I'm carrying. A cardboard box, held together with pieces of string. What's in it? A four-hundred-and-ten-page manuscript.

I keep running. I look around. So this is what SoHo's become...neat and clean and very rich. Give the people what they want. And what they want is SoHo as a tourist attraction—high-tech gyms and up-scale restaurants. Not much else. The cool "buy-in-bulk" underwear shops and electronics stores selling 1950s lighting fixtures have all disappeared. Today you can buy a five-hundred-dollar dinner of porcini mushroom foam with frozen nettle crème brûlée, but you can't buy a pair of Jockey shorts or a Phillips-head screwdriver or a quart of skim milk.

I stop for a moment in front of a restaurant—the sign says PORC ET FLAGEOLETS. The translation is high school easy—"pork and beans." Adorable. Just then I hear a woman's voice behind me.

"That's gotta be him. That's the guy. Jacob Brandeis."

I turn around. The woman is "old" SoHo—black tights, tattoos, Native American silver jewelry. Eighty years old at least. Her tats have wrinkles. She must have lived in SoHo since the Dutch settled New York.

"I'm going to call the police," she says. She's not afraid of me.

Her equally hip but much younger male friend says, "Let's not. Who the hell wants to get involved?"

They deliberately cross the street, and I hear the woman speak. "I have to say: he is really handsome."

That comment doesn't surprise me. Women like me a lot. Okay, that's obnoxious and arrogant, but it's true. The old gal should have seen me a few years ago. I had long dirty-blond hair, and, as a girl in college once told me, I was a "hunky nerd." I was. Until all this shit happened to me and wore me out and brought me down and...

The old lady and younger man are now across the street. I shout to them.

"You don't have to call the cops, lady. I'm sure they know I'm here."

As if to prove this fact to myself, I look up and see a camera-packed drone hovering above me, recording my every step. How could I have forgotten? Drones zoom through the sky—in pairs, in groups, alone. Tiny cameras dot the corners of every building. In this New York, a person is never really alone.

I stumble along for another block, then I stop at a classic SoHo cast-iron building. It's home to Writers Place, the last major publisher left in New York. Hell, it's the last major publisher in all of America.

I clutch the box that holds the manuscript. Dirt streaks my face. My back and armpits are soaked. You know you smell like hell when you can smell your own sweat.

I'm about to push my way through the revolving door when I pause.

I feel like I could cry, but instead I extend the middle finger of my right hand and flip it at the drone.

TWO

ANNE GUTMAN, editor in chief and publisher of Writers Place, greets me with her usual warmth.

"You look like shit," she says.

"Thank you," I say. "Now let's get the hell out of your office and go someplace where we can't be watched."

"Where'd you have in mind, Jacob? Jupiter or Mars?"

"Christ. I can't stand it," I say. "They watch me 24-7."

She nods, but I'm not sure she agrees with me. I'm not even sure she cares. I lean forward and hand her the box.

"What's this?" she says. "A gift?"

"It's the manuscript! It's *Twenty-Twenty*!" I yell. Why am I yelling?

Anne tosses her head back and laughs.

"I can't remember the last time I received a hard-copy manuscript," she says.

Then I look at her intently. I lower my voice.

"Look, Anne. This book is incredible. This is corporate reporting like it's never been written before."

"You know my concern, Jacob," she says.

"Yeah. I know. You don't think the Store is worth writing about; you don't truly think it's morally bankrupt."

"That's not it. I think it may very well be morally bankrupt, but I can make a list of forty companies that are just as bad. I don't think the Store is *inherently* evil. It's a creative monopoly."

"Read my book. Read *Twenty-Twenty*. Then decide."

"I will."

"Tonight?" I ask.

"Yes. Tonight. Immediately."

"Immediately? Wow. That's fast."

Anne smiles at my minuscule joke. I try to remain calm. I'm sure if she reads the book she's going to be blown away. Then again, maybe she won't be. Maybe she'll toss it after a few chapters. What do I know? After all, I've been wrong about this sort of thing before.

Suddenly there's noise. A scuffling of feet. Indistinguishable but loud. It comes from outside Anne's office. Then a very quick knock on the door. Before Anne can say anything, her assistant opens the door and speaks.

"Ms. Gutman, there are three policemen and two NYPD detectives out here with me."

"What do they want?" Anne asks.

"They're here to arrest Mr. Brandeis."

Anne and I look at each other as her assistant closes the door. I'm about to fall apart. As always, she's in take-charge mode.

"You go out through the conference room. Then take the back stairs down and outside. Find a place to stay."

Anne hands me some money from the top drawer of her desk. I turn toward the conference room.

"I'll handle the cops," Anne says.

"Read the book, okay?" I say.

"Damn it, Jacob. Of course I'll read the book."

She walks out her office door. I also start walking. The last thing I hear her say is: "Good afternoon, officers. How can I help you?"

EIGHT MONTHS EARLIER

CHAPTER 1

MY WIFE, Megan, wrote an e-vite to our dinner party that was like Megan herself: funny, sharp, and a touch mysterious:

MEGAN AND JACOB BRANDEIS

INVITE YOU TO OUR

"LAST GASP IN MANHATTAN" PARTY

TUESDAY EVENING, AUGUST 30

8:00 P.M.

322 PEARL STREET

We had invited our eight best friends to have dinner with us in the big goofy-looking loft space that we had carved out of half a floor in an art deco building. If you're thinking when you hear the word *loft* that the space was glamorous, high-tech, and modern, you're thinking wrong. Our very long, very narrow apartment was in what had once been an old insurance company building. After that, it was vacant for five years. Then it was home to a bunch of squatters. Then it was bought by a bunch of would-be writers and artists. Each apartment had a *tiny* view of the East River and a *fabulous* view of the garbage barges docked at the South Street Seaport. We could afford the apartment only because the area at the time (then the Financial District, now very chicly called FiDi) was a no-man's-land. The nearest grocery store was two miles away in Greenwich Village. We could also afford it because we were making *fairly* decent money writing everything from ad copy to catalog copy to an occasional piece for *New York* magazine and the *New York Observer*. Like everyone else in Manhattan who hadn't founded a tech company or managed a hedge fund, we made do. What's even better is that our kids seemed to have no problem making do.

Lindsay was sixteen and attended Spence. When I was a kid at George Washington High, Spence was debutante-snooty. Only a touch of that culture remained, and those types didn't seem to interest Lindsay. In fact, most of her friends seemed to be the Latinos and African American scholarship kids, with a UN ambassador's daughter or Middle Eastern princess thrown in for diversity.

Alex, Lindsay's thirteen-year-old brother, attended a Reform-Jewish prep school, Rodeph Sholom, on the Upper West Side. He pretty much liked his school and liked his friends and didn't hate the subway ride up to the place. We had sent him there because both Megan and I were thoroughly unreligious—she a lapsed Catholic, I a Jew in terms of culture only. But by the end of his first month at the school, Alex had become almost frighteningly interested in Judaism. He studied as much Torah as he did computer science. He studied Chinese, but he also took Hebrew. And of course he made me feel embarrassed that my knowledge of Judaism revolved around three things: (1) food (matzo balls should be hard), (2) superstitions that no other Jewish family had ever heard of ("Touch a coat button if you see a nun"), and (3) the words *be careful,* which we say to anyone leaving our apartment—a plumber, a great-aunt, a Jehovah's Witness.

Alex and Lindsay fought constantly with each other, and when they weren't fighting they were laughing with each other. Plus they read books—real books with real paper pages that you have to use your fingers to turn. These kids were smart, sarcastic, and usually nice. Megan and I really got a kick out of them. I don't want to speculate how much they reciprocated the adoration.

The evening of the party found Megan and me very nervous. But we had our reasons. I poured Megan her third white wine (an unusually enormous amount for her), and Lindsay and Alex put the final touches on the dinner—Lindsay glazed the poached salmon while Alex scattered the watercress over the fish. "I'm doing watercress. Dill is a catering cliché." Great chefs talk tough.

"Live and learn," I said.

Megan took a sip of her wine and spoke. "Maybe we should have entitled this evening the 'Last Dinosaurs in Manhattan' party."

I laughed and said, "Maybe," but I knew what she meant. All eight guests were people whose jobs were simply not very important anymore. In a piece I had written the previous month for Salon.com, I had referred to this category of worker as "leftover people in our new high-tech world."

Yes, the friends who'd be eating our salmon that evening were folks waiting to be—as the British would say—"made redundant." I had been thinking of that scene in the movie *The Tall Guy* in which the boss turns to his assistant, played by Jeff Goldblum, and says, "You're fired. F-U-C-K-E-D. Fired!" If I sound heartless, I don't mean to be. It was a fact of life, and it was happening all over the country.

The night was a kind of debutante party for those "coming out" of the workforce.

Sandi Feinblum, the assistant style editor at the *New York Times*, was taking a buyout. She had been assigned to the "traditional" hard-copy newspaper. But the only people who still preferred the printed *Times* were slowly but surely showing up on the obituaries page.

Wendy Witten and Chuck McKirdy were editors of a wine magazine and a golf magazine respectively; neither publication had transitioned successfully from a newsstand presence to an Internet presence.

We had also invited an executive from Sotheby's auction house and his very nervous, prescription-druggy wife. He was quickly being strangled into oblivion by websites like eBay and iGavel.

One woman had already gotten the ax. A former travel agent. All the people who once used her services were now making their own hotel reservations and printing their own airline tickets. In essence, she had been replaced by William Shatner.

One guy, Charlie Burke, was in a business that was about to be eaten by Fox. When that meal took place, he would probably be known as the last guy on earth who had ever managed an independent broadcasting company. His syndicated sitcoms would be just another part of neo-con broadcasting.

And finally there was Anne Gutman, editor in chief of Writers Place. Anne still managed to make a living editing and occasionally publishing a few nonfiction writers such as Megan and me. But she knew—we all knew—that she was the exception to the electronic rule.

Shit. The unemployment office could have set up an application desk in our dining room. What's more, Megan and I would have been first in line.

CHAPTER 2

YES, WE were in trouble.

From the outside we still looked prosperous—the crazy-looking loft (full of interesting, artsy "found objects"), the two good-looking teenage kids, the August rental on Fire Island.

But the fact was, we were hurting badly.

To our shock, Anne Gutman had turned down the book that Megan and I had been working on for almost two years. Our proposed project was entitled *The Roots of Rap*. It traced the history of rap music from blues through early rock and roll, then doo-wop, and ultimately the past twenty-five years of rap and hip-hop.

"I just don't have the funds anymore," Anne had said. "I had money when you started the project, but I've just been squeezed too hard by the Internet.... Then, of course, there's always the Store....I just can't afford to take big risks anymore....I could shove it into self-publish, but the guys in research told me you'd be lucky to sell five hundred copies."

The Store. This online colossus was becoming a huge player in the world of publishing. And in every other part of the consumer world as well.

The Store stocked what people wanted. Then, because it controlled pricing, it pretty much told us what to buy. It's where we all went shopping for our toasters, tractors, Tide, soy sauce, jeans, lightbulbs. If somebody on earth manufactured something, anything, the Store sold it. Potted oak trees, cases of wine, automobiles…all usually at a lower price than the brick-and-mortar source.

The Store's publishing arm was churning out e-books, and every once in a while they'd hit upon something really popular. *Okay,* Megan and I thought…*if you can't beat 'em…*

So as soon as the painful impact of Anne's rejection sank in, we did the only thing left to do. We moved over to the opposition: we flipped open our laptops, quickly pulled up the Store page, then clicked over to "Independent Publishing." We had no other choice. Why the hell not? Megan and I were sure we had a bestselling e-book.

Within less than a *minute* of logging on, I was having my first e-mail conversation with my "contact rep."

At the beginning, our e-mail conversations were all warm hugs and wet kisses. A few rewrites. Our promise to start a Twitter account, a Facebook page, an Instagram profile—the usual social-media journey to the bestseller list. It was going great…only a matter of time until Megan and I would be looking at book-cover concepts.

Then came the not-so-inevitable kick in the balls.

With one tap of the Send button, the Store destroyed our plan. They suddenly rejected *The Roots of Rap.* No reason was given. Their e-mail sounded like a ransom letter: *Your project is no longer viable. The Store.*

My index finger raced to the Reply tab. *Hey, folks, what gives? All of a sudden? This idea is a winner waiting to happen. This book could really live online. It's about music. You know, music downloads. The YouTube clips. The cross-ref…*

Came a one-line response: *We are as sorry about the outcome as you are. The Store.*

It was clear: the Store was finished with us. Or so they thought.

But *we* were not finished with the Store. Not by a long shot.

CHAPTER 3

"NEBRASKA! THAT'S nuts!" Chuck McKirdy shouted. "You two will be moving to freakin' Nebraska?"

Megan stepped in and answered the question with her usual patience.

"That's where the jobs are. So that's where we'll be going," she said softly.

"What's Nebraska's nickname? The Cornhusking State?" Sandi asked.

I corrected her. "The Cornhusker State."

"Go, Cornhuskers!" someone shouted.

The chant was quickly picked up. "Go, Cornhuskers! Go, Cornhuskers!"

"Okay," I said. "The annual asshole convention will now come to order."

Megan smiled, then began a little speech. She said it was hardly a secret in our social group that our most recent nonfiction effort had been rejected "not merely by faithful friends who shall remain nameless"—at this point Anne Gutman jokingly hid her face behind her unfolded napkin—"but also…and you're not going to believe this humiliation…even rejected by the Store.

"So with *The Roots of Rap* totally without a future, and Jacob and I—not to mention our two kids— totally without a future, it looked like we were doomed. But just when things looked darkest, lo and behold, the Store came through for us."

We stopped talking. Just for a moment, but long enough to run the risk of screwing up our story. And it was a story, almost a fairy tale. It was a highly fictionalized account of what had really happened.

At that very moment Megan and I were about to tell a very big lie to our closest friends. And even though we had rehearsed it carefully, my stomach was rolling, my chest was filling with acid, and Megan's hands visibly shook. But the starting pistol had been fired. We had to talk. So Megan took off.

"Well, it's sort of crazy what happened next. We thought it was all finished between us and the Store. And Alex and Lindsay even started joking about being so poor that they'd have to decide which relatives to go live with."

I interrupted. "Nobody wanted to go with Megan's family."

She punched me gently. (We had not rehearsed the ad-libs.)

"Anyway, we got a message from the Store HR people, and they…offered…us…jobs."

"Doing what?" Chuck asked. "Writing ad copy or catalog stuff?"

"Well, that's the sorry part," I said. "They're kinda crappy jobs. We'll be working in their fulfillment center. You know, filling orders and getting them out to people. But…" I paused. I was lost.

Megan was not going to let that sentence hang there in space. "But," Megan said, "because the Store is so big and growing, we'll be eligible for promotions and advancements within three months. Just three months."

"And that's the story," I said, hoping that the strength in my delivery would let me recover and seal the deal with my friends.

Okay, they were surprised. Very surprised. And yes, our friends were still spitting out a few farmer jokes, a few Republican jokes, a few Cornhusker jokes. But as I looked around the room I could tell everyone believed me. Someone mentioned a good-bye party. Someone else mentioned a group bus trip to Nebraska. Yes, it looked like everyone believed us.

Well, almost everyone.

I glanced out the apartment window and saw a drone hovering. It was recording everything going on at our dinner table.

I also noticed that Anne Gutman was looking directly at me. We were good friends, old friends. She had a weak smile on her lips. And I could tell that Anne wasn't buying a single word of our story.

CHAPTER 4

OKAY, WE had told our friends a lie. But it wasn't a total lie. I say that as if a partial lie is somehow more acceptable.

Yes, we were moving to Nebraska. Yes, we were going to work at the Store. But here's what we left out:

The Store had not invited us to work there.

The real truth was that Megan and I had made all this happen. And like a lot of things, it all started with a simple idea.

Here's how the bean stalk grew: after the Store had rejected our manuscript, I was burning with anger and resentment. Sure, they thought they could screw me. Well, here's some news. I was going to show them. If I sound like a crazy person, I think it's because I was.

Megan and I would infiltrate the Store. We'd unearth their secrets and their plans. Then we'd write about it. We'd get even. But first we had to get hired.

Some good news (finally): it turned out that getting hired by the Store was incredibly easy. The Store's business was growing so fast that apparently they accepted almost everyone who clicked on the link that sat at the bottom of every Store Web page: "Be part of our team."

I clicked on it one day, and within seconds an application form appeared. The form was hardly detailed, but I was sure it was because the Store would be doing their own investigative deep dive.

When they asked why we wanted to work there, we had planned the perfect answer: we were tired of the New York rat race. Tired of alternate side of the street parking, homeless beggars on every corner, squeezing four people into a crappy walk-up apartment built for two. We had a sincere desire to raise our kids in a proper community, with a real backyard, grass, trees…blah, blah, blah. We were writers. We knew that people outside New York loved anti–New York opinions, and even Megan, usually a very bad liar, followed my lead and fibbed like a pro. It worked.

Two days later I was having an online chat with a "marshal of human resources" who had the male-or-female name of Leslie. Leslie stated the Store's position unequivocally: *You're superqualified for marketing or business positions, but at the moment we can offer you employment in our beautiful new New Burg, Nebraska, fulfillment center.* I was aching to write the book. We were busting to be…well…spies. I was willing to take the job. So was Megan. We made a deal. And the Store made it clear that Megan and I were *not* being assigned to high-level, white-collar corporate jobs. No way. Ours were strictly factory jobs, filling orders and pasting on mailing labels. Yes, it was a truly shitty job. It required nothing more than a grammar-school education and a strong back.

Small computers would hang from chains around our necks. The computers would sputter out orders, and we would find the merchandise, collect it, and bring it to the packaging department (itself the size of a football stadium), then steer our little electronic go-karts back for another pickup. Only this time, instead of, say, a carton of Cap'n Crunch, a tube of hemorrhoid cream, a glass coffee table, and four copies of *Naked Hot Yoga at Home,* we might be fetching a chain for a John Deere hay baler, four jars of tangerine marmalade...you get the idea.

The add-ons were surprisingly seductive. The Store was supplying us with a three-bedroom house. They would also pay half the monthly mortgage of four hundred dollars. A fraction of what we'd been paying for our dingy apartment. We were sure that the Store must have made a mistake. But as we came to learn, the Store never makes mistakes.

Another e-mail said that our new house would be located in one of several Store-built communities. *Most of your neighbors will be employees of the Store.* Excellent: neighbors who might be possible sources for gossip and inside information.

It was starting to sound perfect. But of course, as spies, we were going to find the imperfections in that perfection. I'd be lying if I didn't say we were scared—two long-unemployed New York softies going to battle at one of the creepiest and fastest-growing companies in the United States.

But damn it, the book idea was too good to give up on.

CHAPTER 5

"MAN! THIS is soooo sweet!"

That was Alex's reaction when he first saw our new house at 400 Midshipman Lane, New Burg, Nebraska.

Frankly, we all had pretty much the same reaction.

It wasn't a mansion, but it was...well, man, soooo sweet. The kind of house that a midlevel tech executive might live in, not some guy who was packing toothpaste tubes and algebra textbooks into cardboard boxes. The house was white brick; it was long (very long) and low, with a three-car garage for our leased Acura.

The inside of the house was equally cool. Everything—from the ten-seat U-shaped charcoal-gray sofa in the living room to the crystal-and-bronze chandelier in the dining room—was LA trendy and top of the line. It was, as Megan pointed out, exactly how we would have decorated if we'd been able to afford it. Then we all took off in different directions to explore.

"Jacob, come in here. You gotta see this," Megan called from the kitchen.

By the time I joined her, she had already opened a large pantry cabinet.

"Yeah, okay," I said. "They told us in an e-mail they'd stock the place with some basics."

"Basics? Look. It's every brand we use. Not just Jif peanut butter and Frosted Flakes and Bumble Bee tuna but also Wilkin and Sons gooseberry conserve and Arrowhead Mills pancake mix."

A cabinet in the dining room contained Grey Goose vodka and J&B Scotch.

As we were studying the bar, Lindsay appeared at the dining-room door. She looked a bit confused.

"Look at this," she said. Then she held out the stuffed animal—Peabody the penguin—that she had owned since her first birthday.

"Hey, it's Peabody!" I said. "I thought you said you left him on the airplane."

"I did," Lindsay said. "But this is him. See? He has the tear on his collar and the chocolate stain on his chest. This is Peabody! He was waiting for me on the bed in my new room."

Lindsay looked nervous. I was about to examine the penguin more closely when I heard Alex's voice coming from the kitchen.

"Hey, Dad. There's a bunch of people at the back door."

CHAPTER 6

NOT JUST a bunch. A *big* bunch. Nine of them. Smiling, happy, good-looking men and smiling, happy, pretty women huddled around our back door like a sports team. They even seemed to have a captain—a very attractive woman in her early forties with shoulder-length brown hair and very tight jeans.

"I'm Marie DiManno," the woman said. "These are a few of your neighbors, and we're here to help you unpack."

I said exactly what I was thinking: "That's freaking amazing."

Megan clarified. "He means that's really very nice of you."

Marie added, "We saw the moving van outside, and we all texted each other. That's what friends are for."

I half expected them to launch into the song.

Fact is, we had been so engrossed by the penguin incident that we hadn't heard the moving van pull into the driveway. I looked over the heads of our neighbors and saw the movers. The four of them were dressed in navy-blue jumpsuits bearing the slogan THE MOVERS FROM THE STORE.

As the movers began carrying boxes into the house, Marie walked inside, told us to introduce ourselves to one another, and followed one of the movers up the front staircase.

We hit the receiving line—a group of people right out of central casting.

First we met the good-looking "older" couple. They were both trim and chic, with gray hair and elegant haircuts. They looked like a couple in one of those Cialis commercials.

Then a good-looking African American couple in their early forties, she in an impeccably faded denim shirt, both of them in light blue J.Crew Bermuda shorts.

Then the inevitable young, good-looking blond couple. The college quarterback and the college cheerleader.

And finally the all-purpose sitcom couple—the bald-headed guy with a potbelly and his wife with a wide mouth waiting to shoot out a wisecrack.

"I'm Mark Stanton," said the handsome black guy as he shook my hand. "Welcome to New Burg. This is my wife, Cookie."

Cookie said, "Welcome to the Store, and welcome to the Store *family*."

"That's a lot of welcoming," I said.

If they detected a note of sarcasm in my voice (and I had just meant to be funny, not sarcastic), their faces didn't register it.

I learned quickly that Mark Stanton worked in the fulfillment "gathering" building. (So that's what folks called the job—gathering. I'd be hearing that word a lot in the following hour or two.) It seemed that everyone who came out to help us worked in packing or shipping or gathering merchandise, except

Marie. Marie was "resting" since the unexpected death of her husband. She had no "money-type concerns," she told me, "because the Store kindly provides a resting widow's pension."

The older gray-haired lady wasted no time telling me that "moving to New Burg and the Store will be the smartest thing you've ever done. Where else can you combine such nice work with such nice people in such a nice place? Martin and I had retired to Tampa, and frankly we were having trouble making ends meet. We have a son in Miami who's a drug addict."

She gave me this information as if she were telling us that her son was a dentist.

She continued. "Then Martin applied for a job at the Store. They hired us, shipped us out here just like you folks, and it's...well, it's made life worth living."

Our new neighbors appeared to be high-energy experts at unpacking. Marilyn Fidler, the pretty blond woman, had brought paper with which she proceeded to line the bedroom dresser drawers. (In a million years, Megan and I would not have thought to line our furniture drawers.)

"You want everything to start out as clean as possible," Marilyn said as she helped Megan and Lindsay fill two drawers with sweaters and sweatshirts.

As the busy morning wore on, Alex took me aside and whispered, "Hey, Dad, you know what that Marie lady brought?"

"A great deal of energy," I said.

"No. She had this plasticky kind of shirt cardboard. She showed me how you fold T-shirts around it. She said it makes them stack up nice and neat, like on a store shelf. That's kind of creepy, no?"

"I don't know, buddy. I think she's just a perfectionist."

Alex looked doubtful, then he saw his sister carrying a box of *his* video games. He took off after her.

"Kind of creepy, no?" That's what Alex had said. I had disagreed with him, but I knew what he meant. Charming. Delightful. Friendly. Neat. Tidy. Industrious. Why were all those good things adding up to "creepy"?

Damn it, I thought. These folks are just being good neighbors.

And my son and I are just two typical cynical New Yorkers, too jaded to appreciate the simple life.

CHAPTER 7

NOT ONLY had I made Friday night's dinner, I was also such a cool husband that I was even doing the cleanup. Megan and the kids were outside exploring the backyard.

The meal itself had been a huge success: boeuf bourguignonne (Julia Child's secret recipe), Tuscan potato torta (Mario Batali's recipe), Key lime pie (Jacob Brandeis's recipe). Why Key lime pie? Whoever had stocked our kitchen included a graham cracker crust, sweetened condensed milk, eggs, and six perfect Key limes.

I was on my second Brillo pad when Megan returned to the kitchen.

"Jacob, c'mon outside," she said.

"Soon as I finish."

"No. Now. Right now." Her voice was surprisingly serious.

"Sure, sweetie," I said. But I wasn't moving fast enough for Megan.

"Now! Please. You've got to see this."

This time her voice was urgent. I didn't bother rinsing my hands. I simply wiped off the pink Brillo suds with a dish towel.

"Look up there," Megan said, and she pointed (or so I thought) to the bright starry sky above the garage-door basketball hoop.

"It's a beautiful night," I said.

Impatience filled Megan's voice. "Show him, Alex."

Alex skipped a few feet to the hoop. He squatted, then he jumped and hung from the rim with his left hand. As Alex dangled he pointed to a small instrument made of glass and gray metal—almost unde-tectable against the gray paint of the garage. Then Alex snapped it from its holder. He dropped to the ground and tossed it to me.

"It's a camera," I said. "A tiny camera, like a…spy camera."

Megan, Lindsay, Alex, and I stared at it. We looked like a group who had just discovered a rare diamond. And I guess, in a way, we had.

I broke the silence.

"Son of a bitch!" I shouted. "In New York, they have street surveillance, but this shit is going too far. Cameras right in our own house."

"Jacob, calm down," Megan said.

"Megan! C'mon. People can expect reasonable goddamn privacy in their own houses, can't they?"

"Maybe in Nebraska the laws are different," Megan said.

"No," I said. I was beginning to shake with anger. "You can't ever do something like this in someone's house."

Then I exploded: *"That's illegal!"*

I looked at the tiny camera in my hand, then flung it with all my strength toward the garage door. I heard the crack, the immediate shattering of the pieces.

I rushed into the house. When a man goes beyond mad, he becomes a madman.

Megan and the kids were right behind me.

I looked around the kitchen. I began studying the ceiling and the tops of cabinets. In the tiny space between the Sub-Zero fridge and the appliance garage, where the industrial-size mixer was stored, was another camera. I wedged my fingers into the tiny space and pulled it out.

"*That's* illegal!" I yelled.

I found another camera in the window over the very sink where I'd been doing the dishes.

"*That's* illegal!" I yelled.

In the front hallway was a camera over the coat closet, perfect for recording guests.

"*That's* illegal!" I shouted.

Room to room. Lindsay was sobbing. Megan was as angry as I was.

Over the living-room fireplace.

"*That's* illegal!"

Behind the corner cabinet in the dining room.

"*That's* illegal!"

As I bounded up the stairs, Lindsay said, "They're probably watching you bust up their camera stuff."

"Let them. What the hell do I care? And you know why?" I yelled as I yanked a camera from the medicine cabinet in the kids' bathroom.

"Because *that's* illegal!"

From our bedroom to the attic. From the guest room to the playroom.

"Illegal! Illegal!"

We stood—a sweaty, crazed group of four—in the center of the playroom. The ghost of a video game made an occasional gargle on the TV screen. The silent furnace in the utility room cast a long shadow on the playroom floor. We surveyed the room. We were like the four-man crew of a ship that had survived a terrible storm.

"You think we got them all?" Megan asked.

The truthful answer would have been "No, I don't," but my wife and kids seemed scared enough.

I said, "Yeah, probably."

We sat at the bottom of the basement staircase. We were covered with perspiration. I was gasping for breath. There were a good sixty seconds of silence.

"What now?" Lindsay asked.

"Now we wait," I said. "It's their move."

CHAPTER 8

WE ALL slept badly.

I can't recall how many times Megan and I turned our heads and asked each other "Are you still awake?"

Or how many times I walked into Alex's room and said, "Either lower the music or use your earbuds."

No one was hungry for breakfast. Not even Alex, who's never been known to turn down food.

"How about we all take a drive and check out the downtown area?" I said.

I didn't expect anyone to agree to my suggestion. But Lindsay said, "Why not?" and Alex said, "I guess," and Megan gave a shrug that meant "Might as well." Okay, not an enthusiastic majority, but a majority nonetheless.

It was a quick drive from our house to downtown New Burg. No one brought up the surveillance cameras from the night before. Maybe we felt that if we didn't acknowledge it, then it didn't really happen. Or maybe we were just too spooked to dwell on it.

Ten minutes later we were standing at the corner of Brick Street and Mortar Street.

Alex gently punched Lindsay in the arm and mockingly said, "Brick and Mortar. Get it, dummy?"

"Of course I get it, you idiot," Lindsay said.

"Stop it, both of you," Megan said. "It's too hot to argue."

"Damn. It really is hot. Like a dry sauna," I said.

"Really different from New York," Alex said.

"No humidity," I said.

Not many other people were out walking. We all noticed *that*. Maybe it was the heat. Maybe.

We walked slowly. The combination of the intense heat and the perfect quaintness of the town was somehow hypnotizing. The town looked like an exquisitely built movie set—a movie from, say, the 1950s. A barbershop with a striped pole outside. A drugstore with a large brass apothecary scale in the window. A noble-looking First Bank of New Burg with what appeared to be real marble pillars at its entrance.

We walked silently, my eyes occasionally glancing up toward the street signs and the tops of small buildings in search of surveillance cameras. I was slowly becoming a man obsessed.

Something was strange about this downtown. We all felt it. But Megan was the first to put it into words.

"How many people do you see on the street?" she asked.

We looked around us.

"Fifteen," I said. "Not counting us."

"And how old do they look to you?" Megan asked.

We got it immediately. They were *all* old. Everyone was over seventy, some of them probably in their eighties. White-haired widows in pink-and-white pantsuits. Knobby-kneed old men in polyester shorts and imitation Lacoste shirts. One woman with a walker. One woman in a motorized wheelchair. A few old guys with canes.

"It all makes sense," I said. "That's why this downtown area exists—for the old people who just couldn't make the adjustment to the brave new world of the Store."

While drones hovered overhead, while the Store planned the techno-invasion of all consumer consumption, there remained a group of people who simply were not going to be part of it.

Clearly this downtown area had been created to soothe and seduce the elderly—people who did not want to use a Command key or an Option key. These were people who had to touch the oranges and smell the flowers and try on the shoes before they bought them. So the Store built a little town just for them. The Store knew it would be temporary; that sooner rather than later these old folks would die, and the world would be left to a new generation that could handle an iPad and a laptop and a cell phone at the same time.

We walked the wide wooden sidewalks. Inside the Drug Store, an elderly couple—he in baggy chinos, she in a very loose powder-blue caftan—sat at the counter. They each were drinking a chocolate malted. Behind the counter was a soda jerk from central casting—a bony young guy with rolled-up sleeves, a white apron, and a paper cap.

As we walked past the Jewelry Store, its window filled with charm bracelets and Timex watches, wedding bands and tiny diamond solitaire necklaces, two women passed us. Age guess? Both around seventy-five, both wearing billowing pants that looked like skirts (Megan later told me these items were called culottes). They both had very shiny silver hair and smiled when they saw us.

"Well, if it isn't the Brandeis family!" one of them said.

Before we could respond, the other woman announced our names as if she were a schoolteacher taking attendance.

"Megan, Jacob, Alex, and Lindsay."

"Yes, that's us," said Megan. "But how did you—"

"I meant to come by yesterday," the first woman said.

"I'll be over this week with a walnut streusel coffee cake, my specialty. So nice to meet you all," the second woman said, although they had never told us their names. Then they walked on briskly, still chuckling.

We four also kept walking. When we passed the Hardware Store, two very old men carrying cans of paint, folded tarps, and paint rollers tipped the visors on their baseball caps.

Almost in unison they said, "Welcome to New Burg, Mrs. Brandeis...Mr. Brandeis." Then they walked on.

We walked past a few more stores. The main street of town was almost ending. The last store sign said THE PIZZA STORE. Every shop had the word *store* in its name.

A drone was headed skyward, carrying a stack of four pizza boxes.

Then a big hulking blond guy walked out of the pizza place carrying two pizza boxes. He was wearing cut-off jeans, a white T-shirt, and a baseball cap with the letter *N* imprinted on the front.

"Hey, man, watch the door," he said. His voice was deep and surly. He paused, then he broke into a big wide smile.

"Jacob, my man. I didn't realize it was you."

"It's all good," I said.

"I'm sorry, man. Is this the brood?"

"Uh, yeah. My family."

"Good to see you, gang. Jake's my man."

Then the big guy hit me gently on my shoulder and walked away.

Before anyone could ask, I said, "*No!* I have absolutely no idea who that guy was. But by the way, does anyone know what the *N* on his hat stands for?"

Lindsay had an answer.

"University of Nebraska?"

"No," I said. "It stands for *knowledge*."

All three of them groaned. I didn't even wait for the question Lindsay and Alex were about to ask. I simply said, "Listen. I don't know how they know our names. They just do. Maybe there's, like, a new arrivals section in the local paper. Maybe they all work for Welcome Wagon or saw our names on a church bulletin board."

Or maybe, I thought, *it could be something else.* I just didn't know what.

CHAPTER 9

"HEY, LOOK!" Alex said as he pointed across the street.

I hoped for something interesting, and I guess it was interesting—for him. Alex had spotted the Army and Navy Store.

"Let's check it out," I said.

So with no cars coming from either direction, we crossed the street. The kids crossed the street ahead of us and waited outside the store. As Megan and I stepped onto the sidewalk, we heard it before we saw it: a police car with a flashing light and siren.

A cop, fleshy and pink-faced, stepped out of the car. He was smiling ever so slightly.

"Mr. Brandeis, isn't it?" the cop said. Like everyone else in New Burg, he was determined to be impeccably polite.

"Uh...yeah," I said.

He looked at Megan, tipped an imaginary hat toward her, and said, "Good morning to you, too, Mrs. Brandeis."

"Good morning," Megan said softly.

"Do you folks realize you just broke the law?"

"We did?" Megan said.

"Jaywalking is against the law here," the officer

said. I wanted to say, "You've got to be kidding," but the cop, though polite, was also deadly serious.

"Well, there were no cars. So we thought…" I realized that I was foolish to say anything.

"Mr. Brandeis, a law is a law. A rule is a rule."

I nodded. But the officer wasn't finished talking.

"Jaywalking. *That's* illegal."

Megan and I looked at each other. I saw the fear in her eyes.

"Maybe in New York City they flaunt the law," he said. (I thought this would be a bad time to tell him that the correct verb was *flout,* not *flaunt.*)

He went on. "But here in New Burg, if you don't follow the rules, well…*that's* illegal."

"But…we…"

"No problem, Mr. Brandeis. Let's just call this conversation…a warning?"

He tipped his imaginary hat once again.

"Welcome to New Burg," he said, and he got back in the patrol car and sped off.

We stood silently for a few seconds. We pretended we were looking at the bomber jackets and khaki cargo pants in the store window.

Then my daughter turned and put her arms around me. She hugged me tightly, and I could feel her tears against my chest. It was her brother, however, who spoke next.

"We're scared, Dad. This isn't fun. This is no fun at all."

They were too old for the usual parental bullshit. I couldn't say, "Oh, c'mon, there's nothing to be scared about." I couldn't say, "Whaddya mean 'no fun'? What about the goofball guy with the baseball cap? This crazy old cop was like something from a movie. Nothing to be scared of."

Instead I said, "I know how you feel. I'm scared, too."

Alex put his arms around my side. Megan moved toward me and touched my face. Then Megan spoke.

"Of course we're all scared."

My wife, ladies and gentlemen. Now, there's one smart and wonderful woman.

CHAPTER 10

MEGAN AND I were absolute suckers for old bookstores and old libraries. So when we saw the words NEW BURG FREE LIBRARY engraved on a sign in front of a small redbrick building, we smiled knowingly at each other and headed to the library's white front door.

The library was open. We walked in.

An old-fashioned feather duster sat on the tall wooden checkout desk. But apparently the duster had not been used in quite a while; a thin layer of dust covered just about every surface.

I counted ten rows of dark wood shelves. A random survey of the library collection indicated that there was nothing much that had been published after the 1930s. I saw a lot of Sinclair Lewis—*Babbitt, Main Street, Dodsworth*. I saw a few old bestsellers—*Grand Hotel, Back Street, Saratoga Trunk*. Megan pointed out a big selection of Agatha Christie and a small selection of William Faulkner. But none of the books seemed to have ever been opened. When I took down a copy of *Gone with the Wind,* the spine of the book cracked gently; the pages were pristine.

"Megan! Jacob!" A crisp, stern woman's voice shot through the room.

The voice rang out again: "I'm in the home crafts and culinary section. Don't move. I know where you are."

So we did not move. I just turned to Megan and said, "Oh, shit: we're probably in trouble again."

Walking around the end of the fiction section was a woman about forty years old. Her hair was pulled back. She wore a simple gray linen smock, and her face was so plain that I could not tell if she was smiling or scowling.

"I'm Deb Borelli. I'm the librarian."

"And you seem to know who we are," Megan said.

"Everybody knows everybody in New Burg," she said. Maybe there was the start of a smile on her face.

"I see," I said. As if what she had said was actually an explanation.

"May I answer any questions you might have?"

I had a thousand questions. Why was the library empty? Why was the library dirty? Why were there no books less than seventy-five years old? Why does everybody recognize us and know our names? Why are only old people walking the downtown streets?

"No. I don't have any questions, but thank you," Megan said. "Jacob? Any questions for Ms. Borelli?"

"Oh, please," the librarian said. "I hate the word *Ms*. It tells you absolutely nothing about a woman."

I wanted to say, "Well, that's the whole point," but I was learning to keep my smart mouth shut in New Burg. Megan was much better about it than I was.

"So is it Miss or Mrs.?" Megan asked.

Now the librarian smiled. It was gracious. I was certain that it was also phony.

"Not Miss. It's Mrs."

"Oh, you're married?" Megan said.

"Yes, I'm married."

Ever the charmer, I said, "Well, no doubt we'll meet Mr. Borelli one of these days."

The librarian spoke.

"No. You won't."

Uh-oh—a divorce or a death. I stepped in it again.

"My husband's been transferred," she said.

There was a silence. Deb Borelli's face was vacant. Her eyes looked back and forth between Megan and me. I decided to say something.

"Transferred. What exactly does that mean?"

Her eyes narrowed. Her chin quivered a tiny bit. Then she spoke.

"He's...been transferred."

Never content to make a small mistake, I then turned it into a big mistake.

"What do you mean by 'transferred'?" I said.

"What I mean is: he's not here anymore."

She turned quickly and began to walk away. "You'll have to excuse me now."

CHAPTER 11

WE WERE tired and angry and nervous when we returned to our car. So as I drove we did what every normal American family does: we argued like idiots and got on one another's nerves.

"Why don't *you* sit in the back for a change, Mom?" Alex said. He had a definite snarkiness in his voice. And I really was not in the mood for it.

"Your mother always sits in the front," I said. "That's the rule. So don't start."

"That time we drove to Albany she didn't sit in the front," he said.

Lindsay joined the action.

"That's because you acted like a baby and lied. You said you were getting carsick when you weren't. You've never gotten carsick in your life."

"I get carsick whenever I look at you," Alex answered.

Suddenly (and unexpectedly) Megan exploded.

"Stop it. Both of you. Just stop it. Only imbeciles would argue about where we should sit in the goddamn car."

To ward off a potential escalation, I said, "And

don't either of you make a joke or an insult about 'only imbeciles.'"

Before I or anyone else could say anything, I saw a flashing light in the rearview mirror. It was accompanied by a siren.

"What the hell is that for?" I said. Then, almost reflexively, I pulled onto the shoulder of the road. I shifted the car into Park, and I rechecked the rearview mirror.

Oh, it was definitely a police car, and the red light was still flashing.

Alex and Lindsay were taking turns shouting, "What's happening?" and "What's going on?"

"Don't turn around!" I yelled, and I really had no idea why I said that. I squinted hard, alternating my gaze between the rearview and the side-view mirror.

I could not be certain, but I suspected that the round face and wide shoulders I saw in the mirrors belonged to the same cop who gave us the scary-stern warning for jaywalking.

Why wasn't he getting out of his police car?

The light kept whirling. Then another siren. This one from another car, a different police car. Now this new car pulled in front of my own stopped car. Then the siren stopped. I wasn't sure whether I was supposed to get out of my car...yet I was vaguely recalling that you're supposed to stay *in* your car...on the other hand, if I didn't get out I might piss off the cops. Suddenly a blast of sound erupted from the loudspeaker on the patrol car behind me.

Police info for halted vehicle. Police info for halted vehicle.

Please proceed to place of residence. Re-

peat. Please proceed to place of residence.
Maintain legal speed limit. Proceed now.

"What are we going to do now, Dad?" Alex asked.

At that moment I was feeling virtually every feeling a man could feel. I felt furious, stupid, embarrassed. I hooked on furious, of course, and I fired back at my son.

"Are you deaf? The guy couldn't have been clearer. We're supposed to drive home. You know, our goddamn place of residence. You heard him as well as I did."

There was a creeping numbness in my arms and hands. But I managed to pull out into the very light traffic. As I did, the police car in front of me anticipated the move. He, too, pulled out, staying in front of me. I couldn't pass the legal speed limit even if I wanted to.

Yet in all the chaos and confusion I was suddenly aware that Megan had remained very quiet.

"Whaddya think?" I said softly.

"I think we should do what they ask," she said, equally softly.

Then from the backseat, Lindsay spoke: "Any ideas, Daddy?"

"No," I said.

"Nothing?" Alex asked.

They seemed just short of stunned that the dad with all the answers—"You work with your knees for a jump shot"; "A little more reading and a little less computer wouldn't kill you"—had absolutely no answer.

In almost no time—no time at all—it seemed that we were turning into our driveway. I glanced up at the surveillance cameras, still there. I saw a neighbor trimming the bushes under her dining-room window.

The cop cars stopped in front of and behind me.

I was uncertain whether or not my family and I should exit the car. Then the front patrol car made a U-turn and left the driveway. The one behind me remained.

I was expecting something bad. The police officer behind me stepped out of his car. He walked toward my car. He motioned us to exit. I unlocked the doors. We stepped out.

Yes, it was indeed the same pink-faced asshole who had stopped us for jaywalking, who lectured us and frightened us and pretty much humiliated us.

"So there you are," the officer said with a big fat smile on his big fat face. "The Brandeis family got a fancy police escort home. The New Burg police wanted to prove that we can be your enemy...or we can be your friend."

He gave us an informal two-finger salute and walked back to his car. He opened the car door. Just before he got in he spoke.

"You all have a nice day, now."

CHAPTER 12

THAT SATURDAY night, after a drone had delivered a delicious dinner of veal parmigiana, arugula salad, and pizza margherita from the Pizza Store (we were quickly embracing the various conveniences of living in the world of the Store), Megan and I settled into our "office" in the attic—a tiny corner space where we had decided to write our tell-all book.

People told us the dry heat of the Midwest would be a relief after the humid heat of Manhattan. They lied. Our attic was scorching. The central air-conditioning didn't reach that far up, and the fan served mainly to toss around our index cards and printer paper.

We had chosen the attic in case there were still some cameras we may have missed in other rooms. Yes, a few spycams were most likely hidden in the attic (we're not *that* naive), but after we removed two that were attached to wooden roof beams we thought we had a good shot at privacy.

But who the hell knew with these people?

One lightbulb dangled over the small card table we were using as a desk. The heat was so intense that we had stripped down to our underwear. The ice cubes melted in our iced coffees.

Most of the house felt like it had been built the previous week, but the attic looked like it was two hundred years old: cobwebs and rodent droppings on most of the beams, creaking floorboards, and, in the stifling heat, something we couldn't explain—an occasional shot of very cold air.

More troubling than that, however, was the question Megan asked before we had written a single word of our book.

"How did this happen, Jacob? How did we end up sitting half naked in a hundred-and-ten-degree attic in Nebraska writing a book about some insane company?"

It was a good question, one that I had also been pondering. Unfortunately I didn't have the remotest idea of a good response.

"Maybe we're just destined to write this book," I said.

"Not to be cynical, sweetie, but that's way too strange an answer—like God wants us to write the book."

"Not God," I said. "But I don't know. Maybe fate."

"'Fate' is just shorthand for 'God.'"

"I guess," I said. "But it does seem that everything just kind of came together—the rap book being turned down, our becoming really aware of the Store, then our needing the job and the money. It's like we enlisted in the army for a war, kind of a *holy* war."

"I guess," she said, but it was clear that we were both a little scared. She went on. "If we get caught, we'll be…well, I can't even imagine what they could do to us."

"Ugga-bugga," I said.

"Ugga-bugga is right," Megan answered. No smile. Yes, we definitely were scared. Then she said, "Why don't we just get to work?"

And so we did. Both Megan and I used the same system when we were writing nonfiction. We wrote everything, every little piece of fact or opinion or interview quotation, on index cards. We filed them and sorted them and filed them again. We kept small files of cards as subfiles of large files. Eventually we would have thousands of cards, stored carefully and sorted precisely, in hundreds of plastic boxes (which, of course, we bought from a stationery supplier on the Store's website).

Although, like most people our age, we lived our lives excessively on our laptops, we could not find a satisfying way to put our nonfiction research on the computer. We somehow needed to see the shoe boxes, to riffle through them, to move the index cards and Post-it notes around as new information came into the work.

Oh, we still used the Internet a lot.

The original Indian name of New Burg, Nebraska? Go to Google. (The name, by the way, is an anglicized form of *nom-bah,* the Quapaw word for the number 2.)

Do consumers believe there is a significant difference between items bought online and those purchased in brick-and-mortar stores? Hello, Google. (Turns out that most people don't care.)

That night, however, we were mainly in index-card territory. A number of cards were written about Deb the librarian and her husband, who had been "transferred." There were about ten cards about the guy coming out of the Pizza Store. Brick Street meeting Mortar Street. The surveillance-camera search.

The neighbors who came to help. The cop and his kind "warning." On and on and on.

Our number 2 pencils scratched away, interrupted only by an unexpected whoosh of icy air.

Our shoulders seemed to start aching at about the same time. We arched our backs. We stretched our arms.

Then Megan said, "When did they deliver that box over there?"

I looked around. She pointed to a box marked THE STORE HOME OFFICE SUPPLIES.

"I have no idea," I said. "Is it stuff you ordered?"

"No. I haven't ordered a thing since we got to New Burg."

We walked the few yards to the box. It was snuggled under a wooden slope in the roof. We opened it easily enough and looked inside: two cellophane-wrapped packages of number 2 pencils, fifteen packets of index cards in various sizes and colors, a small cardboard box containing ten Rolling Writer pens, and, weirdest of all, two thick memo pads. One said FROM THE DESK OF MEGAN BRANDEIS. The other was identical except, of course, it had my name at the top.

"Are you sure *you* didn't order these?" Megan asked. "I mean, Jesus, it's exactly the stuff we use."

"Yeah, like the peanut butter and the cereal they had for us." Both of us simply did not want to discuss it.

It was almost 2:00 a.m. And it was clearly time to call it a night.

"Somehow I feel about ten times more awake than I did when we started," Megan said.

"Good. Let's not waste the energy," I said. "Pull up the Store site."

Megan threw me a what-are-you-up-to look, but the site came up, and the page read as it always did:

Welcome to the Store
It's All You Need in Life

I took the laptop from her, and Megan watched over my shoulder as I tapped away.

I went to "The Store for Books." This is how the Store had begun its merchandising conquest of the world—selling books. They maintained the largest collection of books in the world, bigger than the collection at the Library of Congress. Classics, bestsellers, textbooks, kids' books, porn—everything you could imagine putting between two covers.

In addition to all those traditional books was a unique section: "Request a Book You'd Like to See Written." This section of the Store website was filled with title suggestions for books that didn't yet exist— *How to Spay Your Pet at Home* (I swear) and *The Tao of Algorithms* were two of many thousands.

I moved to the subsection headlined with the letter *U*. There, right after the title *The Ultimate Book of Zen Orchestral Accompaniment*, I clicked on "Submit your book request."

I carefully typed in "*Ulysses: The Perfect Sleep Aid.*"

The following sentence filled the screen: "We'll get to your request as soon as possible. Check back frequently."

I looked at Megan, who was laughing. Then we kissed.

The kiss was filled with a mixture of love and sex and fear.

"I hope they have a sense of humor," Megan said.

"We'll soon find out."

"Yeah," said Megan. "We'll check back frequently."

"But for now, let's beat it," I said.

"Yes, let's. I'm getting really cold," Megan said.

I looked at my computer screen. It read: TIME: 2:14
A.M. TEMP: 45 F.

CHAPTER 13

"HEY, IT'S Sunday," I said. "Let's all go to church."

From the astonished expressions on my family's faces and the long silence that followed, I might as well have said, "Let's all go to Mars."

Alex spoke first. "What's up with you, Dad? Are you, like, trying out a stand-up comedy routine?"

I didn't respond, but fifteen minutes later, the kids having opted to stay home, Megan and I—she in a yellow dress printed with white daisies, I in a blue linen blazer—were driving toward the *only* church in New Burg for the eleven o'clock service.

The two of us were not particularly religious. As a couple, the last time we had been in a house of worship was eighteen years earlier, when we got married at the Larchmont Temple. Then we were in a holy place because of love. This time we were going for research.

The church was called the New Burg Church of God, a perfectly okay name but without a touch of creativity to it. You know, like Catholic churches called the Most Precious Blood of Jesus or Our Lady, Sorrowful Star of the Sea. Same with temples whose names always sounded like my grandmother's Yiddish expressions: Anshe Emeth Shalom or Temple Shaaray Tefila.

At 10:55 the church parking lot was packed. Whatever they were selling at the New Burg Church of God, the people of New Burg were certainly buying it. Latecomers like us, arriving only a few minutes before curtain time, had to park at the far end of the lot.

We got out of the car and instinctively tugged at our clothes and patted our hair. Megan and I were strangers in a strange land.

Then we heard a voice.

"Don't worry. You both look just fine."

It was a man's voice—slow, deep, and slightly slurred—and it was coming from the passenger side of a car parked directly next to ours. Megan and I flashed embarrassed smiles, and I said something inane: "Thank you very much. So do you."

"Well, frankly, we don't. See for yourself," said the man.

He opened the car door, stood up, and stretched himself out to about six feet tall. He was dark-skinned, maybe East Indian, maybe Mediterranean. His hair was sloppy, and his sport shirt was wrinkled, but he was also handsome. He had that I-just-swam-in-the-ocean look that a lot of women seem to like.

His female companion moved out from the driver's side. She was pretty hot. She was almost as tall as he was, with long blond hair. Both of them looked about our age.

Something else got out of the car with them— the thick, sweet, beautiful scent of marijuana smoke. I know there's no such thing as a contact high, but if I were ever going to get one, that would have been the time. Our parking-lot neighbors must have been smoking with the car windows rolled up, because the smell of weed was moving toward us like a tiny cyclone.

"My name is Bud, Bud Robinson, and the slightly stoned blonde over there is my wife, Bette—that's Bette with an *e*, not a *y*—and you *do* pronounce the *e*."

I was still processing the spelling and pronunciation of Bette's name when I saw Bud looking at his cell phone. He began reading aloud.

"And you two are Megan and Jacob Brandeis. Jacob, a former writer and an NYU grad. Megan, also a former writer and—woo-hoo—a Stanford grad."

Bette was exhaling from a long hit on the joint they were sharing. Then she spoke. "It's all kinda creepy, isn't it?"

Bud built on her question: "Ya know, how everybody knows everything about everyone else. That's the Store for you."

"Is it all because of the Store?" Megan asked.

We were both being cautious.

The response to Megan's question was a burst of laughter from Bette and Bud. My translation of their laughter was: "Are you two so simple that you couldn't figure that out for yourselves?"

Bette had passed the joint to Bud. He had taken a hit. Then he offered it to Megan.

Megan took it, took a small puff, then handed the joint to me. It was pretty clear that we were going to be late for church.

Bud rubbed his head and spoke.

"Now, the other thing it says on my old handheld here is that you live at 400 Midshipman Lane. *We* live at 420 Midshipman."

"I guess that makes you the only people in the neighborhood who didn't come and help us unpack," Megan said.

"We were preoccupied with recreation, if you know what I mean," Bud said, and he tipped his head toward the new joint he was rolling.

Then Bette said, "I'm just curious. I like asking all the newcomers this question."

"Shoot," I said.

"Have you found the surveillance cameras yet?"

"Well, uh…yeah," I said. Then Megan added, "The first night here."

"I've got some advice for you," Bud said. "Don't even bother trying to remove those cameras."

"Too late," I said.

"The Store'll just sneak them back in. They've probably got a robot drone in your house right now, messing around with all new cameras."

Bud inhaled the weed deeply, and he let it out slowly.

"You folks going into the church service?" he asked.

"I guess we should. Better late—" I said.

"You don't have to go in," Bette said. She then explained that last year they learned that the surveillance cameras took attendance by recording the cars entering the parking lot, not by recording the people actually entering the church.

"Are you sure of that?" I asked.

"Not really," Bette said. "With the Store you can never be absolutely sure of anything."

I realized that I was liking these people. This cool guy and his hot wife. Yet I was afraid to like them too much.

I don't think Bette could read my mind, but she sure could read the situation. Suddenly but calmly she said, "I bet you two are thinking, 'We just met these people. Can we trust them?'"

Megan and I smiled. Nervously.

Then I said, "Well, can we? Can we trust you?"

Bud's voice was full of hearty laughter as he spoke.

"Of course not! Are you crazy? We work for the Store."

CHAPTER 14

MONDAY MORNING Megan and I went to work. At the Store fulfillment center.

Eighteen buildings covering three square miles. Eighteen buildings connected by causeways and tunnels and bridges and trams with miles of escalators and conveyor belts in between. Drones flew above the buildings, and humans in navy-blue jumpsuits worked within them.

NO WORRIES

That was the sign that hung on the walls, on the backs of chairs, on the free soda machines, the free snack machines, the free coffee-cappuccino-espresso machines.

NO WORRIES

That was the sign that hung over the thousands of video monitors, over the entrances and exits, even over the urinals in the men's rooms.

Of course Megan and I had nothing *but* worries. Would we be caught taking notes? Would we be found out?

We had just joined thousands of workers. Hundreds of those workers said, "Welcome, friends" as we were escorted by a smiling young woman to the fulfillment center's underground garage. It was in that massive garage that we saw our first Stormer, a computer-controlled driverless vehicle.

If a golf cart and a Porsche had given birth, their offspring would be a Stormer, an efficient merchandise-gathering machine that plied the lanes of the fulfillment-center buildings. Gatherers like Megan and me jumped on and off to gather what everyone at the Store called the stuff.

It seemed that every kind of "stuff" in the world was in those eighteen enormous buildings. Approximate size? Imagine fifteen Madison Square Gardens.

Did you need a leather three-piece sectional sofa, a watermelon and a melon baller, a Patek Philippe watch, an ironing board, two thousand plastic-recycling bags, red paper clips, or an autographed Mickey Mantle baseball card? Maybe you'd like a low-flush toilet, a package of condoms, a Roku box, a pasta machine, a fifty-thousand-dollar Edwardian diamond tiara, a pound of sevruga caviar, a thousand pounds of manure, a napkin holder, a *case* of napkin holders, a Hershey's Special Dark chocolate bar, a *case* of Hershey's Special Dark chocolate bars, a canoe, a Jet Ski, a box of colostomy bags, a…

If it existed, the Store sold it. The Stormers zoomed around like roaches running from the light. The workers popped up and down like characters in old silent movies.

Megan and I watched it all as our Stormer took us on a "training and orientation" tour. A woman's soothing voice came through our earbuds as we rode along:

"At the moment, you're witnessing the assembly of a packing crate. Watch the merchandise being lifted into the crate. The follow-up accountant checks the order and…"

Every few yards, the voice would resume: "At the moment we're in 'semiperishables,' everything from jicama and avocados to deviled eggs and smoked salmon. The temperature in this area is precisely calibrated to…"

Then a surprise.

We were making a left turn from "photo printing and three-dimensional laser printing" to "all-natural flooring, door saddles, and colonial molding" when a hand reached toward my head and pulled off my earbuds.

The assailant, whom I hadn't yet identified, spoke in a loud stage whisper: "Welcome to Planet Crazy. Please check your brain at the entrance."

It was Bud.

"Holy shit!" I said.

"Watch your mouth, New York boy," I heard a woman say. It was Bette.

Yes, our two pothead friends from the church parking lot.

Bette showed us the face of her standard-issue Store tablet as she said, "We tracked your orientation path on the 'Who's New' page. Take a gander."

On Bette's tablet were two very retouched photos of Megan and me. We looked like models in a 1950s clothing catalog. The caption below our picture read "Say hello to Meg and Jake."

Meg? Jake?

Megan shook her head and said, "And so the madness begins."

"And it *is* only the beginning," Bud said.

"We've got to scoot," said Bette. "We can talk later. We'll stop by soon."

Bette and Bud walked away quickly. And Megan and I slipped our earbuds back in.

The voice of the guide began again, "Now that your *unscheduled visit* is ended…"

Someone had been watching us.

The voice continued, "Please report to assignment area 44 for your first task." The voice clicked off.

The Stormer made a sudden sharp right turn at "smoke detectors, fire extinguishers, and carbon monoxide detectors."

In approximately ten minutes we had arrived at assignment area 44. During that ten-minute drive I had counted ninety-five Store slogan signs.

NO WORRIES

No worries?

In my opinion, nothing *but* worries.

CHAPTER 15

AT THE Store assignment area a bell rang, and a text message appeared on our tablet.

The success of the Store depends on the excitement and involvement of the consumers we serve. Sometimes our friends the consumers are so pleased with the low price and easy delivery of the goods they buy that they become totally immersed. When that happens, our friends at home need some help and guidance from their friends at the Store.

Today, Meg and Jake, you two, as a team, will be representing us as we try to help folks break away from their commitment to the products they're using. In other words, let's get them out of their houses and return them to service. Many of them have been on extended leaves of absence.

Please review the prepared talking points as your Stormer takes you to your first stop. Good luck.

So a Stormer took us to visit Store customers who had become "so engrossed" in Store merchandise that they needed to be "deimmersed and reimmersed."

The objective was to get people to stop using their favorite Store products and go back to work.

Our first stop was a big Tudor-style house. According to the information on our tablets, the thirty-year-old couple living there had not left the place for sixty-five days. That's right, sixty-five days. They had become obsessed with using their small army of Vitamix blenders.

"Man, take one sweet sip of the red cabbage, kale, and blueberry," the husband said at his doorway, holding out a big glass of very unappetizing blue-tinged mud.

"No, thank you," I said.

"Ma'am," he said, offering the same potion to Megan.

I don't think the guy had shaved in sixty-five days. He was wearing a dingy T-shirt and red boxer shorts, both covered with stains the same color as the juice he was offering.

"We're two of your friends from the Store," Megan said.

"And you are friends indeed." It was a different voice, a woman's voice.

Then we saw the woman. She easily weighed 250 pounds.

"Our friends at the Store sold us our Vitamix machines, and those mixers or blenders or whatever they are have just changed our lives."

She, too, held a big glass of liquid. She called her offering a chocolate yogurt ambrosia smoothie.

"Tastes delicious, and it's good for what ails you," she said.

I took the glass. I took a gulp. It was exceptionally delicious. It was also exceptionally sweet and exceptionally rich. I would have bet that she'd been drinking gallons of similar smoothies for the previous sixty-five days.

Megan and I tried to tempt them with the benefits of "getting back to your colleagues at the Store." Their reaction? They invited us into the kitchen to see their "family."

The family consisted of five different Vitamix machines: two CIA Professional Series blenders, two Professional Series 500 blenders, and a G-series 780.

"The G-series is the next generation," the wife whispered confidentially.

They described their lives—if you could call what they were doing living.

The husband ordered his juicing produce—from leeks to oranges to avocados—from the Store. The wife ordered her Chobani yogurt and Mast Brothers chocolate from the Store.

The husband said it perfectly: "The Store makes everything so easy that you never have to leave your house." He paused for a moment and then added, "Well, sometimes you do, but just once. I was playing Pokémon GO." Then he laughed.

They elaborated on this theme. This couple subscribed to the Store's streaming services for movies and TV and sports specials. The Store filled their medical prescriptions ("I have a touch of diabetes, so I gotta have my metformin," the wife said). The Store sold them "a really reasonably priced" Thermador refrigerator in which to keep their overflow of smoothies. The drones delivered their food.

"But what about people, human contact, your friends?" Megan asked.

"Who needs them when you have this?" the woman said.

We left.

Our next stop was only two houses away from the Vitamix couple.

The door was unlocked. So we walked into a big front hall filled with mirrors, clouds of hot steam, and the scent of eucalyptus and menthol. The sounds of exotic music—harp and piano and waterfall—filled the air.

A woman entered, perhaps fifty years old, wearing a long white terry-cloth bathrobe. Her blond hair looked wet; it was pulled back. She asked sweetly if she could help us.

Before I could answer, Megan said, "Wow. You've got some kind of luxury spa in here."

The blond woman spoke: "We think it *is* a luxury spa in here."

She was immediately joined by a smaller version of herself—a thirtyish blond woman, also in a white terry-cloth robe. They had to be mother and daughter.

"I bet you folks are from the Store, aren't you?" the younger woman asked.

We said we were.

"It won't work," the older woman said. "You two aren't the first. They've sent plenty of others. Over the past six months there must have been ten different people from the Store. Sometimes couples, most times women. But the thing is this: they see what we've done with the place, and sometimes they don't want to leave, either. The massage machines, the saunas, even the three attendants…we call 'em the boys. We got them all from the Store, and now the Store says we should get back to work. Well, why should we? They keep extending our paid leave. And…why should we leave all this?"

I suggested that returning to a life of accomplishment and people—the joking, the parties—would be fun.

They laughed at me. They thought I was crazy.

"We have air purifiers, tanning beds, everything we need," the younger woman said.

Then they took us on a short tour of their magical mystery spa, and it was…well, it was a real spa. Another young blond woman was being massaged by a well-built older man. A fat hairy guy sat in a dry sauna. A very old woman sat in a wet sauna.

"Is this a legit business here?" I asked.

"Oh, no," said the older woman. "Just friends and family."

Unsuccessful again. We left the spa. Megan said, "I feel like a Jehovah's Witness."

"What do you mean?"

"Door-to-door but no converts."

Back in the Stormer I gave her a short, sweet kiss. "Ugga-bugga," I said.

"No," Megan said. "The proper expression is…"

She paused for a few moments, and then, almost in unison, we said, "No worries."

CHAPTER 16

THE NEXT day Megan and I were separated…at work. In our strange new world this was a strange new feeling—being alone. Megan and I were always together, especially during the previous few months: working on the disastrous *Roots of Rap,* organizing the move to New Burg, moving in, working in the attic on the new project. Now we were alone, which was unusual for us.

We were each assigned our own Stormer, working in different buildings. That second day I was assigned to "collection housewares," gathering and prepacking wall-mounted plastic-bag dispensers, silicone spatulas, apple-pie-scented candles, and disposable espresso cups.

Megan was assigned to "maternity denim," filling orders for elastic-waist butt-lifting black jeans, stretch-sided white twill jeans, and elastic-waist distressed jeans with "worn, torn, not yet born" holes at the knees.

We drove back home together, of course. Megan did the driving, and I did the writing, filling index cards with notes ("Quick calculation: free cafeteria lunches cost the Store approximately $830,000 daily") and observations ("Pretty sure the 'collection housewares' supervisor has small computer chip embedded in his forearm"), and personal insights ("Stormer check-in staff all nice, polite; Stormer repairmen all suck").

When we arrived home our plan was to check in with Alex and Lindsay, then use the matching treadmills in the basement for half an hour, do fifteen minutes on the StairMaster, and finally cool down with a few icy Sam Adamses.

As I say, that was our plan. Alex was waiting at the open garage door.

No "Hello." No "How was your day?"

His greeting was, "Do you know two people named Bette and Bud?"

"Yes," said Megan, and then, quite sanctimoniously, she added, "We met them at church."

First Alex said, "Alleluia." Then he said, "Well, they're in the dining room, and they just droned in a bucket of Buffalo wings and fries."

We walked into the dining room and were greeted by lots of hugs. Bette and Bud obviously subscribed to the hugging craze that was sweeping the country, including New Burg.

"I warned you we'd be coming by," said Bette.

We told them how pleased we were that they just dropped in, that we had absolutely nothing planned for the evening, and that Buffalo wings were some of our favorite foods in the world.

They didn't seem nearly as hip and good-looking as the previous two times we'd met. Bette seemed pale and wasn't wearing makeup. Her clothes were loose and matronly, and she wore a foolish-looking pink sweatshirt. Bud had a puffiness around the eyes. He was wearing "Dad" pants—baggy, pleated chinos belted high on his stomach.

"Took us exactly two minutes to walk here," Bud said. "Door to door; timed it."

Bette said, "Can you *think* of anything more boring than to use a stopwatch on a walk down the block? Next he'll be counting raindrops."

"By the way," Bud said. "It looks like we were right about something."

"About what?" I asked.

Bud tilted his head in the direction of the fireplace. "The spaniels," he said.

Both Megan and I turned our heads toward the mantel and the early nineteenth-century ceramic cocker spaniels Megan's grandmother had given us.

I must have looked confused.

"He's talking about this," Bette said. She walked to the fireplace, picked up one of the dogs, and turned it upside down. You didn't have to be a CIA operative to spot the surveillance camera that had been drilled into the dog's paw.

"Son of a bitch," I said.

"Please, Jacob," Megan said. "Don't start."

I surveyed the living room and front hall. Yes, the cameras were back, reinstalled, just as Bette and Bud had predicted. Over the front door. Over the hall mirror. Over the hall closet. Over the fake Matisse in the living room. In some of the same places. And in a bunch of new ones. "Get used to it, man," Bud said. "This is the way the Store works. And there isn't anything you can do about it."

He paused. He smiled. Then he said, "Nothing but this…"

Bud leaped up and began singing the teenybop song of the hour, "Jealous." He held the camera-loaded china dog as if it were a microphone. As Bud sang and gyrated and did a third-rate imitation of

Nick Jonas, moving the dog back and forth in front of his face, Megan and I were a little bit too stunned to laugh. Man, the guy was moving with passion.

I don't like the way he's lookin' at you.

He stopped suddenly. He plopped back down.

"I always like to provide a little entertainment for the bastards who have to watch all these videos. You should see my Lady Gaga. It's perfect."

Bette then said, "Of course, you should know that since Bud's wacko performance was recorded on one of the cameras in *your* house, the Store will bring it up in your interview."

"We're being interviewed?" Megan asked.

"Sure thing. Everyone who moves here has a three-hour introductory interview. They call it the in-in. You bring the whole family. The kids. Even a dog or a canary if you've got one. Then they ask about a zillion questions. Some highly personal. Some highly intellectual. And some just plain crazy."

"They're very polite, very courteous," said Bud. "No one seems to know what they do with the results," he said. "But it's nothing to worry about."

From the looks on their faces, we knew it was nothing to look forward to, either.

CHAPTER 17

THE VERY next day Megan, Lindsay, Alex, and I were seated in a large comfortable room.

"Lindsay, let's start with you. Name two things you'd change about your parents if you could."

The walls were paneled in dark wood. The furniture was classic psychiatrist-office stuff: Eames chair, brown-and-black tweed sofa, matching tweed club chair, and, of course, a coffee table topped with a box of Kleenex.

"Jacob, would you ever skip church on Sunday to go to a Major League Baseball game?"

The interviewer was named Justin—a skinny guy with the standard good looks of a TV game-show host. No idea whether he was a real psychiatrist.

"Megan, are you an organ donor?"

Justin said that this was a purely get-to-know-you session. They did it with all new employees and their families. Justin told us something he would repeat a number of times throughout our three hours there. "There are no right or wrong answers." Yeah, sure.

*　　*　　*

"Lindsay, what do you miss most about New York City?"

"The craziness."

"Megan, do you believe that thirteen is an unlucky number?"

Megan said she was not a superstitious person.

"Follow-up, then. Would you live in an apartment on the thirteenth floor?"

"Well, like I said, I'm not superstitious. So I guess I would."

"Another follow-up. You said 'I guess I would.' Does that mean you're not certain?"

Megan said she was certain.

"Alex, same question. Thirteenth floor?"

Alex was ready: "I tend to live wherever my parents live."

"Good answer, my man."

Justin had no paper or pen. He took no notes. I could only assume that we were being recorded or even streamed on video. Had he conducted these interviews so many times that he had it all memorized? Did he just invent things as he went along? Or was it a combination of both?

"Jacob, there are only three flavors available at the ice cream store—pistachio, butter pecan, and chocolate peanut butter cup. Which do you choose?"

I figured I'd show him I was a traditionalist. I answered, "Butter pecan."

Justin's face turned solemn.

"But you're allergic to nuts, Jacob."

I told him I thought it was a theoretical question.

"No. It's a personal question. This is a personal interview. Let's move on."

"But I made the assumption that—" I began.

"Please, Jacob. Let's move on."

And move on we did. The next question was for Lindsay.

"If you could visit just one place in the world for a week, where would that place be?"

Oh, please don't say New York, sweetie, I thought. I shouldn't have worried.

She answered: "The moon."

"Interesting…now, Megan, are you still in touch with any of your friends from elementary school?"

"Megan, tell me one thing about Jacob that no one else in the room knows."

"Alex, what was your favorite toy as a child?"

"Jacob, tell me two things about your wife that you find extremely irritating."

"Megan, what's your ideal weight?"

"Alex, do you care if someone is gay or lesbian?"

"Jacob, if you could only wear a shirt of the same color for the rest of your life, what would that color be?"

And so it went: sports teams, jobs, religion, sex, animals, food, education, the future, the past, and, finally, the Store.

"Is the Store perfect?"

Megan said, "Almost."

Alex said, "I really don't know."

Lindsay said, "I guess so."

"And you, Jacob. Is the Store perfect?"

"Nothing on earth is perfect."

CHAPTER 18

THE CAR ride home from the "testing center." The click of the doors locking. The click of the seat belts fastening. We were like a chorus bursting with the same inevitable question: "So what did you think?"

We all asked it almost at once, and everyone except Lindsay jumped to answer it. Lindsay said she was too fearful of cameras and recording devices in the car to have a conversation. But the rest of us? We couldn't wait to talk about the interview. The hell with surveillance.

Megan said, "It was both better and worse than I had imagined. And I don't think it should have been done as a group. What kind of kid wants to answer tough questions about his parents when the parents are right in the room?"

"I thought it was all creepy," Alex said. "Justin was creepy. The room was creepy. And the questions were stupid. What difference does it make if you want to play the trumpet or play baseball or whether you wish you were taller? I mean, the whole thing was just to make sure you want to be part of this stupid place."

I agreed with all their observations. And I said so. It was creepy and embarrassing...and also exhausting. Hours of questions about your past, present, and future. Then I added a useless comment: "Well, at least it's over." But of course I knew I was lying, and they knew I was lying.

That's when Lindsay spoke. "Is it really over, Daddy? Won't there just be more bullshit? More nonsense? We take down the cameras, and they put them back up. They know you have a nut allergy. They know what toothpaste we use. They…" But then she squeezed her eyes tight. The tears seeped out anyway.

"Come on, sweetie," Megan said, unbuckling her seat belt and reaching toward the backseat. She took Lindsay's hand and squeezed it.

"Look. Once your mother and I…" I started to say, but was interrupted by Alex, whose voice was loud and high.

"Speaking of books: holy shit! Will you look at that?"

I pulled over and slammed on the brakes. To our left was the town library, which Megan and I had visited a few days earlier. Only something was very different: the library had been closed down.

Wooden boards covered the windows. A thick steel chain and a few big padlocks prevented anyone from entering. The flagpoles held no flags. Even the lawn was suddenly scraggly and in need of watering.

"What's going on?" Megan asked.

"I don't know," I answered. "But whatever it is…it's sure as hell not good."

We all looked at it for a few seconds, then I twisted myself around to face all three members of my family.

"Get out of the car. Everybody. Now. This minute," I said.

They looked frightened, but they moved fast. Within seconds we were on the cracked sidewalk in front of the derelict little building.

"You think there's a bomb in the car, Dad?" Alex asked.

"No," I said. "But I'm sure there's some sort of hidden recording device."

Their faces were filled with anxiety.

"Listen, and listen carefully. This town isn't a game or a joke. This place is scary as hell. From now on—and I really don't know what else to say—from now on we've all got to be very, very careful."

I watched as Alex fought to hold back his tears.

I watched as Megan drew the children close to her.

"I'm sorry, Daddy," said Lindsay. "But I'm really scared."

"That makes three of us, sweetie," Megan said.

"No," I said. "That makes four of us."

CHAPTER 19

WE HAVE friends whose apartments have been burglarized. They all say the same thing: "It feels like we've been violated."

I was learning how those friends must have felt. It seemed like every time we left our house, somebody or some*thing* from the Store came in. When we arrived home in the late afternoon after our "interview," we discovered that it had happened once again.

We walked into our house, and Megan said, "Looks like we're having barbecue for dinner." Sure enough, on the kitchen counter were a platter of pork ribs, a bowl of mashed sweet potatoes, and squares of buttered cornbread.

The only thing that amazed me was this: we weren't amazed. We were beginning to realize that being violated was part of life in New Burg.

Our intruders must have had a busy time in our house. The broken hinges on the coat closet had been tightened; the clean clothes in the laundry room had been folded and put away. Megan said, "This is sort of sick. Someone—a person I don't even know—is touching...well, touching my underpants, and it's just perverted."

"Violated," I said. "It makes you feel violated." Megan shook her head.

Then Alex spoke. As was often the case, he was standing in front of the open refrigerator.

"Hey, Mom, remember how I asked you to drone in some Mountain Dew the next time you were droning in groceries, and you said no?"

"What I actually said was…no way. It has too much sugar in it."

"I read that it has one cup of corn syrup in every twelve ounces," Professor Lindsay added.

"Well, whoever's been sneaking around here doesn't seem to agree. There's two six-packs of Dew in the fridge."

Upstairs the beds had been made. Our bathroom cabinet had been stocked with Megan's special prescription soap. The…then I stopped taking inventory and said, "Oh, shit. I gotta go see something."

I ran up the attic stairs. To our "book office." And sure enough, our messy piles of index cards had been straightened out. A new box of toner sat on the floor next to the printer. And—holy shit!—they had put an air conditioner in the tiny window near our work desk.

"Megan," I shouted. "Come up here!"

"I can't. Someone's at the back door."

By the time I'd made it down both flights of stairs, Megan and Lindsay were walking quickly toward the kitchen.

"Did you see on the monitor who's at the door?" I said.

"Who do you think? It's Fred and Ethel."

"Who are Fred and Ethel?" Lindsay said.

"Forget it, honey. It was before your time," Megan said.

"Hell. It was before *our* time."

Megan opened the door for Bette and Bud. Hugs and kisses all around.

"Heard you were having barbecue tonight. Thought we'd invite ourselves over. But we come bearing gifts, too," Bud said.

"Homemade peach pie and a bowl of *real* whipped cream," Bette said.

We didn't bother asking how they knew what our dinner plans were. We had already learned by then that the magical Store tablets disseminated whatever information they wanted people to know.

We settled down in the living room, and all four of us had a glass of Jackie D, as Bud called the Jack Daniel's bourbon he seemed to love so much.

"Nothing like an icy Jackie D and ginger ale on a hot night."

Damn it, I thought. *I have a question, and I'm going to ask it.* Yeah, I knew the surveillance cameras were whirling away. I knew there was no such thing as privacy in our own home. I didn't really care. So I asked.

"When you guys are away from your house, like shopping or at work…well, do people come in and do stuff? Change stuff? Like make the bed or put new grouting in the bathtub?"

Both Bette and Bud chuckled. But I could swear that there was a kind of nervousness behind their laughter.

"When we first got here stuff like that happened all the time. But then it stopped, and I think it's 'cause they figured out we're too ornery to care," Bud said.

"We're not the cooperative types by nature," Bette added.

A strange pause stopped the conversation. Then Bette broke the silence.

"Of course, this is New Burg. So you can't be sure when we say something that we're telling the truth," she said.

Another awkward pause. Megan took a sip of her Jackie D. Then she spoke.

"And of course you can't assume that Jacob and I are telling the truth, either."

"Well, I guess not," Bud said.

Then all four of us laughed.

Megan didn't have to say anything else. I knew what she was thinking.

Ugga-bugga.

CHAPTER 20

BETTE AND Bud went home right after dinner, but we were happy to see that half a peach pie remained. Alex and Lindsay wandered into their worlds of Facebook and Instagram. And Megan and I went to work in our newly air-conditioned attic office. It was almost eleven o'clock, but we had the energy of two people who were just beginning their day.

"This is the thing I've been wanting to show you all night," Megan said as she tapped furiously away at her laptop.

"Don't look over my shoulder," she said. "I want to have it all up on the screen."

After a few more seconds of my pretending not to look over her shoulder, she said, "Okay, now you can look. But understand. This isn't one big document. I simply cut and pasted a bunch of stuff I had downloaded and put all the pieces in one file. I'm calling the file LOLB."

"I give up. What does LOLB stand for?"

"Lots of legal bullshit."

"Oh, I should have been able to guess that," I said sarcastically, but she was ignoring me.

"Go ahead, now," she said. "Take a look."

It was extraordinary.

Bottom line: twenty-seven states had passed legislation that was clearly designed to be favorable to the Store. Oh, sure, the words *the Store* were never mentioned, but Megan and I knew what was going on.

The Connecticut General Assembly had passed what was listed as a "consumer beneficiary act." It prohibited any "land-based establishment" (that meant any brick-and-mortar store) from "reissuing pricing to coordinate with online offers without a seven-day interval."

Translation: if the Store had a Black & Decker power drill on sale for twenty-nine dollars, the town hardware store had to wait seven days before it could lower its price to match the Store's.

In Chicago, the aldermen had passed an act that was "designed for the financial improvement of the low-income housing access incentive," allowing the city to give "free-of-charge electronic tablets and computers to all households with incomes below twenty-four thousand dollars. Within the first three months, said tablets and computers will only be able to access websites with retail marketing content."

Translation: the poor people of Chicago could get crappy free computers programmed only to allow them to visit sites where they could buy stuff. That would mean supermarkets and other big box stores, but it would overwhelmingly mean that they'd be clicking on the Store site, buying all sorts of shit they couldn't afford and getting deeper into credit card debt.

The pro-Store amendments and acts and laws rolled on and on.

Not surprisingly, Nebraska had more pro-Store acts than any other state. It was as if Nebraska were preparing for a day when the Store would rule the state. The legislature in Lincoln had enacted environmentally dangerous rules in preparation for a time when the skies would be so blackened by drones that millions of trees would have to be cut down.

In Florida it was assumed that Cubans would soon be flocking in huge numbers to South Florida, so why not pass a law that allowed "temporary" immigrants to be paid less than minimum wage? That's what the state senate in Tallahassee did.

The new air conditioner was working hard, but it could not stop our blood from boiling.

"This makes me want to vomit," I said.

"And that's putting it nicely," Megan said.

Megan said that she would forward me the entire file immediately. Then she very wisely suggested that we hand-copy the information onto index cards and erase all electronic evidence from our computers. We both assumed that electronic spying was more likely than conducting a home invasion in order to steal hard copy. (Yeah, I know. Never assume.)

"When I say 'erase,' I mean *erase,*" Megan said.

Not a problem for us. One of Megan's "freelance from hell" jobs was writing a ten-page instruction booklet called "Ten Computer Hacks That Anyone Can Learn." So she knew how to scrub a computer *completely* clean, way beyond the useless "Clear History" procedure that most of us amateurs use. (Yeah, I know this, too. There's no such thing as completely clean.)

Before I dug into the LOLB file, I pursued a Store-related project of my own. I had taken on the job of assembling information on the original founder of the Store. You'd think it would be easy to google and surf your way to a pile of facts about Thomas P. Owens, but information was shockingly scarce. Owens was born in Lorain, Ohio, in 1939. That made him around seventy-eight years old now. He was living in Arizona, and he owned another residence in New York City. He had founded the Store about twenty years ago. It was a sloppy-looking, primitive website where Owens sold books, office supplies, and, of all things, long-forgotten candy brands like Necco Wafers and Bonomo Turkish Taffy.

The business (then called Your Store) was successful enough to rate an article in the *Wall Street Journal* and *Crain's New York Business*. In 1998 Owens sold the Store to an investment group.

And I couldn't find a damn thing about the guy from that day on.

My fingers were dancing on the keyboard when Megan said, "Have you read the file on the LOLB stuff?"

"Not yet. I'm about to. I was just doing some follow-ups on Thomas P. Owens."

"Yeah. Well, drop everything, buddy, and step over here. This is going to knock your head off."

CHAPTER 21

**CONFIDENTIAL
READ THE FOLLOWING BEFORE
PROCEEDING**

This electronic communication is for your eyes only. It will self-destruct within an hour of its opening. It is immune from forwarding, printing, and alteration. It is photography-immune. While some readers may wish to copy part or all of this communication, any publicized content will be categorically denied by the sender.

RECIPIENTS: Senator Kathleen Langston, Senator Julio Ramiro Munoz, Senator Franklin Peterson, Senator Dominick Roselli

FROM: Senator William Ward

SUBJECT: Constitutional Amendment XXVIII

This will serve as the final follow-up to our conversation of last Tuesday at the Four Seasons Hotel.

At that meeting it was decided to advance the

cause of a constitutional amendment abolishing all sales tax on consumer goods purchased over the Internet if more than 50 percent of the goods in any given purchase are manufactured in the United States.

I am pleased to report that I have had several conversations with Roger Kendrick, CEO and president of TheStore.com. He has endorsed the idea enthusiastically.

Gathering votes for a constitutional amendment is no small task, yet polls that TheStore.com has conducted privately indicate that it can be accomplished. As such, I am suggesting we create a call-on list of our Senate colleagues and, further, that we designate two of us to visit the Oval Office.

I have made arrangements for our specific group of five to meet secretly Sunday evening at 8:00 p.m. in suite PH3 at the Ritz-Carlton in Georgetown.

Accomplishing our goal of passage of Amendment XXVIII will be great for America, great for TheStore.com, and great for the five of us.

WW/pb

As I read the secret memorandum on the computer screen, my arms and legs were actually shaking. The only thing I could say was the ever-useful "Holy shit!" And I said it more than once.

"Is this for real?" I asked.

"For real."

"Double holy shit!"

Members of the US Senate were plotting to add an amendment to the Constitution that would make the

Store the most important and profitable company in America—and probably the world.

I grasped Megan's shoulders gently. "How'd you get this?" I asked.

Without missing a beat, she said, "I hacked it."

"You hacked it?" I said. "When did—"

"Don't, Jacob. Don't ask. Don't worry about it. I just learned," she said.

This skill seemed way more advanced than the information in her computer hacking booklet.

"Megan, this is serious shit. We could get killed for this," I said.

She stood up and faced me.

"No, Jacob. This is serious shit because five senators are totally screwing with the people of the United States. This is serious shit because the Store is on some weird goddamn track to…I don't know…take over the world. Are we going to do this research right or not? If the answer is no, then let's get the hell back to New York and forget about New Burg and the Store and our book."

I moved in closer to Megan. I hugged her, and I put my face down into her neck and kissed her.

"You're right, of course," I said. "And you're married to a wuss, and you don't deserve what I—"

"Oh, stop it. We're going to do this. We're going to look into this until we either break the Store wide open *or* they…"

She hesitated, just for a moment.

"Or they what?" I said.

"Or they kill us."

CHAPTER 22

OUR JOBS at the fulfillment center were backbreakingly painful *and* mind-numbingly dull—load the Stormer with merchandise, and when the vehicle could hold no more stuff, unload it at the packing center. Then do it again and again and again and...

Quite quickly, however, Megan's job became much easier than mine. You see, Sam Reed, the group manager who handed out the loading assignments, had taken a very smarmy liking to Megan. So while I was usually assigned to lifting and packing cow manure, industrial-size sacks of cake flour, even barbells, Megan was mostly assigned to books, cosmetics, and greeting cards.

Sam called Megan "my sweet Irish colleen" and "my copper-haired beauty." He usually rested his skinny hairy hands on her shoulders when he spoke to her, and once he even suggested that it was unnecessary for her to keep the top button on her Store uniform closed. This suggestion was followed by a creepy "Guys love playing peek-a-breast." Yeah, Sam was a class act.

If this were another company, Megan would have been lodging a complaint with human resources, but we kept reminding each other that the long-term purpose of our jobs was to gather not just Bose headphones and Huggies and folding chairs but also information that would tell America the truth about the Store.

Megan and I were driving home from work the day after we had barbecue with Bette and Bud.

"Am I losing all sense of time in this crazy place?" Megan asked. "Or did we not just have dinner with Bette and Bud?"

She was reading the evening schedule on her tablet.

"Yeah," I said. "Barbecue plus half a bottle of Jackie D."

"Well, guess what? There's a message here. They have a seven o'clock reservation at the Minka Japanese Restaurant in town, and they're expecting us to meet them there for dinner," Megan said.

"How'd they know we were free?" I asked.

"How? You know how. Everyone's schedule is published, and I guess we failed to put something down for seven o'clock. So they rightly assume we're free."

An hour later we were sitting at the Minka with Bette and Bud as well as a huge platter of sushi, a plateful of chicken teriyaki, and some deep-fried pork cutlets. A person might lose his mind living in New Burg, but he'd never lose weight.

"Is Minka the name of the people who own the store, do you think?" I asked.

"No," said Bette. "Minka is a basic farmhouse-type building style that the Japanese use. When I designed the restaurant I thought the rustic look would be very soothing."

"When *you* designed it?" Megan said. She did not

do a very good job of hiding her surprise that this simple-sounding woman in her simple yellow sundress was…an architect?

"Yep. I know I don't seem the type. But I am an architect."

It turned out that Bette had planned and designed almost half the stores and restaurants in New Burg. She had a degree from Carnegie Mellon. She had done an internship at Skidmore, Owings & Merrill.

"And I suppose you're chairman of neurosurgery, Bud?" I said with a laugh.

"Afraid not. Bette's the brains of this duo. I'm a security guard at the chemical warehouse at the fulfillment center," he said.

"We drive past that warehouse on our way to work every day," I said.

Bud said, "Because of my security pass, me and Bette were able to get in and see you both on your first day at the job."

"Now, listen," Bette said very gently. "I have a favor to ask of you two."

"Sure," Megan said. "Anything."

"Oh, this'll be easy," Bette said. "Just don't go telling other people you know that I'm the architect—"

"Or that I'm a security guard."

"But other people must already know," Megan said.

"Some do. Some don't," said Bette. "We believe the less said the better. That should be the eleventh commandment in New Burg."

Shit! They were nervous. They were about as paranoid as anyone could be, even in New Burg. So whether they were friends or not, whether they were spies or not…I had to ask.

"What are you two so afraid of?"

There was a pause.

"Everything. Absolutely everything," Bud said.

After that answer, there really wasn't anything more to say.

Near the window a drone hovered in the air. Had the window been open, the drone could have snatched a piece of sushi.

Bette and Bud looked at each other. They smiled at each other. Then they waved hello to the drone.

CHAPTER 23

IT WAS the first week of school. And we were dreading it.

We knew how Lindsay and Alex felt about leaving their teachers and their friends back in New York—that we'd been selfish in uprooting them. We knew because they never let us forget it.

We also knew that as two savvy, jaded New York kids, they were bound to be negative and sarcastic about a high school in Nebraska. So we were prepared for the worst when they came home from their first day at New Burg High.

"How was school?" Megan asked—steeling herself for the complaints, the accusations, the guilt.

"Kind of cool," said Alex.

"Way cool," Lindsay added. "Do you know that they give every kid a brand-new cell phone? Look!" She took one out of her backpack. "And we can load it up with all the apps we want—free. Anything that isn't X-rated."

"Plus look—we each got our own new laptop," Alex added. "So you can junk the one I brought with me."

That laptop, state of the art a year ago, didn't hold a candle to the new one Alex had in his hands, outfitted with all the best bells and whistles Silicon Valley could create. Alex showed me that the laptop had a flexible screen that could be creased and rolled into a cylinder. When he showed me that it had "retinal access," so you didn't need a password, I thought I had landed in the year 2040…or maybe the year 2040 had already landed in New Burg.

Okay. So it stood to reason that any school connected to the Store would be a mecca of high-end electronics. So much for the first day, as both kids disappeared into their rooms to explore their new gadgets.

But day 2 surprised us even more.

They still loved it.

I mean…they *really* loved it.

They loved it like nothing they'd ever loved before. Even the ridiculously expensive private schools they had attended back in New York.

They loved the teachers. They loved the students. They loved the classes. They loved the school sports teams, the school colors, even the food in the cafeteria. ("Dad, they've even got an authentic sushi chef.")

As the days went on, we kept hearing about "this cool computer science teacher" and "this cool soccer coach" and "this cool girl with this really cool ladybug tattoo on the back of her neck."

Megan and I were silent for the first week or so. But something was clearly wrong.

"Okay. Here goes," Megan nervously said to me one night. "I never thought I'd say this in a million years. But I think the kids are liking school way, way too much."

Ordinarily we would have laughed at such a wacky observation. But she was right. And it scared us.

"Could they be lying to make us feel good?" I asked.

"They rarely lie. And they rarely care how we feel," she said.

"The other thing is that they seem to have so many more friends than they did back in New York."

And that was true. Alex and Lindsay were bringing home new friends every day. Kids with big wide smiles on big, good-looking faces. I had taken to calling them the Smileys. Smiley Jason, Smiley Andrew, Smiley Emma...

"I know I'm going to sound like a crazy lady," Megan said. "But teenagers *shouldn't be so happy.*"

Our kids were changed, all right. But it was starting to feel like a change for the worse.

Our conversation came to a quick halt when Alex walked into the room.

"Hey," he said. "When's dinner? I've got to be at my friend Nathan's in half an hour. By the way, did Lindsay tell you about the Life Program e-mails we both got?"

"Life Program?" Megan said as she put the vegetables in the microwave. "Sounds like a plan for healthy eating."

"No. It's awesome—really," said Alex. "We took a bunch of tests on the second day of school, and they have some people who figure out from the tests, like, what a kid would be good at. And they arrange your whole school experience—that's what they call it. Like, for me, they said I tested really well to be a doctor. So they want me to join Chem Club and get training for the New Burg Emergency Rescue Unit and take a bunch of special bio courses. And—if you can believe it—they said that Lindsay would be, like, a marketing genius when she grows up. So she should take all these extra courses they give in—I don't know, like, why people buy stuff and want stuff and dimbographics—"

"Demographics," Megan said.

"It sounds way too early in life to start planning that sort of stuff," I said. There was no anger in my voice, but there was certainly some anxiety in my heart.

"It sounds great to me," Alex said. "I mean, Dad, come on. You can't ever get started early enough. And these people at school know what they're doing."

Who was this kid talking? What happened to Alex?

"But Alex," Megan said. "You're just beginning to live your life. You can't know what you want to be or do or…"

"Yeah? Why not, Mom? Even Lindsay agrees. It makes a lot of sense."

He was smiling. He was wearing the same smile I saw on his friends. It was the charming but vacant smile, the "all's right with the world" smile. The New Burg smile.

"Call me when the food's on the table," he yelled as he left.

Alex was gone. Megan and I looked at each other. We didn't say anything for a few seconds.

Then I said, "Okay. Okay. I know it sounds a little crazy. But maybe we're overreacting. This could be a very good thing. It makes some sense."

"I kinda disagree. Jacob, the thing is called Life Program. Lindsay and Alex are kids. They're barely adolescents. And they're being *programmed*. *For life!*"

"Let's stay calm. Like I said, it could be a good thing."

"Do you really think so?" Megan asked.

I shook my head. Confused. Concerned.

"No, I don't."

Megan spoke again.

"Are they trying to take our kids away from us?"

I shook my head again.

"That's crazy, right? I mean...they couldn't really do that. Could they?"

Could they?

The microwave beeped. Megan called to Alex and Lindsay. They came running in quickly.

Both of them were smiling.

CHAPTER 24

THERE WAS a good reason why Megan and I had been selected to "help out" at the Special Arts Gathering. But we didn't know it at the time.

The shindig was to be held in the Executive Reception Hall. The guests: big-deal artists, designers, writers, and philosophers as well as some of the seldom-seen movers and shakers from the world of the Store.

The Executive Reception Hall was a dead ringer for Versailles: Fragonard-style murals, ornate (and probably authentic) Louis XIV furniture, gold-and-crystal chandeliers. At one end of the huge room was a stage with a lectern.

Mingling among the celebrities were around a hundred people who worked at the Store. I recognized nobody, but they were easy to spot. They all wore electronic ID badges that read: I'M WITH THE STORE. WELCOME.

After the guests had their fill of Champagne and hors d'oeuvres, the chandeliers flickered and the guests took their seats. Megan and I and the other six "helpers" scurried around like rats, collecting dirty plates, glasses, and napkins. Then we stood behind the seated assembly and watched.

A very attractive young woman wearing a very attractive navy-blue suit approached the lectern.

"Isabel Toledo," Megan whispered to me.

"That's her name?" I whispered back.

Megan rolled her eyes.

"No, idiot. That's who designed her suit."

"Oh."

"The Store Talks to the Arts lectures have been a huge success so far," she said. "Today, for the fifth in the series, we're delighted to have with us Dr. David Werner, the world-renowned economist and Kinkaid professor of economics at Harvard University."

The woman recited a few more of Dr. Werner's credentials and ended with this: "Dr. Werner's talk is entitled 'The Hidden and Surprising Influence of Art and Music on the Economic Recovery.'"

Then Dr. Werner took the stage: a frail-looking man of around seventy-five in a dark gray suit and bright blue bow tie.

We would quickly discover that there was nothing frail about him.

At first he said nothing. He took his time surveying the audience, his face stern, his head moving slowly from left to right. Then he spoke.

"I have been called upon to speak about art and music. And I am sure we would all enjoy a discussion on such noble pleasures. But that's not what I'm going to talk about. And if you don't like what I have to say, well, that's just too damn bad."

A few in the crowd looked at one another, some with concern, some with confusion. The woman who had introduced Dr. Werner abruptly stood from her front-row seat and left the auditorium. Dr. Werner continued.

"Let me make my point very clear at the outset."

There was a pause. Then his voice boomed out over the crowd.

"I don't like you! At all! Any of you!"

There were a few scattered laughs in the audience. But Werner quickly silenced them with a swat of his hand.

"No—don't laugh," he continued. "In fact…" Another pause, and then even louder than before, "You all sicken me. This place sickens me. The Store makes me puke."

People in the audience looked at one another. Eyebrows shot up. Mouths shot open. A murmur. A few whispers.

I heard someone say, "It must be a joke."

But something inside me knew this was not a joke. This fire-and-brimstone preacher was there to preach.

The question was, would anyone other than Megan and I agree with him?

"Just look at the evil that you and the Store have unleashed," he shouted. "Not content to manipulate the general public by underselling and eliminating all competition in a free capitalist system, you and the Store have also become the world's primary gatherer of personal and private customer information."

The murmurs were growing louder. An occasional hiss shot out of the audience. I heard some hearty angry boos.

"The Store has captured the minds and wallets of America because it follows and records everything Americans do. They know what people search for, long for. They know and analyze everything people do online—whether tawdry or respectable. They know what Americans eat and when they eat it. They know what people watch and when they watch it. They even know when people screw and whom they screw…"

Megan and I looked at each other in amazement. This Werner guy was hurling bombs of truth at the audience—things we truly believed.

But the audience was having none of it. Two hulking thugs in cheap black suits appeared at either side of the stage.

But Dr. Werner wouldn't let up. With every sentence, he left Megan and me with faster heartbeats and happier hearts.

"The Store has lobbyists in Washington, DC, that number in the thousands," he said. "And a network of spies and counterspies who have infiltrated every state in the union, perhaps every country in the world," he added.

"I can only assume that the most basic protective agencies of government—organizations such as the FBI and the CIA—are complicit."

Megan and I looked around. Many in the audience were standing, shouting at Werner, "Get the hell out of here." Those who stayed seated were stamping their feet.

"And worst of all," he began—but he never got to finish.

The two black-suited thugs rushed toward him and lifted him up by his armpits, hauling him offstage. As he tried to wriggle out of their grasp, the audience cheered.

"Don't say anything, Jacob," Megan said. "Don't look at him. Don't look at me. Don't smile. Let's just clear these dishes as if nothing had happened."

Of course she was right. Even the slightest reaction on our part could betray us as the rebels we knew we were.

"But I've got to meet this guy."

I worked my way to the front of the huge room,

to the door that led to an offstage area. The pretty woman in the blue suit was in serious conversation with the two beefy-looking guys who had carried Werner off.

"Excuse me," I said. "I was wondering if you could direct me to Dr. Werner."

The three of them looked at one another for a moment.

"He's gone," the first man said.

"I know. I saw him…uh…leave the stage. I was hoping I could—"

"Gone," said the second man.

"Well, do you happen to know which way he went? Maybe there's a chance I could—"

"No," the woman said, cutting me off. She made a gesture with her hand.

"Dr. Werner…is not with us anymore."

CHAPTER 25

IT'S 1984 ALL OVER AGAIN!
BARBECUE AT BETTE AND BUD'S
SUNDAY, 5:00 P.M.

That was Bette and Bud's e-vite.

Megan's reaction was the same as mine.

"Did it ever *stop* being 1984 in New Burg?" she asked.

Whatever the year, we showed up with a chocolate-marshmallow pie in our hands and a bunch of index cards in our back pockets.

"I think you already know at least half the folks here," Bette said.

She was right. Many of the twenty-odd people at the barbecue had helped us on moving day. One of them was suddenly standing right next to me.

I'm embarrassed to say that I remembered Mark Stanton because Mark and his wife, Cookie, were the only African Americans in that collection of white New Burg faces.

"My man Jacob," said Mark Stanton.

We bumped fists, and I said, "Where's Cookie?"

Mark shrugged, a vague nonanswer.

Meanwhile Megan was talking to Marie Di-Manno, the widow who seemed to have been the chief organizer of the help on our moving day.

A pretty woman distributed rum-laced drinks in plastic cups. Two handsome guys I didn't know played a lazy man's game of badminton.

For a moment I considered this: there were worse things than standing and sipping a cool drink on a warm Nebraska Sunday afternoon.

But that happy moment passed quickly. I also knew that there was a video camera beneath the picnic table and at least three other cameras attached to the gutters of the house. I recognized one of the men tending the charcoal grill as one of the two guys who had hustled Dr. Werner offstage. I watched audio-video drones swooping in and around small groupings of party guests. And I couldn't help but wonder why Mark Stanton had not given me a simple straight answer when I'd asked about his wife.

It took us about an hour to devour all the steak (excellent) and ribs (extraordinary) that Bette and Bud had served up. By 7:00 p.m. we had polished off the last remnants of chocolate-marshmallow pie and coconut cream cake. Two blackberry pies had also disappeared. The video cameras were recording lots of people groaning in satisfaction.

Who knew that the evening was just beginning?

One of the guests, a nice-looking mom type who worked at the fulfillment center, tapped a spoon against a coffee cup and spoke.

"You all know me. I'm Lynn Harris. And you all know what time it is, right?" she said.

Everyone except Megan and I seemed to know.

Everyone else began applauding and letting out whoops and cheers.

"That's right. It's the perfect moment for Store Talk," she said. Then she looked directly at Megan and me.

"I think our new neighbors need to be told about Store Talk. Don't be scared, you two. We pick a bunch of topics that are sort of meaningful to New Burg and the Store. Then we put the topics in a little bag, pull one topic out, and have a discussion. We keep doing that until we all get tired or somebody gets nasty."

Lynn laughed. Then she added, "I wrote out the topics this time."

I couldn't keep my mouth shut, of course. "You thought up the topics and put them in the bag or you were *given* the topics and put them in the bag?"

One of the guys who had been playing badminton said, "Little bit of each. It doesn't really make any difference where the topics come from."

"It sounds like a lot of fun," Megan said.

I was both proud and nervous to be married to a wife who could lie so convincingly.

"Megan, you draw the first topic," Lynn said. Then she added, "And Jacob, you can read it to us."

The crowd applauded, and Bud yelled, "Go on, Megan. Pick a good one."

In a few seconds, Megan handed me a piece of paper.

Then I read the first Store Talk subject to the crowd.

"Pawnee Preservation," I read. Then I added, "Maybe it's supposed to say 'reservation,' not 'preservation.'"

"No. It's right," said a chubby middle-aged guy. "There's a big to-do about this Indian burial ground they found when they started digging for the new water fluoridation and vitamin-enhancement plant. Some folks think it should be left alone, and some folks think, oh, what the hell. The Indians—"

"Native Americans," Mark Stanton said, correcting him.

"Yeah, Native Americans…are all gone."

"Well, I don't think it's rightly our decision," said Marie DiManno. "The Store people should decide stuff like that."

Now Bette spoke. She was cheerful, but her voice was firm: "Right. Why should we have a part in any decision?" Sure, Megan and I realized Bette was being sarcastic, but I wondered how many others did.

I watched as Bud gently tapped his wife's hand, a kind of "Calm down, honey" gesture.

"Give us another topic, Megan. Try to make it a bit less controversial," Bud said.

"I'll try my best," said Megan. Soon I had another phrase to read.

"Cornhusker football!"

Where I come from, a sports "discussion" could lead to screams, threats, and pistols at dawn. I soon found out it wasn't much different in New Burg.

"They're a bunch of freakin' losers this year," said one slightly paunchy guy who, ironically, was wearing a Nebraska T-shirt.

"They're looking like winners to me," said the security guard from the Werner lecture.

Then Bud spoke up. His voice was a little too loud for comfort.

"Yeah, they're winners. As long as they don't play Ohio State, Michigan State, Penn State, or Wisconsin." Laughter from most of the group.

But one young guy disagreed enough to stand up and say angrily, "Who the hell are you? Joe Buck?"

Another young guy shot up and said, "Watch your language, Carl. There are women here."

"Let's all stay calm and friendly," Lynn said. "It's only football."

A new voice yelled, *"Only? Only football?"*

I watched as one couple headed toward the driveway.

Lynn spoke. She was clearly nervous. "I'm going to have Megan keep picking until we get something that we can have a civil discussion about."

The group had quieted down, but almost no one was smiling.

Lynn put the bag in front of Megan once again.

Megan pulled out a slip of paper and handed it to me.

I read aloud, "Dr. David Werner."

A few "Who?" and "Who's that?" murmurs came from the crowd.

I answered. "He's the guy who spoke at the arts gathering the other day. He's the guy who was dissing the Store."

"I heard about him. He's a lunatic," one woman said.

"My wife was helping out at the place. She said that the guy was a maniac. They even had to pull him off the stage."

The crowd was stirring now. Mumblings of people exchanging ideas. Some of them pretty loud.

"He sounds like a real asshole."

"Yeah. If you live here, then you know what the deal is. You go with the Store. It's their town."

"Well, I can't say I agree with this Werner's point of view, but he does have the right to—" said one foolishly courageous woman.

Some other woman shot back immediately: "He

sure as hell doesn't have the right to come in here and shoot off his mouth. He's probably one of these egghead types who's jealous of our lives here."

Then Bette stood up. Her voice was calm but strong.

She said, "I think Werner made a lot of good points."

A sudden silence came over everyone. Bette surveyed the crowd quickly, her face a mix of confusion and anger.

"What's wrong with all of you? Are you so afraid of the Store that you can't even express an opinion at a backyard barbecue?"

"We're not *afraid*. We're happy," yelled Mark Stanton. "Is that so awful?"

Bette responded immediately. "Lemme ask you this. Is your wife, Cookie, happy, too? Is she so happy that we never see her anymore?"

"Bud, get your wife to shut up," an older man shouted.

Lynn Harris then joined the noise. "There's no place in all of America that's as good as this. Forgive me if I just take my shopping bag and leave."

Lynn Harris and her husband and another two couples walked toward the driveway.

"Don't you get it, Bette? We like living here. We think it's pretty damn perfect," said one of the badminton guys.

And then it happened.

Bette looked directly at Megan and me and said, "You guys know what I'm talking about. Right? We've got to get some limitations put on the Store. Our lives are *our* lives. You agree with me? Right?"

We didn't answer.

Bud joined her. "Come on. You know she's right.

You know that. Don't you? Jacob, Megan. Say something."

But we didn't.

We had a horrible choice. Megan and I could say what we thought and blow our cover, or we could simply lie and move ahead with our book.

Then Mark Stanton lost his very smooth coolness and shouted. "This is all bullshit, Bette. We'd have nothing if we didn't have the Store."

People were agreeing loudly, and more people began leaving. Some left quietly with a few polite farewells. Others left curtly, without so much as a good-bye.

"What should we do?" Megan said quietly to me.

"We should try to remember everything that's happening here right now. Then go home and write it all down."

CHAPTER 26

CARS WERE leaving the driveway quickly, as if they were fleeing a disaster. Only Marie remained. She was talking to Bette and Bud.

We heard Marie say, "Thanks for the party. But you guys'll have to learn when to keep your mouths closed. I'll come get my bowls tomorrow."

And then there were four. Bette and Bud. Megan and I.

"Well, thanks," I said. "It was really interesting. Fun and interesting."

Bette looked at Megan sadly.

"Did you really think so? The problem is—" but she was interrupted by a man's voice coming from the other end of the backyard.

"Excuse me, folks," the man said. Now we saw two police officers—one male, one female. They were walking toward us.

"We got some complaints about noise coming from a party here," the man said.

Bud—gruff and unhappy—spoke up. "It's only a barbecue. How noisy could it be?"

"Are you the owner of this residence?" the male officer said.

"Yeah, we both are," said Bette.

"Well, it might be time to send the guests home and start the cleanup," the officer said.

"We're the only guests left," I said.

"And we were just leaving," Megan added.

Both of us gave dumb little smiles to Bette and Bud. The police began heading back toward one end of the yard.

"Wait. Wait. Wait," Bud shouted. "Megan, Jacob. I just want to say one thing to you guys."

There was a pause. Bette was looking at the ground. Bud's eyes were wet.

"Promise me," Bud said. "Promise me you won't become like the rest of them."

Before I could say anything, Bette spoke.

"Bud, honey, don't ask them to make promises they can't keep."

CHAPTER 27

MEGAN AND I had plenty of juicy material to transcribe when we got home that night. We stayed up until well past 2:00 a.m., which may not have been the smartest idea. The next day was Monday, our early day. On Mondays we had to check in at the fulfillment center at 7:00 a.m.

"We've got a few minutes," I said to Megan as we turned in to our designated entry gate. "I'm going to see if we can stop by and see Bud at the chemical warehouse."

"They'll never let you visit a site that's not approved for you," Megan said.

She was probably right, but I wanted to give it a try. Plus I have enormous faith in my own powers of bullshit. So we gave the hundreds of surveillance cameras quite the workout. With the help of the Store Driving Assist app we pulled up in front of a security gate at the chemical warehouse around fifteen minutes later.

My electronically embedded entrance pass did not budge the steel gate. But it did, apparently, notify three security guards that people who had not been properly cleared were trying to get in.

"You folks lost?" said the small nervous-looking woman, accompanied by two male guards, who came out front to meet us.

"No. We know we're at the chemical warehouse. I wanted to drop by for a second before work and deliver a message to our friend Bud."

Megan spoke up. "We work at the fulfillment center."

"What's Bud's last name?" the woman asked.

"Robinson. Bud may not be his real first name. It could be a nickname."

The woman was pressing keys on her tablet.

"Nobody named Robinson here. Bud or otherwise," she said.

The two men were also pressing keys on their tablets. One of them said, "Wait a sec. Was this guy a security guard?"

"Where'd you see that?" the woman asked.

"He's on the T list," he said.

"Yes, he's a security guard," I said.

"Yeah, the T list," the woman said. "He and his wife are being transferred."

"What the hell does that mean?" I said way too loudly. I was feeling the same angry confusion I had felt when the librarian told us that her husband had been transferred, with no explanation.

"It means that the husband and wife have been transferred. Sometimes they send transfer candidates to the main office, in San Francisco, for debriefing before reassignment," one of the men said. Then the woman spoke.

"If I were you two, I'd get over to your jobs at the fulfillment center. You don't want to be late, Megan. You don't either, Jacob. Put in a good day's work. Then get on home to make a nice dinner for Alex and Lindsay."

We were becoming so used to everyone knowing everything about us that we weren't surprised that she knew our names.

All Megan and I knew was this: less than twelve hours after their barbecue, Bette and Bud were being transferred or had been transferred or were being debriefed before they were transferred.

Megan and I decided that we would be late for work.

CHAPTER 28

WE PULLED into Bette and Bud's driveway like two highway patrolmen on a chase. Even the brakes screeched as we made a fast stop and then walked quickly to the front door.

Doorbell. Short wait. A thirtyish woman, pretty enough, in jeans and a turquoise T-shirt, a headband holding her blond hair back. Since so many of the residents of New Burg looked like they could be related, I thought that possibly this woman was related to Bette. A cousin, maybe?

"Hey," I said. "Sorry to bother you so early in the day, but is Bud or Bette around?"

"Who?"

"Oh, we're the Brandeises. I'm Megan. He's my husband, Jacob."

"Hi," she said sweetly. "But what I meant is, who is it you're looking for?"

I was becoming as confused as the woman. "Bette and Bud Robinson. They live here."

"You must have the wrong house. I'm Tess Morris. My husband, Peter, and I just moved in here with our kids."

"When?" Megan asked. "When did you move in?"

"We flew in last night. We slept on some air mattresses, and the moving truck is out back, unloading our furniture. A few new neighbors even came by to help. I thought you might be part of that group."

There was a pause. All three of us were feeling awkward.

A man—quite tall, dark curly hair—walked in behind the woman at the door.

"Hi," he said. "I'm Pete Morris. We just moved in. What can I do for you?"

Tess Morris explained what our visit was about, that we were "mistakenly looking for a couple who don't live here."

"They were living here yesterday," Megan said. "We went to a barbecue…right here, early last night."

"I doubt it," said Pete. He was developing that "Are you crazy or what?" attitude. "There's not even a barbecue grill out back. I looked. And the rooms are all freshly painted. Come on in. You can get a whiff of the fresh paint."

We stepped inside. We'd been in this front hallway before. When Bette and Bud lived here it was painted a pale mint-green color. Now it was beige. I looked through the narrow passage that led to the kitchen. I saw Marie DiManno carrying a large cardboard moving carton. A moment later I watched Mark Stanton carrying a big crystal lamp.

"Yeah," I said. "The paint *does* smell fresh. The place looks great. But I've got to ask just one more time. You two never heard of Bette and Bud Robinson?"

"No. Never heard of them," Pete said.

Megan to the rescue.

"Well, whatever. Welcome to the neighborhood. We'll be by with a pie or a casserole or something. Really. Welcome," she said.

"Thanks," Tess Morris said. "I think this town is going to be perfect for us."

Just before we turned toward the open door, I said, "Yes. I think this place will be absolutely perfect for you."

CHAPTER 29

WE STIFLED any ideas we might have had about looking into Bette and Bud's disappearance. We had heard at the fulfillment center that there were two debriefing centers, one in San Francisco and one in Atlanta. But we didn't know how to begin, let alone where to begin. And with our day jobs at the Store and our night jobs on our book project, we were already running on only four or five hours of sleep a night.

The day job was stupid. Megan and I never got tired of complaining to each other about it. The work was hard. It was uninteresting. It was boring. Driving our Stormers around the vast fulfillment center was also surprisingly exhausting.

But the job had important advantages. We could fade anonymously into the routine of the thousands of people who worked at the Store and move easily among our fellow workers. Megan's sweet personality made her especially adept at getting people to relax and open up, sometimes with some juicy inside information about the goings-on at the Store. But even that was scary. Were our informants telling us the truth? Were they reporting back to some higher-ups that we were digging around for information? Who the hell ever knew what the real deal was at the Store?

And after just weeks on the job, in spite of the aches in our backs and the dullness in our brains, we were on our way to a great book.

"Look," I would often say. "A year from now we'll be back in New York, sitting on top of the world."

Megan would agree. Then she would say that we were going to be found out, that she and I and Alex and Lindsay would disappear from the face of the earth. We'd talk. We'd even cry sometimes. And then we did the only thing we could: we'd get back to work on the book.

So when the notice went out on everyone's personal message boards that the job of assistant group manager, reporting to Sam Reed, was available, Megan and I never even considered applying.

A few days later, while loading twenty cartons of environmentally friendly lightbulbs and three hundred cases of Fancy Feast Classic cat food on my Stormer, I received the following text message from Megan:

Unbelievable! They promoted me to the Asst Mgr job!

When Megan and I spoke at lunch, I said that I was shocked; she hadn't even applied for the job.

Megan said, "I would have been shocked, too… *except* our asshole manager Sam Reed is the one who told me about it. He said it was mainly his decision. He said it's because I have 'such a sweet attitude.'"

"And such a sweet ass," I added.

We both laughed. But let's face it. This kind of thing never makes a husband happy.

Megan and I agreed that the best way to proceed would be to act grateful to Sam and try to create more opportunities to get information for our book. So at the little congratulatory party for Megan (a few hundred people, exquisite Lafite Rothschild Bordeaux, and the same little caviar treats they'd served at Dr. Werner's rant), when Sam raised his glass to toast Megan and said, "Who'd have thought we'd welcome so much sunshine from New York?" Megan smiled.

Then she said, "I can't think of a nicer place to shine than right here in New Burg."

And the Oscar for best performance by a woman in a leading role goes to Megan Brandeis.

I couldn't help but think—at least for a second— that tomorrow Megan would be behind a desk and I'd be behind the wheel of a Stormer. Then I glanced toward the front of the room and watched Sam Reed and Megan. They were posing for photos. Phone cameras were clicking all over the place. I watched as Sam put his arm around the back of Megan's waist. I watched his hand inch slowly down to a place it shouldn't be. I watched and waited for Megan to push Sam's hand away. It didn't happen. Maybe she had to let Sam hold her. But then again, maybe she didn't.

My paranoia was not over the edge, but it sure as hell was heading in that direction.

I decided that all would be well for a while. Maybe I was being stupidly influenced by all those signs around the fulfillment centers that said NO WORRIES.

CHAPTER 30

"ALEX, YOU can turn off that damn camera *right now,*" Megan said. Her voice meant business.

We had both spotted Alex and Lindsay in our workroom-office, hiding behind a stack of old issues of the *Wall Street Journal*. They were making yet another video of us on their flat-vids, the little slim steel contraptions that let them text, phone, record, and edit videos.

For the past three days they had been shooting us nonstop. They shot us having coffee in the morning. They shot us on the phone, at the supermarket, washing the car, everywhere but in the shower and on the john—and I wasn't even sure we had escaped that humiliation. They told us, "We even have lots of great shots of you guys sleeping."

They said it was for a school project called Home Sweet New Burg.

"It's a collage-type thing," Alex explained. "Lots of quick cuts, you know? A really cool music track. Maybe Beck. Just like a really interesting documentary, you know?"

I *didn't* know. And the incessant filming was getting on my nerves.

"Okay," Lindsay said. "If you don't care about our school project, we'll just sit here quietly."

"Of course we care about your school project," Megan said, taking a deep breath. "But your father and I are working now. You know how important *our* project is."

"So we can't just sit here quietly?" Alex asked.

"Why would you even want to?" I asked.

Both Alex and Lindsay still had their standard New Burg smiles, but when Lindsay replied, there was a definite edge to her voice.

"Yeah. You're right. Why would we want to?"

She turned to Alex. "Let's go," she said.

And they disappeared out the door.

"Were we too harsh?" Megan said.

"No," I said. "It's unnerving—this sudden interest the kids have in hanging out with us."

"Maybe it's just a sign that they're growing up. They want to be with us."

"I never wanted to be with *my* parents," I said.

Megan said, "I'm not surprised. I've met your parents."

"Now, *that's* harsh."

"They just like to hang out with us. Is that so terrible?"

"I don't know," I said. "It seems that a lot of the time they spend with us they're not exactly... interacting. They don't talk very much. When we're online, when we're reading. They even come up to the office and..." I struggled for the words.

Megan said, "And hang out."

"No, not just hang out. Watch us. I feel like they're watching us."

She laughed. Then she leaned in and kissed me.

"The only things watching us," Megan said, "are the drones and the surveillance cameras."

"And now the drones and the surveillance cameras are watching our children watching us. Look. I'm worried. Sure, they love school. They love their friends and their teachers and…well, here's the thing. This project is a perfect example. They are so intense about it, so into it…it's like they're turning into…I don't know. They're just not the Alex and Lindsay I know."

"I understand, but it was bound to happen," Megan said.

"That they'd become strangers?"

"No. That they'd grow up."

We both returned to our laptops. But not for long. There was a knock, and suddenly Alex appeared in our workroom.

"Oh, honey," Megan said nicely. "No more video. Please."

"No," he said. "No more video. But there's something I've been wanting to say to you both." The smile was still on his face. So how bad could it be?

"Go ahead," I said.

"This book you two are doing…"

"What about it?" Megan asked.

"Stop it. Stop doing it. Stop writing it."

"Why?" I asked.

"Please, just stop it," he said.

And again I asked, "But why?"

"It's a *bad idea*."

The ever-present smile suddenly and completely left his face. Alex walked to the door. Then he turned and spoke one final time.

"A really bad idea."

CHAPTER 31

ON MONDAY morning Megan's boss, Sam Reed (known to Megan and me as Sam Slimeball), informed Megan that he and she would be attending a five-day conference for Store supervisors. It would be held at the main office, in San Francisco.

On Monday night I dreamed that Megan and Sam Reed were standing naked in the fulfillment center, loading a two-thousand-count carton of Trojan Ultra Ribbed lubricated latex condoms onto a Stormer that I was driving.

Okay, I know it was a fairly sick and predictable dream, but the next morning I told Megan that it might be a great idea if I tagged along on the San Francisco trip. After all, workers who had just started at the Store were automatically entitled to five vacation days.

"Don't waste your vacation time, Jacob. What's more, you're patronizing me. I'm no little girl. I can take care of myself."

"Look, we both know he's going to try to jump you when you two are away together," I said.

"Yeah, I'm sure he'll try to pull some shit. But I've put him in his place before, and I'll do it again…and again…and again."

"C'mon. I'll buy myself a cheap ticket and go. Maybe between the two of us we can get some really hot info for the book. Just tell Slimeball that I'm coming. I won't be in the way. Tell him we've never been to San Francisco, and we always wanted to climb Nob Hill."

"Well, first of all, that's a lie. We *have* been to San Francisco," she said.

"Big deal. Twenty years ago, when we were barely out of college and totally broke," I said. "Camping out in Golden Gate Park, eating lunch at soup kitchens, walking—"

Megan cut me off before I really started to stroll down memory lane.

"Okay. Much as I hate lying, I can live with that lie. But I know Sam's going to have a shit fit when I tell him you're joining us."

"Good. That makes me feel even better about going."

Megan turned out to be absolutely right about Sam Slimeball's reaction. He was pissed and disappointed and tried like hell to dissuade her. He said point-blank that this was an "opportunity" for him and Megan to really get to know each other.

Megan told me that she said, "That's exactly what I was afraid of: you want to really get to know me better."

Her response to Sam Reed's comment sounded a little too aggressive to believe, even for a strong woman like Megan.

But what the hell. Like I said, Megan wasn't lying. If that's what she said she said...then that's what she said.

I sure hoped I was right about that.

CHAPTER 32

IT TURNED out that Megan and Sam were booked on a separate charter flight with a big group of executive-level people from the Store. That group was flying out of Omaha, the airport where my family and I landed when we first arrived here.

Me? I was leaving two hours later from NBU— the airport code for New Burg, Nebraska.

If you accidentally happened upon New Burg International Airport, or—amazingly—had to fly out of the place, you'd think it was just another sleepy Midwest airport, home to a few business flights, a few private planes, some commuter flights, and a handful of crop dusters. If you ignored the two jet runways all you'd see is a smallish ramshackle wooden terminal. Like most everything in New Burg, the building is quaint and small and designed to be cute—in this case, sporting gray weathered shingles and storm fencing around a parking lot that could accommodate only around a dozen cars.

But like almost everything in New Burg, looks usually prove to be wildly deceiving.

I parked and removed my suitcase from the trunk. It is one of my really stupid affectations that I refuse to use a suitcase with wheels. Every time Megan and I are at an airport, whether it's Rio or London or New York, she never tires of pointing out the many men younger than I am who are easily rolling a wheeled suitcase.

The doorway to the simple wooden terminal was not automatic. It actually had a doorknob. I turned it. I walked inside, and a woman dressed in a red skirt and a blue blazer, a woman who looked like she might have stepped out of a 1950s television commercial, greeted me.

"Welcome to NBU, sir. May I see your boarding pass?" she said. She was neither sweet nor sour. She was perfectly New Burg polite.

I showed her the boarding pass. After she examined it she handed it back and gestured to a closed door behind her.

"Use this escalator here, sir," she said. This door *did* open automatically. I stepped aboard the escalator, and I swiftly descended. Within moments I was in the most elaborate modern room I'd ever entered. It had things you'd find in other airports—moving sidewalks, flashing arrival and departure signs, steel desks that seemed to signal airline gates—but the sidewalks were faster, the signs brighter, the steel desks taller.

Everything seemed bigger than normal, better than normal. The walkways were wider. The dome-like ceilings were higher.

I looked at the departure board, yet I saw nothing that indicated flights to San Francisco. No SFO. Lots of LGAs and JFKs and LAXs. But nothing to help me. The suitcase was beginning to feel heavier.

Then a woman—attractive, young, not wearing a uniform—approached me.

"Mr. Brandeis? Jacob Brandeis?" she asked.

"Yes, that's me."

"Wonderful."

"Yeah, it is wonderful," I said with a smile. She ignored my joke. I was beginning to realize that almost everyone in New Burg ignored my jokes. Maybe I just wasn't very funny.

She was holding a small electronic device. She looked down at it and then spoke.

"I see you're scheduled for the next flight to San Francisco. And that your wife left approximately two hours ago on a United flight from Omaha. And that you are traveling with two children," she said.

"Well, you're sort of right. My wife is traveling with a different group. But I was booked here by the Store."

"Right," she said, as if I had just told her that the sky was blue or the sun was hot.

"But you're scheduled to fly with two children, Alexander and Lindsay Anne."

"Yes. They're our children. But they're at home. They're in school," I said.

I was becoming nervous but not panicked-nervous. I was also noticing that almost every other person or group of people in the airport was being interviewed by a similarly attractive young woman using a handheld device. The only difference was that these other people seemed happy, almost giddy, in their conversations.

"Well," she said. "There has been some sort of mix-up. Let me try to straighten it out."

She punched some buttons.

Then she confirmed what she'd previously told me.

"No. The children should be with you. They must have Store child care and Store nutritional catering. They cannot be left alone."

"You see," I said, "they're old enough to be left alone. We've left them alone many times. They're perfectly capable.... The girl is—"

I was preparing myself for a big-time run-in with this woman. Suddenly she spoke, this time with a ridiculously wide grin.

"No problem, Jacob. No problem."

She then hit a few more keys on her handheld and continued speaking.

"Child-Care Look-In Assistance has been contacted, and both morning and evening meals have been arranged for nutritional standardization and accurate drone delivery."

All I could get out of my mouth was "Good. That's good."

"Gate 11," she said with that damned stupid smile. "Your San Francisco flight leaves in forty-five minutes. Enjoy."

Then she added, "Be at peace."

"By the way," I said. "What's the airline I'm flying?"

She smiled. Then she spoke.

"As I said, Mr. Brandeis. Be at peace."

CHAPTER 33

A LOT of things about San Francisco were unchanged since our visit twenty years ago. The charming cable cars still struggled up the hills, and the Golden Gate Bridge remained awesomely beautiful in its strange industrial orange paint.

Yet many other things had changed enormously. It wasn't just the hundreds of new forty-story buildings scraping the heavens or all those Silicon Valley billionaires jamming up the traffic with their Porsches and Mercedes.

One group of changes was particularly frightening to Megan and me. It was as if the little town of New Burg had been exploded into a giant chic city.

Government-placed CCTV cameras and Store-placed surveillance cameras were posted everywhere: on top of traffic lights and building entrances, on the refrigerated cases in delis, hidden in the stained-glass windows of Saint Mary's Cathedral, even on the doors of the bathroom stalls in AT&T Park.

Miniature audio pickups dotted every coffee-shop table and every department-store counter and every hotel room. There were audio recorders in the taxis, the buses, the cable cars. There were cameras in the restaurants, the parks, the ferry to Alcatraz. Lots of people wore surgical masks, not merely because of the filthy air, I thought, but also because it helped hide their identities.

Just as depressing and creepy were the heavens above. That sunless sky was no longer just the result of the notorious San Francisco fog. No, the skies were also dark because they were thick with surveillance drones and delivery drones and research drones. The new San Francisco made me very scared, but it also made me very sad. I had seen the future, and it clearly belonged to the Store.

And oh, yes. One other thing had changed during this trip, and that other thing had nothing to do with San Francisco. It had everything to do with our obnoxious boss, Sam Reed.

Sam Reed, the same guy who couldn't keep his hands off my wife, the same guy who spoke to me as if I were a mongrel, had suddenly turned into my best bud. For no apparent reason.

"Hey, Jacob, I scored some tickets for the Giants-Dodgers game tonight. How about Megan does some shopping at Gump's and takes in a museum or two while we do the game? Then we can all meet up for a late dinner." Huh?

Here's another equally creepy and unexpected burst of humanity from Sam:

"Look, Jacob, I can't invite you to join Megan and me for tomorrow morning's lectures and meetings, but I can hook you in to the afternoon trip to Napa that they planned for us."

Both Megan and I were super suspicious, to say the least—Mr. Hyde was morphing into Dr. Jekyll way too easily.

Back at the Fairmont, where I was changing for our ball game, we discussed "the new Sam Reed."

As always, Megan didn't care that the surveillance cameras were recording our every word. She let fly with her opinion.

"He's up to something," Megan said. "There's no way someone like Sam can turn into Mr. Nice Guy overnight."

"Let's not push the Cynical button so fast," I said. "Maybe he's just sort of getting to know us, and he thinks, like, we're funny and smart and decent and—"

"Don't kid yourself, Jacob," Megan said. "Remember when we asked him about Bette and Bud yesterday? He just click-clacked his iPad, and in about ten seconds he said, 'Nope. Just transferred. Not here for a debriefing. Never were.'"

"Maybe that's all the info he got."

"Oh, come on. His voice turned to ice. His Mr. Nice Guy act totally folded. I think he was genuinely happy telling us that Bette and Bud were nowhere to be found. Think whatever you want," she added. "But I don't trust him one teensy little bit."

"I guess you're right," I said. "But we might as well enjoy the new Sam while we can. You know, before the old Sam reappears."

"You enjoy him," she said. "I'm not moving in too close."

I slipped into my jeans, and Megan pinned her hair on top of her head. As she dabbed on some eye makeup and pulled a fairly snug navy-blue T-shirt over her head, I couldn't help but think about her and Sam.

We both certainly knew him as a first-class sleazeball, but wasn't it just possible that he had settled down? Megan wasn't buying it "one teensy little bit." I sure didn't like the guy, but Megan actually hated him.

Or at least that's what she wanted me to think.

CHAPTER 34

THE MOST important event of the San Francisco conference was a totally mind-boggling surprise— a presentation by Thomas P. Owens, founder of the Store.

The fact was that nobody in the organization really knew Mr. Owens. Everyone seemed to believe he was in seclusion. One source said he was on a ranch in Brazil. Another said he had a twenty-room penthouse in Sardinia. We investigated every lead, and everything led to a dead end. Almost no one had ever met the guy.

Because of our secret book, Megan and I had some pretty hefty files on Owens. But even after we read all the information we had accumulated, even after we analyzed every business article about him, even after we tracked down and briefly interviewed a woman who claimed to be his illegitimate daughter, we knew just as little about Owens as everyone else did. Whether he was hiding behind a curtain somewhere in New York, in his hometown of Lorain, Ohio, or in the Land of Oz itself, nobody seemed to know. Yet everyone seemed to care.

I had no business being at Gallery 16, the terminally hip modern art gallery and exhibition hall where Thomas P. Owens was to appear. But I lucked out.

My new best friend, Sam Reed, had arranged for me to attend. A young doctor (at least I think he was a doctor) came to our room and administered an injection into my left elbow. He told me that the injection registered on a supersurveillance board and would allow me three-hour clearance and access to the event. Sam told me that this was standard procedure for admission to Owens's appearances.

When Sam, Megan, and I arrived at Gallery 16, Sam suggested, "You make yourself semi-scarce. You know, stand in the back with a few other illegal interlopers." Both Megan and Sam laughed a bit, but I obeyed. I made myself semi-scarce with a bunch of waiters and Store photographers standing on the sidelines. Meanwhile Sam and Megan were in the high-class seats—first row, on the aisle.

From where I was standing I had an excellent view of the eighty or so management members who filled the other seats. The men wore either blue blazers or dark suits. The women wore either dark slacks or modest dark dresses.

But the conservative clothes and the traditional New Burg smiles (even Megan had pasted a smile onto her face) could not disguise the fact that the room was electric with excitement. People were embracing. Some looked on the verge of tears. Everyone was talking excitedly. There is really only one way to describe it: this crowd was waiting for the Messiah.

Finally a woman walked to the front of the room. She stood directly in front of an Andy Warhol blue *Queen Elizabeth II* print. The audience became completely silent. The woman turned toward the audience and flashed the New Burg smile. I quickly recognized her as the woman who had presided over the disastrous Dr. David Werner lecture. She was apparently the official hostess for all off-site meetings at the Store.

I could not resist speaking to the female stranger standing next to me.

"That woman is wearing an Isabel Toledo dress," I said.

"Oh, good," she said, then she moved a few inches away from me.

The onstage woman spoke: "I must say that I share your exhilaration and anticipation at this very rare opportunity to meet and greet the Store's founder and conscience, Mr. Thomas P. Owens."

The applause was wildly enthusiastic.

"As such, you can imagine that I then share your deep disappointment in learning just a few minutes ago that Mr. Owens will not be able to join us this afternoon."

The moans, the shout-outs of "What?" "Why not?" "What happened?"

"Mr. Owens sends his deepest apologies and his warmest wishes for a fruitful and invigorating conference in the Bay Area. Please enjoy the beverages at the various bars, and don't miss the omelet and crepe station and the blini and caviar station."

The hostess walked away and into the groups of people that were forming around the room. The New Burg smiles had all but disappeared. Some people held one another. Others bowed their heads. A handful of them were dabbing at their eyes; they were actually weeping. Is this what happens when you're expecting the Messiah and he fails to show up?

I almost could not believe what I was seeing, and

when I glanced toward the first row I truly could not believe what I was seeing. Megan and Sam.

What the hell was happening? Megan was crying. I also saw that Sam Reed had his arms around her. Apparently he was trying to comfort her.

Sure.

CHAPTER 35

I DIDN'T have time to be pissed off about the warm hug Sam had just wrapped around Megan.

No. I had something much bigger to be pissed off about: Megan and I had been summoned for "an in-depth interview and analysis" at the Store headquarters.

"It's no big deal," Sam told us. "They knew Megan was here, and of course they found out immediately that you had come along, Jacob. So it looked to the senior interview committee like perfect timing."

"But they asked us every conceivable question in the world when they interviewed us back in New Burg," Megan said. "Does everyone get this interview treatment? Or is it just those of us who might be a little out of control?"

"Not *everybody* has this interview. There's no pattern to who gets it. It's kinda random," Sam said. "Look. It's only around an hour, and everyone's really nice, and it's just for their records, and—"

"And I guess we can't say we won't do it," I said.

The stern, nasty voice of the "real" Sam Reed returned.

"I wouldn't recommend it."

So that afternoon Megan and I sat in a very large, very stark conference room containing nothing but four comfortable leather chairs and a small glass coffee table on top of which sat a silver pitcher of coffee, another of tea, and four bottles of mineral water.

Our interviewers were a man and a woman. Like everyone employed by the Store, they were unfailingly polite and friendly, but they did not offer their names when we shook hands. The two of them looked like they were in their twenties. They looked more like graduate students, and in fact I wondered if Megan and I were so unimportant in the great scheme of the Store that we were just practice interviewees for these "kids."

The woman said, "Let's begin. But I should mention that you may find the first few questions a bit…shall we say…obvious or ridiculous." Then she read from her laptop.

"From the following list, select the group you would most likely want to be part of: A, the Church of Scientology; B, the Ku Klux Klan; C, the Store."

"Before I struggle to answer, let me just say you were almost right," I said. "The questions are…shall we say…obvious *and* ridiculous."

"Well," the young man said, "wait till you hear the next one." Then he read from his laptop.

"Of the many wonderful foods available at the various markets and delivery services in New Burg, what would you say is your family's favorite?"

It didn't take a degree in psychology to realize that the whole "ridiculous" conversation was meant to disarm Megan and me, turn the interviewers and the interviewees into old friends. So the four of us chuckled along for a few minutes.

But within five minutes, the nature of the questions began to change.

"So a writer like you, Jacob, can't be very satisfied gathering products down at the fulfillment center. You must be doing some writing in your spare time."

I had barely given my evasive, bullshitty response when the woman interviewer asked: "What private writing project are you working on now, Jacob? Something personal? Something autobiographical? Something about your employer? You can be honest with us."

Yeah. Sure. I would cut off my hands at the wrists rather than tell them the truth. So I said, "I am writing, but it's nothing important, nothing that's really come together. In a way it's autobiographical. I'll let you know as I get a little further into it."

With her smile in place, the young woman said, "I'm sure you will. That'd be great."

The young man leaned in toward us with that phony-looking concern usually found in insurance salesmen and annoying uncles.

"The children—Alex and Lindsay. How are they adjusting to their new environment?"

"Really well. They love school. They've made friends," Megan said.

"Yeah. The kids are probably doing better than Megan and I are."

The two interviewers looked unpleasantly or pleasantly surprised (it was hard to tell those two expressions apart in New Burg). Megan shot me a look that more or less meant, "Don't be such an asshole."

The young man got us back on track immediately.

"I understand that Alex is pretty much the star of the junior boxing team."

Alex? Boxing? The star? The only sport Alex was

ever interested in is played on a big soft sofa. The equipment is an electronic device, and that device is attached to a television monitor.

"In the spirit of honesty," I said. "Alex's boxing is complete news to me. Did he tell you about this, Megan?"

"Oh, he may have mentioned it once. I'm not sure," she said. As I said, she was not a good liar.

Then the young woman spoke.

"Perhaps he kept this information from you, Mr. Brandeis, because he knows of your abhorrence of rough contact sports like boxing and football."

"I've never discussed that subject with Alex."

"But my statement does correctly reflect your beliefs. You are opposed to boxing in principle."

"Well, yes. But I've never discussed that with Alex or anyone else. I mean, it's a belief, not…I don't know…not an obsession or a cause or a passion or…"

"If we could, let's return briefly to another subject. Mrs. Brandeis, do you assist your husband on the book he's writing?"

I stood up. And I was furious.

"What the hell are you talking about—'the book your husband is writing'? I just told you that I have some thoughts about writing a book. I'm not actually writing a book! I gotta tell you, I don't even know what the purpose of this interview is. I realize that with all your cameras and spies and shit you know a lot about what we do. But this is all crazy. Absolutely crazy."

The woman suggested we take a break, and I stupidly realized, belatedly, that the two mirrors against the mostly bare walls of the room were most likely two-way, that we were being watched during the interview.

"No. We don't need a break. Because we don't need an interview," I said.

"Jacob, please. Let's try to cooperate," Megan said, and frankly I couldn't believe she was saying it.

Then the young man spoke.

"We really don't have much more to cover—a few questions about a police raid at a house party you attended, and then—"

"The interview is absolutely over," I said. Now I was screaming. "We're leaving."

Megan was still seated. I glared at her. She slowly stood up and picked up her pocketbook from the floor.

"Do whatever you want with us," I said. "Transfer us. Put us in jail. Shoot us. Whatever. We are out of here."

CHAPTER 36

MEGAN HAS two kinds of anger: anger that screams and anger that doesn't speak a word. There was no predicting which one was going to erupt. I had guessed that after my behavior at the interview there would be a lot of shouting and swearing and declarations of "I don't care if I'm making a scene." As is often the case, I turned out to be wrong. Dead wrong.

Megan was completely silent as we walked back to the hotel. That's precisely the kind of anger I didn't want. I wanted her to scream at me and tell me how stupidly I had acted at the "interview." I wanted her to get it out of her system, and by doing that to force me back into the frightening world of the Store.

"Okay, okay," I said, trying to force some reaction from her. "I was a complete fool. I should have listened and answered and played along."

She said nothing.

"I know our whole future depends on writing this book. I know I've seriously jeopardized it. I know I behaved like an idiot. And I know you have every right in the world to be pissed off at me."

Still nothing.

The very normal creepiness of the San Francisco

streets only made things worse. This was a big, beautiful city version of New Burg: the drones clogging the sky, one of them clearly assigned to Megan and me; it moved like a big electronic umbrella over our heads. Then there were the tiny video cameras embedded in building walls and stop signs and the rims of trash cans. The trash cans themselves were models of Store efficiency: drop a piece of paper or plastic into the mouth of the garbage container, and the item was silently sucked into a below-ground recycling system.

It was all perfect and neat and scary as shit…at least to me.

Suddenly Megan stopped walking. Her head was bowed. I stopped also.

"Listen to me, Jacob. This is important for you to understand. I'm *not* angry at you. I love you. But it feels like you've just gone over the edge. And I understand that. This new world, this new place, these new rules…they're very hard on you. But your behavior makes things impossible for the rest of us—for Lindsay and Alex…and for me."

"But it was so outrageous what they were doing in that interview room," I began.

"Yes. Yes. It was outrageous. I know that, and you know that. But this sudden inability you've developed—the fact that you simply can't hold your temper inside you for…for…well, the only way I know how to put it is 'for the greater good'—has become kind of a problem. I'm worried."

"Don't worry," I said. "I know that everything will—"

"Turn out all right? No. You don't know that at all." Couples who are really invested in being couples can always finish each other's sentences.

Megan kept talking. "I'm worried about what

you've turned into. We're all *on* the edge. But I think you may have gone *over* the edge."

I put my arms on her shoulders. I moved in a step to hold her, hug her. She began to cry. Nothing big, just short little bursts of sobs.

Shit! Was there any truth in what Megan was thinking and feeling and saying? Was I becoming a strange new person in this strange new world? Yeah, for sure I hated this insanity of complete automation—no books, no pens, no humans manning the trolleys and trains. I was not adapting. I was still always reaching for paper money to pay for things, yet in this new world only cards and cell phones tendered valid currency. I missed everything about my old life. I wanted to watch a crappy Knicks game on a TV set, not see the game on some handheld interactive screen. I wanted to go to the supermarket and squeeze the honeydew melons and get suckered into buying cereal we didn't need. I didn't want to push some buttons and have our pantry reload automatically.

Even as I held Megan close, I looked around and could not feel calm. There were so many people on the street wearing masks and earphones and environmental-protection jumpsuits. The very air had a perpetual scent of a combination of rubber and ammonia as well as just a touch of something floral. I called it gardenia vomit.

Megan looked up and smiled at me. "Gardenia vomit getting to you?" she said. Then we continued to walk.

"Christ," I said. "I hope I haven't screwed things up for us."

I was hoping Megan would say something like "Of course not. Everything will be okay."

But she said nothing. We kept walking.

We were at the hotel now. The drone that was trailing us drifted skyward. In-hotel devices would be taking over our surveillance.

The doorman opened the door and spoke cordially. "Welcome back, Mr. and Mrs. Brandeis. There are two people waiting for you in the lobby."

CHAPTER 37

"HEY, BRANDEISES! Over here!"

It was a woman's voice, happy and loud.

"Look to your right. We're over here," shouted a man.

Megan's own voice suddenly changed to little-girl wonder.

"Oh, my God! It's Bette and Bud!" she shouted.

Oh, my God. It *was* Bette and Bud. They both looked a little younger, a little thinner, a little...well, a little "cooler" than they did back in New Burg.

We hugged. We kissed. We did that thing you do when you hold a person at arm's length and then lean back and look at him or her from head to toe. Bette, Bud, and I sat on a sofa; Megan sat on a big club chair.

"You guys look terrific," I said. And I meant it. It felt like six months since they'd left New Burg, and now they were looking around ten years younger.

"You really do look terrific," Megan said. Since Megan was the thoughtful brains of our outfit, she added, "I mean, you always looked good, but you've both lost weight, and Bette's haircut is *très* chic, and...I dunno...everything. Like, your skin is healthy, and these clothes are all Ralph Laureny."

I guess she finally ran out of compliments to hand out. Megan turned silent but kept on smiling. It should have been a perfect time for Bette and Bud to tell us how terrific we both looked.

"Well, Megan looks as beautiful as ever," Bette said.

"She certainly does. Looks even younger than when we last saw each other," Bud added.

Uh-huh, I was thinking. *Keep going, folks. Tell me how great I look.*

Instead Bud smiled and said, "Now, you, on the other hand, Jacob, look like you've been working too hard. Are they working you too hard?" He chuckled.

"No. Hard but not too hard," I said.

"And he's lost about ten pounds since the last time you saw him," chimed in Megan. "Without trying to lose it."

"What? Are you three ganging up on me? Maybe I need a makeover."

I laughed, but nobody else laughed. I was pissed off, but nobody seemed to notice.

"Listen, Jacob," said Bette. "I'm a big proponent of watching your weight, but too thin is just as bad as too fat."

Megan said "Amen." I looked at her with that what-the-hell-is-going-on-here look. She smiled and said, "It's all for your own good."

I was thinking that whenever someone said that something was for your own good, it never really was. But even more, I was thinking how hurt and angry I was that Megan jumped on the "Doesn't Jacob look like shit" bandwagon.

Fortunately a waiter came to take a drink order (on his electronic pad, of course; I think I was the last person in America who still used an old-fashioned lead pencil).

Megan asked for a vodka and tonic. Bette ordered Diet Coke. Bud ordered club soda ("and don't go putting any lime twist in it, ya hear?"). I ordered a Chivas on the rocks.

"You guys on the wagon?" I asked.

"Not really," Bette said. "We're just trying to cut back. That's always good advice."

I wondered why she felt she needed to call what she said good advice.

Megan then told them that we had tried to locate them when we'd arrived in San Francisco.

"Well, we didn't come to San Francisco when we *first* got transferred," Bette said. "They sent us to San Diego."

"San Jose," Bud corrected her.

"Oh, all these saints," Bette said. "Clara, Monica, Anita, Diego, Clemente. I can't remember where I am half the time."

"So tell us," Megan said. "What are you doing here? It seems like you just disappeared from New Burg overnight."

"Well, we *did* leave New Burg overnight," Bette said. "Some exec at the Store called and said they'd send a car to take us to the airport and have a private company plane at the airport to whisk us away to…" She hesitated for a moment. "San Jose.

"So that's where we're living and working. Only about an hour from here. I'm at the fulfillment center in San Mateo.…There ya go, another saint's name," she added.

Bette and Bud looked at each other with bright eyes and broad smiles. In fact it seemed like they hadn't stopped smiling since the moment we'd spotted them.

I should have dropped the subject. I tried, but I couldn't.

"Look. We're your friends. You were our best friends in New Burg. Tell us what happened," I said, perhaps a bit too intensely.

"What happened, Jacob, is what we told you," said Bud, the smile gone from his face. "They called. They said they wanted us to get ready. The plane was ready. So *we* got ready. And we got transferred."

I was becoming very impatient. My voice shot up pretty loudly.

"Who the hell is 'they'? Who is the 'they' that called? And why did it have to be overnight, immediately? And what exactly does it mean to be transferred? Answer me. Tell me. You two just disappeared. That's not normal! That's not natural!"

"Calm down, Jacob," Megan said.

Bette spoke. "It seemed perfectly natural to us."

"It's not!" I shouted. "It's not perfectly natural to be flown off in the middle of the night to a new place. That's not how things happen in this world."

There was a long pause. I took a big gulp of my Scotch. Then Bud spoke.

"That's exactly how things happen in *this* world. And if for some reason it doesn't seem perfectly natural to you, that's fine. But it does seem perfectly natural to us."

The Refill button on the coffee table in front of us was flashing. We all ignored it, and the flashing eventually stopped.

Bette tried to restore order. Her sweet little voice came into the conversation as if nothing unpleasant or argumentative had been said.

"So," she said. "That's how the transfer happened. A private plane, a zip-zip-zip out to San Jose."

"All in a few hours?" Megan asked. "That's amazing."

"Actually, it's kinda creepy," I said. Megan reached out and patted my hand gently. I was becoming an expert at saying the wrong thing. And Megan was becoming an expert at bailing me out.

"I don't think it's creepy," Megan said. "I think it actually sounds kinda cool."

"And that plane ride sure was luxurious. Just six seats on the plane, a full kitchen, a bar..." Bud began rattling on.

"Pipe down, Bud," Bette said with a chuckle. "I'm sure the Brandeises have been on a private plane."

"Well, if you think that, then you'd be wrong," I said. Bette and Bud laughed so hard you'd have thought Joan Rivers had left me that punch line in her will.

The laughter stopped. But our old friends never stopped smiling. The anger and cynicism they had both harbored about the Store seemed to have completely evaporated. Here they were in their cool clothes and their smiley faces, happy in their jobs and happy in their lives.

We finished our drinks.

I did ask them how they knew Megan and I were in San Francisco.

Bud casually replied, "Oh, you guys know how everyone in the Store knows everything about everyone else."

"That's part of the charm of it," Megan said.

"Yeah. A big part of the charm," I added.

I don't think either Bette or Bud knew for sure whether I was being sarcastic or not.

We chatted for a while about our kids, their new house, Bette's new haircut. Then it was time to say good-bye.

We all stood up and said how great it was to catch

up. It felt like old times. Bette and Megan hugged each other. Bud hugged Megan. Then, just before we went our separate ways, Bud turned and gave me an unexpected hug as well.

"Don't forget," he whispered in my ear. "You never know for sure whether you can trust us."

CHAPTER 38

MEGAN AND I watched Bette and Bud leave. We sat silently in the lobby. After a few minutes I said, "I'm sorry, sweetie. I'll be better. I'll control myself." Then I made those little quotation marks with my fingers and said, "I'll get with 'the program.'"

Megan nodded gently.

Nighttime had sneaked up on us. It was eight o'clock, and I was hungry.

"You want to go get some food? We haven't had anything since breakfast."

"Sure," Megan said. It was not a good, solid "Sure," but it was a yes nonetheless.

"Should we text Sam and see if he wants to join us?" I asked.

"No," she said. "There's some important meeting of big shots that he has to go to. We're on our own."

After consulting the concierge, we headed south to the Nob Hill Café. "Nearby and reasonable," he had said. "You've sure got our profile," I had answered.

"Yes, I do," said the concierge, and I realized he wasn't joking.

The night had that chill that everyone says is special to San Francisco. So we walked quickly.

It was the usual crowd: tourists, natives, people in surgical masks, drones overhead, and, of course, our personal drone hovering over Megan and me. Megan never seemed to mind the surveillance. It always made me furious.

As one of the WALK signs changed to DON'T WALK, I said, "Let's go. We can beat this light."

"No," she said. "I hate it when you cross against the light."

"C'mon. I'm cold."

We started to cross. Our drone was keeping up with us. It swooped in low, very low, almost hitting us.

Immediately there was the sound of a car horn. We saw a huge SUV, a Chevy Tahoe, a foot or two away from us. We managed to stop short and avoid it. The low-flying drone was not so lucky. The drone slammed mercilessly into the driver's side of the SUV. The crash was deafening. The crash was hideous. The Tahoe crumbled into a broken smashed mess of steel. Immediately fire began raging under the hood of the vehicle. People gathered around the crash; others ran from the blaze. The fire spread almost instantly throughout the rest of the Tahoe. The battered and squashed drone was trapped in the rear part of the SUV, snug against the disfigured, bloody faces of two small children. The two kids in the back and what looked like the mom and dad in the front burned like fireplace logs, as if gasoline had been poured on them, and then—*boom!*—they ignited.

Megan and I and four other people tried to get to the passengers, but the heat was unbearable, and it was clearly too late to help.

We heard distant sirens and a few crazy-sounding old-fashioned fire engine bells. As we watched, we realized to our horror that there was another child in the way-back section. That kid was also on fire.

A car marked SFPD arrived with three police officers inside. Then we heard an insistent, relentless beeping noise from above. Within a minute, two massive drones swept down to the scene of the accident. Each drone had mechanical claws dropping from its base down to the twisted, burning mess below. One drone clamped its claws onto the front of the SUV. The other drone performed the identical maneuver at the rear. Together they lifted the entire vehicle, including our personal drone—part of this awful piece of steel sculpture—into the dark city skies. It seemed like a strange mechanical ballet as the burning SUV was lifted up and up and up, looking from a distance like a flying piece of slowly dying charcoal.

The few people who remained on the scene watched until the SUV disappeared. The three policemen told people to move on.

I walked toward one of the cops.

"I saw this all happen, Officer. I was even sort of involved. Let me—" I said.

"Please move on, sir. It's over."

"Jacob, please. Let's go," Megan shouted.

"But—" I said.

Suddenly there were the sounds you usually hear when a truck backs up—that irritating *beep-beep-beep*. Sure enough, the sound was coming from two trucks, but they weren't backing up. They were driving straight down Mason Street very slowly. Each one looked like a very modernist marriage between a garbage truck and a sleek luxury bus. Big heavy steel scrapers—like enormous spatulas— were attached to their fronts. They gathered debris—scraps of metal, burned luggage, a Coca-

Cola cooler—and then lifted it into construction bins attached to the trucks' sides.

Then it was over. Totally over.

The people dispersed. The streets were clean. The trucks drove away. Five people had died brutally, yet it was as if nothing had happened.

"I feel like I just stepped in and out of a nightmare," I said to Megan.

A lone policeman's voice: "I thought I told you folks to move along."

We weren't hungry anymore. We headed back to our hotel. A new drone—a replacement drone—was now assigned to follow us.

"That was fast," the concierge said. We said nothing.

Back in our rooms, we immediately turned on our computers. Local websites? Nothing. National websites? Nothing. AOL? CNN? Nothing. We turned on the television. TV news? Nothing.

The next morning the *San Francisco Chronicle* was delivered to our hotel room door. The Metro section? Nothing.

Nothing. Nothing. Nothing. As if the accident had never happened.

CHAPTER 39

"I HAVEN'T heard a word about it," Sam said.

Megan, Sam, and I were on our way to the San Francisco airport. The taxi driver had barely closed the car trunk when I asked Sam if he'd known about the SUV accident the night before. He didn't.

"That's unbelievable," I replied.

Megan gently but firmly disagreed with me.

"C'mon, Jacob. It was pretty awful, yes, but not *that* newsworthy. I mean, it wasn't 9/11," she said. I was fairly outraged that Sam laughed at Megan's uncharacteristically tasteless joke.

The check-in machines spat out our tickets, and when I looked at mine it said SPEED-CHECK. I assumed that we all were going to go through speed-check, but it appears I was alone in receiving this convenience.

"Well, aren't *you* special?" Sam said with another laugh, and I headed toward the speed-check area with—okay, I admit it—a slightly smug farewell: "See you at the gate," I said to Megan and her boss.

Good luck turned into bad luck in approximately five seconds. The moment I showed my boarding pass to the guard, he asked me to step aside and join him at "the desk." That desk turned out to be a small, cheap-looking card table parked in front of a metal door bearing the sign SECURITY: APPROVED PERSONNEL ONLY. A middle-aged woman wearing one of those uniforms that's supposed to remind you of the police smiled at me and then spoke.

"Were you in San Francisco for business or pleasure, Mr. Brandeis?"

"Uh, both."

"What type of business was it?" she asked.

"I work for the Store. They were having a national meeting."

She pushed a few buttons on her computer, scrolled down a few pages, and then spoke again.

"I don't have you listed at that meeting, sir. There's a Megan Brandeis on the—"

"She's my wife," I said. I glanced up and saw that Sam and Megan had already passed through "normal" security, but speed-check had me waiting. Then the security woman signaled to another agent, who was holding an electronic wand.

"If you don't mind, Mr. Brandeis, this officer is going to screen you electronically."

I did mind, of course, but this was no time to make a scene.

The wanding procedure took less than fifteen seconds.

"That's fine, Mr. Brandeis," the woman said. "Now we'd like to continue the screening privately. This officer from airport security would like you to accompany him through this door to an examination booth."

"What? Are you kidding me?" I said.

"No, sir. I am not. It's a normal procedure, for your own safety as well as everyone else's. Just through this door behind me," she said.

"But why?"

"It's just a procedure, sir. If you care to continue with boarding, please cooperate."

"But *why?*" I asked again.

"Sir, please," she said. By this time the other agent had opened the SECURITY door. Before I walked through the door I looked out toward the area where Megan and Sam had been standing. After a few seconds I spotted them. Sam was talking on his cell phone. Megan was talking on hers.

The agent holding the door open spoke for the first time.

"We're losing patience, sir. Please come with me."

CHAPTER 40

SWEATING. PANTING. Dry-mouthed. That was me, the last passenger to board United Airlines flight 5217 from SFO to Omaha.

My boarding pass was clenched between my teeth. My shirttail was flying like a miniskirt over my chinos. And I only hoped to God that I had remembered to put my laptop back in my carry-on after the twenty-minute security check.

Immediately I ran into my traveling companions, Megan and Sam…in first class. To add insult to injury, they were both sipping Champagne.

"We thought you missed the flight, man," Sam said. "We were worried."

I couldn't figure out whether he actually *was* worried or whether he simply was trying to *sound* worried.

"What happened, Jacob?" Megan asked. She probably thought that I had done something to cause the delay.

A flight attendant behind me said, "We're ready for takeoff, sir. Please take your seat."

"Yes, ma'am," I said. I guess I was getting used to taking orders.

"I upgraded Megan and me to first class," Sam said. "But we'll trade seats. You sit here with your wife. I don't mind flying in the back." Before I could protest his generous gesture he had grabbed my boarding pass and headed through the curtains to the back. I settled in next to Megan, and we both remained silent throughout the safety instruction video.

Megan broke the silence only seconds after "…and we do hope you enjoy the flight."

"Jacob," she said. "I was worried about you. So was Sam."

"Well, you couldn't have been *that* worried. I saw you two on your cell phones," I said, sounding a lot like a six-year-old.

"We just assumed you had gone to the men's room or gone to pick up a sandwich or something. Oh, Jacob," she said, her eyes full of concern and her hands reaching to touch my shoulder and arm. "I feel terrible. What happened?"

I was about to tell her when a voice came through the loudspeaker.

"This is your captain, Brian Heller. Before takeoff we have some final luggage checking to take care of. It shouldn't take more than a few minutes. Then we'll be off to lovely Omaha, where the temperature is…sixty-three degrees. Thanks for your patience."

Almost immediately, two flight attendants appeared at my seat.

"Mr. Brandeis?" the male attendant asked.

"Yes."

"I understand that this is not your originally assigned seat."

More grief, I assumed.

"Well, a friend of mine gave me his—"

"Yes," the woman attendant said. "No problem, Mr. Brandeis. However, the captain…" There was a pause. Then the male flight attendant chimed in.

"The captain would like to examine your carry-on luggage, sir. Is this backpack the only luggage you brought aboard?" he asked as he lifted the backpack resting on my lap.

"Well, yeah. But why does he need—I mean, I've never had this happen before."

"Please, sir," said the attendant.

"Jacob, please, just do it. I'm sure it's nothing," said Megan.

The two flight attendants took the backpack, and they brought it through the open cockpit door.

"I'm going to see what's going on," I said to Megan, and I started to unbuckle my seat belt.

"Just stay put," Megan said. She spoke firmly. She seemed amazingly calm herself.

Within a few minutes, the male flight attendant returned with the backpack.

"Thank you for your cooperation, sir. No problem," he said.

"What were you looking for?" I asked with a touch of impatience.

"Just a precaution, sir. Thank you. Can I get you some Champagne or fresh-squeezed orange juice, sir, when we reach our cruising altitude?"

"No, thank you," I said.

Captain Heller's voice again: "Flight attendants, please prepare for takeoff."

The plane taxied down the runway, and we were off.

"Tell me what happened in that speed-check place," Megan said.

"You and Sam saw it," I began.

"No, we didn't. We didn't know anything was wrong."

"Okay, okay," I said. "They took me off the line. They brought me into a special room, and two guys searched me. It was…forget it. The details are kinda gross."

"Gross?" she said. "What happened?"

"I had to strip down to my underwear. So I stood there, practically naked, and they wanded me… everywhere—my ears, my neck, my armpits, my crotch. They both had rubber gloves on, and one of them put his hand…"

I paused. For some reason I felt like I was about to cry.

"Oh, forget it," I said. "You can imagine the rest."

"Oh, my God," she said. "That's horrible. No wonder you're so upset."

I closed my eyes and opened them about five minutes later. Megan had taken out her laptop and was busily tapping away at it. When I looked out the plane window I saw at least forty drones flying alongside the plane. They looked like huge black-and-gray birds in a formation flying south for the winter.

"Holy shit!" I said.

"What's the matter?" Megan said.

"Out the window. Around a million drones."

Megan glanced out the window for a few seconds.

"Oh, Jacob, please. They're delivering merchandise."

I was silent for a few seconds. Then I turned and looked at her squarely, face-to-face, close in. I spoke.

"You think I'm crazy, don't you?"

There was only a momentary pause, but that moment felt like an hour.

"No. I don't think you're crazy. I think you're tired."

"But the drones—"

"Jacob. C'mon. Like I said. They're just delivery drones. There's nothing to be afraid of."

CHAPTER 41

SUITCASES, LAPTOP cases, carry-on luggage, shopping bags. Megan and I arrived through the back door and into our kitchen late that evening. Back home in good old New Burg.

Okay, Lindsay and Alex were way past the stage when they might welcome us yelling, "Yay! Mommy and Daddy are home!" when we returned from a trip. But the least they could do was come down and say hello. Instead our welcome-home greeting consisted of a shout from Alex in his room.

"Who the hell is downstairs?"

"It's us!" Megan shouted.

"Oh, hi," Alex yelled back.

I walked to the bottom of the hall staircase.

"Where's your sister?"

"How would I know?" Alex yelled.

I swore to myself that I wouldn't get angry.

"I'm up here," came Lindsay's voice. No hello. No welcome back. Just "I'm up here."

So much for swearing that I wouldn't get angry.

Megan joined me in the hall.

"Couldn't you guys come down and say hello?" she shouted up the stairs.

"In a few minutes" was Alex's answer. Lindsay's response was even worse: "Can't. Busy."

Megan shook her head and walked into the kitchen, but I didn't move, except to sit down on the bottom hall step. I used my hands to try to wipe the heavy perspiration from my face. It was not a particularly efficient method. Then I buried my wet face in my wet hands. The feeling I had on the plane returned, the feeling that I might at any moment burst into tears.

A sense of confusion. A kind of sadness that was mixed with anger. Megan's impatience. Bette and Bud's transformation into smiley faces. The SUV accident. The drones crowding every piece of sky that I walked under.

I stood up and climbed to the third step. And I screamed.

"Get down here right now. Right now! Do you hear me? Right now." I couldn't stop yelling. I couldn't stop the words from tumbling so fiercely out of my mouth.

"Are you hearing me? Are you two deaf? You two are wanted down here immediately!"

My daughter and son appeared.

They looked confused.

My arms and hands were shaking. My stomach tightened. My legs and head ached.

By now Megan had also appeared.

"What's wrong, Jacob?"

"What's wrong?" I bellowed. "Our kids couldn't even come downstairs and say hello to us. That's what's wrong."

Deadly silence.

"What's the big deal?" Alex said. But I did not have the energy to continue my rant.

"What's happening to you, Daddy?" Lindsay said.

Instead I said quietly, "Never mind. Just go back to whatever you were doing." They looked at me suspiciously. Then they turned and went back upstairs.

I looked at Megan. "I worry that we're losing the kids," I said.

"I worry that we're losing you," she said.

I thought I had spent all my anger and energy, but suddenly I could feel it building up again. The tension returned to my limbs. The throbbing returned to my head.

"Megan," I said. "I'm going upstairs to do some work on the book."

"Well, what about the luggage and dinner and checking e-mail and—" she was rattling away. I interrupted.

"No! Not now. Leave me alone. I'm going upstairs to do some work on the book. I'm fresh right now. I want to work now." I picked up my computer case and began running up the stairs, two steps at a time, three steps at a time. I was outside the workroom door. In my head I heard the umpire shout.

Safe at home!

CHAPTER 42

I PULLED open the attic workroom door with so much energy that a screw popped out of one of its hinges.

The workroom was totally overwhelming me with dry heat. I actually loved it. I loved that my eyes burned and my skin exploded with sweat. I pulled off my shirt like a fighter who was late for a match. I used my shirt to blot the sweat from my face and hair and neck.

I spread my notes—scrawled on scraps of paper, the backs of envelopes—across the dusty floor. I hadn't felt this excited in days. The anger within me had been replaced by an almost uncontrollable energy.

I zipped quickly through my computer notes, transferring important topics and facts onto the ever-growing pile of index cards. As the pencil lead wore out or broke, I'd grab a new one and keep going. I could not write fast enough.

I wasn't clear, but I think my plan was to get as much done as I could before Megan showed up to tell me that what I was doing was wrong. It wasn't too many hours away from tomorrow, when I'd once again be lifting gallons of apple juice and boxes of mi-crowave ovens and cartons of hedge clippers and…

And then I had an idea that I knew was great. I also knew that if Megan had been there she would not have agreed that it was so great.

I would actually start writing the book itself. The notes could wait. Sure, there was a lot more research to be done, a lot more investigating, a lot more index cards to put in a lot more shoe boxes. But I finally understood the phrase "I thought I might explode!"

I began typing.

Who actually created hell? Some say it was God. Some say it was the devil himself. But if you've ever spent time in New Burg, Nebraska, you would quickly discover that it was neither God nor the devil. Hell was created by a company called the Store.

I pounded away for another half an hour. Maybe longer. I don't remember. I stopped only when I heard Megan open the door and enter.

"Jacob, it's an oven in here. Turn on the air conditioner," she said.

"I will," I said. But I kept typing.

"What are you doing? You're typing like a crazy man," she said.

"I'm doing what I said I'd be doing. I'm working on our project."

"No need to be nasty," she said. "Jacob, you are so sweaty. You look like you've been swimming."

I wanted to say, "Stop talking, goddamn it. I'm thinking." But I ignored her and just kept writing. Finally I stopped. I just stopped. I was a race car that had suddenly run out of gas. I let my head drop to my wet chest. I was breathing heavily. Megan looked concerned.

She ran her hand across my bare back as she sat in the chair next to mine.

"Are you okay?" she said.

"In a way," I answered.

"In a way? What does that mean?"

"I'm not sure," I said.

Megan flipped open her laptop, and I eventually gained enough composure and energy to click over to my e-mail. I looked at the long stack that had accumulated since I first checked it early that morning in San Francisco. My eye immediately went to the e-mail with the subject line written in big red type. URGENT STORE MGMT SF, CA.

I opened it.

Hello, Jacob Brandeis,

We are sorry to inform you that your presence at the Store fulfillment center in New Burg, Nebraska, is no longer required at this moment.

We are sorry for contacting you on such short notice, but circumstances have prevented us from doing so sooner.

In keeping with our ongoing philosophy—No worries— we will be in touch soon with more information regarding your future with the Store.

The e-mail was unsigned.

"Holy shit!" I said softly.

"What's the matter?" Megan asked.

"Holy shit!" I said it again.

"Jacob, what's going on?"

"I think I just lost my job."

CHAPTER 43

FROM THAT moment on everything was different.

Megan and I still awoke early every day. But while she left for her supervisory job at the Store, I went up to our attic office and worked on the book.

I made it my job, and it turned out to be a job that I really loved. I was fueled by my disgust for my former employer, and I was especially fueled by the fact that I had been fired in a painful, careless way. So working on the book was almost like a drug for me. As I slapped away at the keys and constantly rearranged index cards, my heart beat fast and loud. When I made phone calls to informants I hoped could help me—former Store employees, former suppliers, a retired judge in Denver whom the founder, Thomas P. Owens, had briefly clerked for—I was quick and smooth and mildly aggressive. I was, I thought, doing God's work. And other than an occasional break to use the bathroom or nibble on a piece of cheese like a happy rat, I spent all day at my desk.

I was happy at my unpaid freelance job, but I was not happy with my family and my life with them.

All three of them never seemed to tire of reminding me that they had warned me about my behavior.

Mind you, they were never mean when the subject came up, but it came up way too frequently.

"How many times did I tell you to calm down and get with the program?" Megan would say.

Then Alex would chime in: "I told you, Dad. I told you more than once that you were losing it."

Megan would circle back around and say something like, "Yeah, even the kids noticed. First we made them change their lives by bringing them out to the middle of nowhere. And when, miraculously, they adjusted—when they even liked it—"

"We *loved* it," Lindsay said, correcting her.

Megan continued: "When they *loved* it, *you* couldn't adjust to it. You had to go mess things up."

We had that conversation, or some variation of that conversation, almost every night and more often on weekends.

If I argued, if I protested, they didn't seem to care. They argued louder and bigger than I could. The refrain they said over and over was, "Why don't you just go back to your office and write your book?"

More than a few times at the beginning of my "retirement" I'd catch the children recording me on video. I might be up in the workroom, deeply involved with the manuscript. I'd stop, feeling the presence of someone who had come into the room, then turn around and see Lindsay or Alex filming me.

"Why? Why?" I'd yell, and their answers would be something between evasive and credible.

"It's for a project on our home life."

"This flat-vid had an upgrade. I'm just trying it out."

"Alex and I are doing this for a video scrapbook. You'll be dead someday, you know."

I would yell, "Just stop it. Please just stop it," and

they would roll their eyes with impatience. The children would tell me to "chill," and Megan would tell me pretty much the same thing. "What they're doing is harmless, for God's sake."

Eventually I pretty much grew used to it. I knew, of course, that I should be in charge. I should insist that they stop. I should take the damned flat-vids away. I should argue louder than the three of them. But the simple fact was that all I really cared about was the book.

The more I got pissed off, the more I worked. And because of all that angry energy, the book was moving really fast. It moved even faster when I began the second part, the eyewitness part—based mostly on my phone calls, research, e-mails, letters, and, of course, my own experiences.

Bette and Bud's "transfer." Bette and Bud's barbecue. The no-show founder at the meeting in San Francisco. My treatment at airport security.

My days were filled with energy, and because Megan was usually tired from her supervisory job, I became the book's full-time writer. Megan became the part-time editor.

I usually worked on my manuscript until around 2:00 a.m. Then I checked to make certain that my writing had been saved onto a red flash drive. Once I knew my words were safely recorded I yanked out the flash drive and kept it with me at all times. Quite simply, it never left my sight. That red flash drive was titled simply *Twenty-Twenty*. And someday soon I would be printing its contents—the start of something I was already thinking of as *Store Wars*.

Knowing that this manuscript was safe and growing kept me as calm as I could ever hope to be. I was not angry at the constant carping from my family about "losing it" and "not getting with the program." I was not angry when my children committed my most ordinary moments to video. I was not even angry when Megan quietly opened the bathroom door a crack and made a video of me drying off after a shower.

All I really cared about was the book.

CHAPTER 44

BEEF BRISKET in a sweet-and-sour onion-tomato sauce. Good and lumpy real mashed potatoes. Emerald-green peas mixed with tiny little bits of prosciutto.

It should have been a perfect meal.

"Now, listen," I said. "If you want me to have dinner with you, put every video and recording device away. Agreed?" I said.

"Agreed," Lindsay said.

"I didn't hear you, Alex," I said.

"Agreed," he said. Okay, his voice was sullen—but he said it.

"Megan? What about you?"

"You expect me to take the oath?" she said, only slightly annoyed.

"Yes, ma'am."

"Are you crazy?" she asked.

With a smile I said, "Possibly."

"Oh, my God," Megan said. Then she took a big breath, let it out, and very softly said, "Agreed." She waited. Then added, just as softly, "And you *are* crazy."

Dinner began.

"No wine for me," I said. "I've got work to do."

Alex asked that Lindsay "please pass the pot roast." Lindsay corrected him and told him it was beef brisket. Megan told them not to start arguing.

As I was taking my first taste of the buttery mashed potatoes, Lindsay said, "How's the book going?"

"Like you care," I said. Why was my voice so venomous, so sarcastic? I often joked with the kids (and Megan) in a funny, teasing way, but all the "how to raise your child" books always advised against anger and sarcasm.

"Jacob," Megan said. "Lindsay was asking a perfectly reasonable question."

But I could not stop.

"Yeah, *you* think it's reasonable. But I know it's *not* reasonable."

Alex looked down at his dinner plate. Lindsay took a big gulp from her water glass.

"My book. My book. My book." I was shaking my head. What was the matter with me?

"Maybe you're spending too much time working on your book, your book, your book," Alex said.

I stared at him with open, angry eyes.

"We've told you. The three of us. Give up on the book."

Then Lindsay spoke loudly, with volume and irritation in her voice: *"You just don't understand!"*

In a scary, soft tone, I said, "Oh…but that's where you're all wrong…I absolutely do understand.

"I understand what a magnificently evil, powerful machine the subject of my book…"

"Our book," Megan said, correcting me.

Now I was really pissed.

"No, Megan. It's *my* book. You and *your* children have done nothing but try to get me to stop. Well, I've got news for you. I will not stop. I know what a powerful machine the Store is. No one knows as much as I do. No one has looked at it so closely."

I stood up, and in my mind I was as inspiring as King Arthur addressing the Round Table, as wise as Christ at the Last Supper.

And for the first time I realized that Megan and the kids might be right: I was crazy.

"Yes. They'll come for me. Like soldiers, like Nazis, in the middle of the night. They'll take me, and they'll take my book."

There was no structure to my thoughts. As the ideas came to my head I vomited the words out into the air.

"They know what I'm up to. They know everything. The Store is more powerful than anyone or anything. Nobody can escape it—especially a little nobody like me. The surveillance cameras. The recording devices. The spies at work. The spies in the San Francisco hotels. The drones. The neighbors who are not really neighbors. The friends who are not really friends. The family who…" I had to stop there.

Alex's eyes had not moved from his downward stare at his plate. Lindsay's hand was shaking as it held her water glass. Megan's eyes were wet.

"I am *not* prepared for their arrival. Nobody can be. But I will be strong about it all. The exposé will go on. They can steal my book. They can burn my book. But the truth will come out.

"You three are wrong. You preach at me to stop. You plead with me to stop. But you three are totally wrong. Totally.

"What you don't understand is this: *I do understand!*"

CHAPTER 45

"GET THE hell off my property," I screamed.

"Brandeis, we are here to enforce a town and state request," said one of the two men banging their fists on our front door.

"I said get the hell off my property."

It was three o'clock on a Saturday afternoon. Cold and cloudy, and the weather was not made pleasanter by the fact that my family and I were barely speaking to one another.

"Brandeis, let us in or we'll have to use force," said the same guy.

Both men wore cheap-looking gray suits. One guy was tall and white and blond. The other guy was tall and black and bald. Both of them were annoyingly handsome. Both of them were alarmingly large. I figured that neither of them was from New Burg, because neither of them was smiling.

"Let them in, Jacob," Megan said. "Why are you always fighting, always causing problems?"

I took a deep breath and began unlocking the door. The second I had completed the job, precisely when the door was unlocked, the blond guy put his hand through the open space and pushed me violently into the hallway. I fell to the floor. The bald guy was carrying a sledgehammer, which he used to smash the knob from the door. One quick and powerful movement. That door would be staying unlocked.

"What's this all—" I started to speak but was immediately interrupted by the bald-headed guy.

"Jacob Brandeis, sir?" he said, exactly as I imagined an army sergeant leading basic training would say it. I was pulling myself up off the floor.

"I'm asking you what this—" I tried again. The blond guy spoke next.

"Answer, sir. Are you Jacob Brandeis?" He was even more hostile.

"Look—" I tried yet again.

"Jacob Brandeis? Answer me, sir. Answer me *now!*"

Megan decided to answer for me.

"Yes. He's Jacob Brandeis." Her voice was cold, precise.

The bald guy said, "Your computer, Brandeis."

"No," I said.

"Give us your computer, Brandeis."

"Maybe you didn't hear me," I said.

The blond guy now: "Your computer, Brandeis."

Then, like a little kid, I said, "You can't make me." I was nervous, and, of course, I felt like a sniveling six-year-old in front of my family.

"It's in his attic workroom," Lindsay said. Like her mother's, my daughter's voice was quiet but stern.

"You *cannot* come into my house like this and ask for me to give you *my* things."

"Yes, they can, Jacob," Megan said.

At that moment the blond guy grabbed hold of my upper arms with his hands and pulled me from the stairway landing. He flung me to the hall floor. The bald guy ran up the stairs, hurdling every three steps.

The other guy was right behind him. I stood up and was about to follow them.

Megan yelled, "Stop your dad!"

To my astonishment, Alex made a lame attempt to push me back down. I ran up the stairs and arrived in the attic at the same moment one of the intruders was folding the power cord around my closed laptop. The other guy was making uneven stacks of every piece of paper—scraps, printouts, index cards—on my desk. I briefly noticed that neither of the men had taken Megan's computer.

CHAPTER 46

"DO YOU have any other electronic equipment, Brandeis?" the bald guy said. The skin on his head glistened with sweat.

I just looked at him.

"Do you?" he repeated.

"You know as well as I do what I have," I said.

"Check," the guy said. He and his colleague each took plastic garbage bags from their briefcases and emptied the contents of the wastebaskets into them. They also swept the three unsorted, uneven stacks of papers from my desk into their bags. Then they pulled some loose planks from the steep incline under the roof. All they found was asbestos padding. Of course, I hoped they'd die from being so close to the toxic material.

The bald guy and the blond guy then saw an unlocked trunk. They flipped open the top. Nothing but old CDs (Ludacris, anyone?), old college books (*Middlemarch,* anyone?), and old children's drawings ("My Dad mak god raveoli"). They felt the inner sides of the trunk for secret panels. They seemed very pissed off that they found nothing incriminating. For me it was a small pleasure, but it was a pleasure nonetheless.

Megan and Alex and Lindsay appeared at the doorway. Megan shook her head gently. The children? I don't know. I'm not sure. Were they smug? Were they sad? Did they find me pathetic? Foolish? I couldn't tell, and I regret to say that I was on the verge of not giving a shit.

"Brandeis, we've finished our search-and-gather," said the blond guy.

"Search-and-gather?" I said. "That's what you call it? It's a basic violation of every American privacy law. But frankly, I don't give a shit. It's exactly what I was expecting."

I surveyed the strangely uncluttered room. The men stood next to their respective black garbage bags. The bald-headed guy read aloud from a large card:

"Jacob Brandeis, the town and city of New Burg, in the state of Nebraska, have rightfully collected, with approval from the offices of the Nebraska Department of Justice, item or items that are considered of governmental consequence to the people of the state. This material may or may not be returned to you upon completion of examination."

There was a pause. Then, continuing to read, the bald-headed guy said:

"Do you understand the statement I have just read to you?"

"Sure," I said. "And you can all burn in hell."

CHAPTER 47

IT WAS precisely 5:00 a.m. I carefully got out of bed.

Megan seemed to be sleeping soundly, making tiny sharp nasal sounds somewhere between snoring and loud breathing. I quietly opened the bedroom door and stepped out, closing it behind me. Then I briefly held my ear to the door of Alex's room. Heavy snoring. Then I listened at the door to Lindsay's room. I wasn't absolutely certain that she wasn't awake, but no light drifted into the hallway from under her bedroom door. I was pretty sure that my three housemates were asleep.

I walked up the stairway to my barren workroom. Then I removed the red flash drive from my jeans pocket. I snapped the little piece into Megan's laptop and typed:

TWENTY-TWENTY
The True Story of the Store
by
Jacob Brandeis

I pressed Save, then ejected the red flash drive and returned it to my jeans pocket.

I had stashed my backpack behind two stacks of old *Businessweek* magazines. The backpack itself was filled with a change of clothing, a toothbrush, toothpaste, a yellow legal pad, two pens, a bottle of Lipitor, a fifth of Jack Daniel's, and my iPad, newly loaded with a bunch of classic novels and the first two seasons of *House of Cards*.

I was ready to go.

I closed the door to my workroom and headed down the attic stairs. As I passed by a closed bedroom door I heard a stage whisper: "Daddy, where are you going?"

It was Lindsay.

"I'll be back in a little bit. Don't worry," I said.

The breathy, rasping whisper followed me downstairs: "You really are crazy," she said.

Only I could hear my response.

"So I've heard."

CHAPTER 48

I TOSSED my backpack and a six-pack of Fresca on the passenger seat. With all the surveillance cameras hanging from trees and stoplights, I couldn't race away, but let's just say that I challenged the speed limit.

Where was I headed? The only destination I had in mind was "anyplace that isn't this place." Away from my absurd family and town. I was, deep down inside, also hoping to escape from myself—from my overwhelming fear and paranoia.

I quickly arrived at Interstate 80, the highway that runs from California to New Jersey. I had no idea whether to head west or east. Then I thought: *Hey, what about the ski instructor who taught the kids two years ago, when we were on vacation in Vail?* Amy and I had become very friendly; Megan thought we had become way too friendly, which, just to let you know, was absolutely untrue. I could call her. She'd remember me. Then my brain returned, and I realized she would have no memory of who I was.

Bette and Bud were obviously out, and with the pathetic realization that I had no close friends west of the Mississippi, I headed east on I-80. At least I had a former college friend in some Chicago suburb, and I was pretty sure that my cousin the kidney specialist lived in Saint Louis.

The highway was surprisingly busy for just after 5:00 a.m. My guesses: trucks hauling pigs and cows to slaughterhouses; tankards filled with corn oil, a Nebraska specialty; high-striving yuppies off to their cubicles at the Store.

The farther I drove, the better I felt. The better I felt, the more certain I was that my book, *Twenty-Twenty,* was marked for success. *The timing is absolutely perfect,* I thought, slamming both fists on the steering wheel as I reached the outskirts of Lincoln.

By seven o'clock that morning I was about to cross the state border into Iowa. It was then that I had what could modestly be called a brainstorm: I would call Anne Gutman, my editor at Writers Place. Sure, she had screwed me over a little by rejecting my and Megan's music book, but I knew Anne had faith in me. And I knew she would see how hot my manuscript was.

Yes. *Twenty-Twenty.* The phrase "marked for success" kept running through my mind. "Marked for success," like George Orwell's *1984.* His exposé of a cultural nightmare was off by thirty-six years.

Twenty-Twenty would be right on target.

CHAPTER 49

ONCE ANNE Gutman got over the initial shock of hearing my voice on the phone, she said something I hadn't heard in a long time.

"You're in luck." Then she added, "I have a friend who lives east of Des Moines in a sweet little town called Goosen Valley. Her name is Maggie Pine, and five years ago she did a magnificent coffee-table book for me on Mennonite quilts."

Thirty minutes later I was sitting and eating warm blueberry muffins in a kitchen in Goosen Valley, Iowa. The kitchen had an oak Hoosier cabinet and a collection of nineteenth-century mixing bowls, and Maggie Pine had a sweet face that would prompt a normal human being to trust her. I guess I was no longer a normal human being, because the charming kitchen seemed cold, and Maggie's sweet face felt unfriendly... at least to me.

While Maggie went upstairs to wash her face and "run a brush through my mop," I walked around the backyard herb garden. The basil was sparse and dying. The rosemary plants were still standing tall. And a little plant sign that said BORAGE (I had never heard of it) stood beneath a giant ugly clump of weedy-looking green leaves.

On the walk to her tiny newspaper office at the *Goosen Register* (Margaret Pine, editor and only full-time reporter), my new friend and hostess told me how "wonderfully helpful" Anne Gutman had been to her when she was "assembling and writing my quilt tome."

"She had me to New York City two times, and she put me up in a hotel on Fifth Avenue with a view of Central Park, hardly a place to think about Mennonite quilts, but I managed."

As we walked through the small downtown, I was amazed at how much it resembled New Burg. But this town was real, and by "real" I mean "really real." The ice cream parlor had a hand-lettered sign above the door that said FOUR GREAT FLAVORS. The library exterior was a harsh mixture of old brick and new aluminum siding. Even the bookstore, called Good Books and Good Things, had a window that held not only books but also other items for sale: china teapots made to resemble cats, school supplies, jars of orange marmalade. New Burg wanted to be just like Goosen Valley; it just couldn't do it.

"Is there enough news in this town to fill a weekly newspaper?" I asked Maggie as we sat in her storefront office and she zipped quickly through her e-mail.

"Well, we do the usual. One of the local teachers, he does the high school sports news. Everyone cares about that. Then I have a part-time woman who does the social news, such as it is. That's birthday parties and anniversary parties and church news. But...now, don't you go thinking we're just a bunch of farmers. We have a monthly book club and read important books, and I don't mean *Fifty Shades of Grey*. A retired doctor wrote a very thoughtful piece on eldercare and dementia. And when I did an editorial endorsing same-sex marriage, only two e-mails to the editor criticized me. Thirty-four others cheered me on."

I threw my hands up in the air.

"You got me. Clearly Goosen Valley is the Paris of the Midwest. And I don't mean that sarcastically. I wish New Burg had been more like this town," I said.

"Look," Maggie said. "Anne gave me a brief synopsis of your problems, at least as she understands them after a short phone conversation. All I can say is that I hope you make peace with yourself. You can stay at my place until you're ready to move on, Jacob. And with any luck…"

Suddenly from outside I heard a very big thud. It was mixed with the sound of a buzzing motor. My head snapped toward the storefront window.

"Not to worry," Maggie said. "It's just a drone delivery."

CHAPTER 50

THAT NIGHT Maggie Pine fed me honey-glazed roasted chicken, lump-free mashed turnips, and, of course, corn on the cob made perfect with lots of butter and salt.

Maggie was a very pretty red-haired woman, but this pretty woman and this great-tasting meal did not make me long for Maggie. It made me long for the old days in New York with Megan and Alex and Lindsay around the table. I really wanted to phone my family, but I stopped myself every time the idea tempted me. I knew it would be a stupid thing, a really stupid thing, to contact them. Tomorrow I'd be back on the road again. Maybe I'd feel different. Maybe then I'd call, or the next day…or the next…or…

The guest bedroom in Maggie's house was straight out of a bed-and-breakfast catalog: a canopy bed with a whole bunch of decorative pillows. The room was also a kind of Mennonite quilt museum—one quilt on the bed, two folded at the foot of the bed, and five others on an old steamer trunk under the window.

I tried reading one of the books I'd grabbed from Maggie's shelf, *The Good Earth*. It only made me wonder how they figured that book deserved the Pulitzer Prize back then.

I tossed. Then I turned. Then I tossed some more. I remembered what my mother used to say: "When you can't sleep, it means you've got a guilty conscience." I got up and out of bed.

When I walked to the window I could see the dark images of "downtown" Goosen Valley, a model of Americana, complete with steeple and water tower. Closer to my window were the branches of a tree that Maggie had identified as an ancient black walnut. The sun was just rising, darkness outside beginning to build to light. Two tiny stars, still hanging on in the morning light, sparkled through the branches of the black walnut tree.

Everything was peaceful for a moment. Even me.

CHAPTER 51

MAYBE I had slept a little bit. Maybe for a few minutes? A half hour? Maybe I had just fallen asleep sitting on the window ledge? Maybe...oh, what the hell difference did it make? Here I was on a chair near the window in Maggie Pine's guest bedroom. And it was suddenly morning. And I was sort of awake. And I could really use a shower to get totally awake.

As I walked to the little bathroom attached to the bedroom I noticed a small framed antique sampler hanging on the wall. It said that it was created by a girl named Marie D in the year 1822. It was a line from the Bible:

Watch therefore, for ye know neither the day nor the hour wherein the Son of man cometh.

I sure couldn't argue with that.

The bathroom had no shower, only a tub. Bathing in a tub never made sense to me. I'm not a guy who likes soaking in his own dirty water. So I did my best to wash away the previous day's dirt and sweat by kneeling in front of the bathtub faucet. I let the water run, and I bent my head forward to wash my hair. Then I alternately soaped myself up and splashed myself off to get rid of the soap.

On the small table near the tub were the perfect props for such a quaint little bathroom: dried flowers in a Mason jar, an engraved antique silver hand mirror, and a matching silver comb. Also on the table was a tin of Yardley talcum powder—lily of the valley.

I dried myself with a big white towel, then I made a decision that was, for me, a daring one. I doused myself with a lot of the floral-scented powder.

Because I'd left the bathroom door open, I had no trouble hearing the knock on the bedroom door. Then the door squeaked open.

"Jacob," I heard. "Jacob. It's just me, Maggie."

"Hold on," I yelled back. "I just took a shower… er…not a shower…I just took a bath. What's up?"

I asked this question with a slight nervousness in my voice, all the while wrapping the towel around me and securing it as firmly as I could.

Before I went back into the bedroom, I glanced at myself in the old mirror over the sink. I tell you—not with phony modesty—I was not a particularly handsome sight: chest hair made grayish white with talcum powder, along with my ridiculously skinny arms and equally skinny legs.

"Almost caught me," I said to Maggie.

"I'm sorry. I should have waited for you to answer the door."

"It's okay. We're friends," I said, and I'm sure I had one of those grins that's usually called sheepish or stupid or both.

"I brought some coffee and a little flask of orange juice." As she spoke she gestured toward the table next to the narrow bed. Sure enough, there was a wooden tray with a delicate little cup, steam rising out of it, and a small cut-glass container of orange juice.

"You look tired, Jacob," Maggie said.

"Yeah, I'm not even sure that I fell asleep. When that happens you really know you had a bad night."

At the foot of the bed was an undershirt. I slipped it over my head, but I then suddenly worried that by moving my arms into the armholes I'd be pulling in my waist and end up losing my towel.

"Here," Maggie said. "Let me help."

She walked toward me.

"Hey, you used the lily of the valley stuff," she said. "I like that so much. It reminds me of my grandmother."

"Great. I very often remind girls of their grandmothers."

She laughed, and she stretched the undershirt over my shoulders. All the while I held on to the towel knot.

Maggie was about to pull the undershirt down over me when she brushed her hand hard against my chest. A fairly small puff of white powder erupted.

She put her hand back on my chest. Then she spoke.

"So whaddya think?" she said.

For a few moments I said nothing. And for those same moments she did nothing.

Finally it was Maggie who spoke.

"I guess not," she said.

"Well…" I paused. Then I added, "I guess not."

She walked to the bedroom door and told me to drink my coffee and take my time. She'd be downstairs. She'd make some toast. Or did I want something else? She could make some corn muffins. No; toast was fine. Actually I never eat breakfast. Cereal, maybe. She had some old Rice Krispies. No. No, thank you...then she suddenly walked out of the room and closed the door behind her.

I don't think I breathed a sigh of relief, but I was relieved. I was also sad.

I must have looked ridiculous: my undershirt half on, my towel coming undone. I brushed as much of her grandma-smelling powder off me as I could.

It was my intention to sip my coffee, drink my orange juice, and take my time getting dressed.

But that was not going to happen.

CHAPTER 52

"JACOB! GET down here! Now!"

It took me a moment to recognize Maggie's voice.

Suddenly I heard sirens. Bright light poured through the bedroom window.

"Jacob! Please! Hurry!"

I left my peaceful view of a Goosen Valley morning. Wearing only my white undershirt and white boxers, I ran from the bedroom and shot down the stairs two at a time.

In the small front hallway was Maggie Pine with a crowd of people, at least a dozen of them, two or three of them spilling out through the open front door. It took me only a few seconds to realize that this was neither a fire response nor police activity. These were people I actually knew: Megan, Alex, Lindsay. Surrounding my family were Sam and Bette and Bud. Holy shit. There was the neighborhood leader, Marie DiManno.

The faces that were familiar to me but also nameless were the young man and woman who had "interviewed" us in San Francisco as well as the two thuglike men who had appropriated my laptop and private papers only a couple of nights ago in New Burg.

"What in hell is going on?" I said—quietly, full of confusion, amazement.

"We're all here to help," said Maggie.

Oh, my God. So Maggie was in on it, too.

"What the hell is this?" I said. My eyes and head whirled from one face to another. The faces were sad-looking, serious.

"Help with what?" I was yelling now.

Lindsay stepped forward and took my hand in hers. She spoke the way you might address a three-year-old who's dropped his ice cream cone.

"This is an intervention, Daddy."

I snapped my hand back from her grip. "This is bullshit!" I said.

My anger was apparently a signal for the two thugs—the bald guy and the blond guy—to step forward and prepare to hold me back. As they moved, I could see through the door. A news truck. A sound truck. Four men and two women. Two of them wore headphones, two of them held boom mikes.

This intervention was being filmed.

The interview woman stepped forward and stood beside Lindsay.

Her voice was dramatically soft and sweet. "Let's try to stay calm. Maybe we can go somewhere to talk quietly. Is that possible, Ms. Pine?"

"Of course. Let's move into the dining room. I fixed it so there'd be room for everyone."

As the crowd moved, joined by some of the film crew, I was almost shoved bodily past the staircase and into the dining room.

Maggie had pushed her old pine dining table against the wall and arranged the chairs—the regular dining chairs and a bunch of folding chairs—in a semicircle.

"I'm in my goddamn underwear," I shouted.

Megan touched my shoulder and tried to nudge me gently into the center chair. This was the first time my wife had spoken.

"Sweetie, don't be so formal. It doesn't matter what you're wearing."

"Of course it matters," I said angrily. "It only doesn't matter if someone is crazy…if someone is a goddamn mental patient. All of you, get the hell out of here."

No one reacted. No one lost his or her temper.

So that was it? They thought I was crazy, and they were going to treat me as a crazy person?

Only for a moment did I think they might be right. I thought it as I looked down at my bare legs, at the filthy soles of my naked feet, at the glazed look on my children's faces. Bette was silently mouthing words. A prayer, maybe? The two interviewers were taking notes on their handheld devices. The thugs were seated on either side of me. Just in case.

But the thought of madness evaporated as fast as it had appeared. I was angry. I was foolish, perhaps. But I was certainly not crazy. And I suddenly knew more than ever that the manuscript had to get to Anne Gutman. And I knew just how to do that.

CHAPTER 53

"WE ARE all worried—very, very worried about you, Jacob."

Bud was talking.

"You know it, Dad," Alex said. He crossed in front of his mother and sister, stood in front of me, and, facing me, placed his hands on my shoulders. This was definitely not Alex's style. Who the hell was this kid?

Meanwhile the sound guy held the boom over whoever might be talking. Three cameramen moved softly around the room, one of them filming whoever was speaking, another filming "reaction shots," the third concentrating entirely on me.

Bette, Lindsay, and the woman interviewer from San Francisco all contributed to the intervention. They carried the theme of caring and understanding and the need for help to a nauseating level. Literally, my stomach rumbled. My chest ached with anger. Perhaps the most over-the-top piece of madness came from Lindsay.

After she carried on tearfully about my inability to focus on my family, my wife, and my children—"the people who are here to bring you joy"—she looked squarely into my eyes and said, "I want my father back."

I wanted to scream at my daughter, "You make me sick." Instead I stood up and spoke in a calm, normal tone: "Please. Why don't you all just leave me alone?" Then I yelled at the top of my lungs: "Please!"

At that the two thugs standing behind me moved closer, just in case I needed to be subdued.

My crazy brain was suddenly elsewhere: I needed to find a way to escape. I had to find a way. What I considered a compelling and important book a few days ago I now thought of as something way beyond a masterpiece, a book that would conquer evil and deliver freedom before it was too late. Was I just another crazy man, or was I carrying what was essentially the fifth Gospel?

I wasn't sure. But I had to keep fighting.

The interview guy from San Francisco stood up and moved smack-dab in front of me. He spoke slowly and deliberately and kept inserting an especially maddening phrase into his speech: "Do you understand me, Jacob?"

I shook with anger. My eyes filled with tears. My undershirt was drenched with sweat.

"We are here to help you. Do you understand me, Jacob? We are going to bring you back to New Burg and enter you into a treatment and behavior renewal clinic, where you will relearn the concepts of joyful living. Do you understand me, Jacob? We all believe—your family, your friends, specialists from the psychotherapy group at the Store—that within four or five weeks you will be better and stronger and happier. Do you understand me, Jacob?"

As he spoke, the intervention group began surrounding me. Despite their soft words and pitiful faces, they were scaring me. I felt strangely like the victim of a lynch mob.

"We'll be with you, Daddy," Lindsay said.

"I love you, sweetie," Megan said.

"I warned you about that book, Dad," Alex said.

The two thugs were on either side of my chair now.

Bud spoke in almost a whisper.

"It'll be the best thing for you, Jake. Don't be mad. Don't be angry."

The tears dribbled out of my eyes. I could taste the saltiness sneaking into my mouth. I could see my naked knees shaking.

I knew it was because of my sheer fury at their brazen intervention.

They thought they had convinced me of the wisdom of their mission.

My tears came harder now. I stood up. The thugs put their hands firmly around my elbows and wrists.

"Stop it! Please stop it!" I yelled.

I sat down, and I quietly said what I had to say.

"I understand. I do. I thank you all. I'll do what you want me to do."

CHAPTER 54

IT WORKED.

Man, I thought. *If I'm still alive next year when they give out the Oscars they've got to give one to me.* Bette and Bud and Marie dripped tears like three waterfalls. My kids and my wife hugged me and thanked me. The woman from the San Francisco interview called me a good man. The bald-headed thug called me a wise man. Maggie Pine said she hoped I'd be a forgiving man.

"I was brought into this intervention at the very end," she added.

"Does our friend Anne know about all this?" I asked.

"Oh, no. Only this small intervention group knows about it," she said. Maggie shared a knowing smile with Megan, two bitches in cahoots. The blond thug standing beside me joined in the sickening smile.

Maggie walked off toward the kitchen. The blond guy said he needed to speak with me. This bastard who had invaded my home and stolen my things was now talking like the sweetest guy on earth.

Megan and the kids paid very close attention as he spoke.

"So here's the plan, Jake."

Jake?

"One of our people will drive your car back to New Burg. Now, there are a few other cars that we brought along. One will take your family to their house. So you and I and Cue Ball…"

I stopped paying attention right there. The bald guy was called Cue Ball? Does a bald guy like being called Cue Ball? And aren't cue balls usually white? This guy was black. And he must have a real name, a given name…

"Mr. Brandeis, are you listening?" the blond guy asked.

Mr. Brandeis. No more Jake. No more last name only, as it was when he stole my laptop, wrecked my office, set me off on this madness.

"Yes, of course," I said.

"As I said, you and I and Cue Ball will drive back to New Burg in our own car. It will have a driver and a driving assistant…"

I spoke: "You mean a driver and a guard."

"No. I mean a driver and a driving assistant, should anything happen to the driver."

Okay, Jacob, go back to acting like the cooperative patient they want. Just keep it up. Play nice. And, most important, figure out how to escape.

"We should get going," the blond guy said. "Do you have anything up in your room that you absolutely need?"

"*Absolutely need?* Maybe you noticed that I'm standing here in my underwear."

"Okay, let's go up and put your clothes on."

"What are you gonna do? Zip my fly?"

That wise-guy line put me back on his shit list.

"Let's go," he said.

"You need coffee," Maggie Pine yelled. She was carrying a large tray that held a big pot of coffee and a lot of paper cups. We walked a few feet to the dining-room table.

As she handed the blond guy a cup, she said, "Cream and sugar?"

"Just black," he said.

"Me, too," I said. "We're going up to get my things. Then we're leaving."

"I thought so," Maggie said.

In my best sarcastic tone of voice I said, "By the way, thanks for everything."

"Sure," she said. "Just be sure to check the bathroom cabinet. Make certain you didn't forget anything."

"I will," I said.

CHAPTER 55

I SLIPPED into my jeans. I slipped into my army-green T-shirt. I slipped into my old red-and-white Nikes.

The blond guy gave the inside of my backpack a thorough search. The most illicit thing he could find was my bottle of bourbon.

I glanced out the window. It was full morning now, and I realized that what I had earlier thought were stars twinkling through the branches of the walnut tree were—*Holy shit! Of course!*—surveillance cameras.

"I need to slap some water on my face, and I need to pee," I said.

"Yeah, sure," he said. I guess we were friends again. "Only leave the door open."

I walked into the bathroom, left the door ajar by a foot or so, turned on the faucet to a quick drip. I hoped it sounded like a guy urinating.

When I opened the linen closet in the bathroom, I glanced from top to bottom—Martha Stewart towels, Crabtree & Evelyn soap, Caswell-Massey body lotion. Sort of what I expected. What I didn't expect was a two-foot-tall cabinet below the lowest shelf. When I pulled open the drawer, it turned out to be a false wooden front. It fell to the floor.

From the bedroom: "That's the longest piss I've ever heard. What'd ya do, have a few Buds before bedtime?"

I don't know if he said anything more. By that time I had seen the window at the rear of the closet. Under the sill was an attached rope ladder as well as a small envelope. The envelope had pencil writing on the front: GOOD LUCK. MAGGIE. Inside the envelope were my car keys.

I unrolled the rope ladder out the window and down the side of the house.

It took me around thirty seconds to make it to the ground. It took another thirty seconds to get to Maggie's garden. I knelt down and dug up my little red flash drive. It was wrapped in aluminum foil and was near the huge borage plant. Exactly where I had buried it yesterday morning.

I ran to my car. A quarter of a tank of gas. I took off. No headlights on. No seat belt fastened.

As I drove away from the house all I could say, over and over again, was "God bless Maggie Pine."

CHAPTER 56

FEAR. CHAOS. And hell. Not necessarily in that order.

Okay, I made it out of the insane intervention, but I was in a huge pile of trouble. I got an idea of how huge the minute I drove out of Maggie Pine's mud-and-cobblestone driveway. The auto-info—the car speaker that came on automatically when the Store had an announcement that they wanted broadcast immediately—blasted out at me:

"A person of suspicious and possibly harmful nature is at large. His last known location was the Nebraska-Iowa border. His name is Jacob Brandeis. Male, midforties, white. He is wearing red-and-white shoes. Photos and more details of subject are available on all electronic devices, electronic billboards, and electronic posters. If you see Jacob Brandeis or anyone resembling Jacob Brandeis, text STORE 134."

This announcement, which would be repeated every five minutes, was replaced by a Jay Z song played backwards.

If I had any doubt that I was a crazy man on a crazy flight, less than two miles away from Maggie Pine's house was a large electronic poster, a composite of a white male in his forties. He didn't look harmful, but he sure as hell looked exactly like me—right down to his scruffy T-shirt and two-day growth of beard.

The first thing I realized was that if I had even a slight chance of succeeding in this escape I had to ditch the car. By now, I was a major expert on how the Store operated, and I knew that the Store would be quickly broadcasting more information: GPS coordinates, car description, license-plate number, locations of former friends (a few) and current friends (not many). The Store would be relentless. I was a weak little rabbit being chased by the psycho equivalent of the United States Marines.

What the hell could I do? Run through the Iowa cornfield like some asshole in a bad B movie?

It was a small miracle that my sweaty, dirty hands could hold on to the steering wheel.

Suddenly Jay Z was interrupted by a repeat of the previous announcement. They were going to find Jacob Brandeis. A guy who wrote a book was as big a threat as a kidnapper or a terrorist.

When the auto-info ended, no other sound returned. The digital speedometer and engine gauges went dead. The car kept moving, but the brakes were feeling shaky. Not failing completely, but failing. The Store had, remotely, disconnected anything that could be disconnected.

Amazingly, after what I estimated to be around five miles of driving, I still had not seen another car—one truck and two tractors, but no car. Of course I assumed that this lack of traffic was part of the plot to capture me, and it seemed like just the sort of creepy, scary method the Store would use. I also knew that it was only a matter of time before the drones would be sailing over me.

I saw four more electronic posters and two electronic billboards with new and enhanced photos of me. One even had a separate rendering of my dirty red-and-white sneakers.

I kept driving, and I kept thinking that some great mother of an idea would hit me. But the only thing that hit me were those posters and those now incessant auto-info broadcasts.

This was truly hell on wheels.

Shit, man. I was a goddamn fugitive.

CHAPTER 57

YOU HAVEN'T tasted the putrid combination of fear and depression until you've stood in the Greyhound bus station in Carolton, Iowa. A tattered billboard half a mile earlier had said BUS STATION. GO GREYHOUND. And it was the first sign of hope that I had encountered since I had escaped the "intervention" at Maggie Pine's house.

I left my car in the rear of an abandoned gas station on the outskirts of town, although it was hard to tell where the town ended and the outskirts began. Then, with my head down, I shuffled toward the bus station. It was a small gray wooden building that looked more like a small saloon in an old western.

Inside, the station was almost empty except for a good-looking teenage boy, blond, skinny, rimless glasses. He sat behind the small counter. The kid was reading on an iPad, and I'm sure he hadn't noticed me enter.

On one of the two wooden benches was a pudgy middle-aged woman knitting. I assumed she was waiting for a bus, but she didn't have a suitcase or even a pocketbook. She was just sitting and knitting.

On the other bench sat a man around seventy years

old. All I need to tell you about him is that he smelled distinctly like a dirty men's room.

I got the young guy's attention, and he very politely asked, "Where you going, sir?"

"Well, when's the next bus coming by?"

"It should be here in an hour," he said. "But that depends on if the driver stopped in Walkersville for some liquid refreshment."

"Where's the bus headed after here?"

"Next stop is Garrettville, then Independence, then it goes straight to Springfield, Illinois," the man said.

"That's where the Simpsons live," I said.

He smiled. "You're not the first person to make that joke."

"I guess I'm not. It's just—"

Then the old stinky guy spoke. He didn't yell, but his voice was strong enough for the young man and me to easily hear him.

"I think that's him," the old man said to nobody in particular.

The woman who was knitting ignored him completely. A woman who's knitting is not usually interested in talking to a bum who smells of piss.

"That guy is the guy," the old man said. He was looking directly at us. He was also clearly drunk.

"Mister," the old guy said. "Aren't you the guy… you know…the guy?"

The woman finally spoke. "Hush up," she said. "You old souse."

The old man looked at the slow-moving ceiling fan. Then he seemed to lose interest. But I was extremely interested.

"Before I buy my ticket to Springfield, is there someplace I can get a soda and a sandwich around here?" I asked.

"A soda?"

"You know—a pop, a Coke."

"Yeah. Four doors to the left is Cappy's. It's not bad if they have the pork shoulder today."

"I'll be back in five minutes," I said. As I headed to the door, the lady who was knitting looked at me carefully. The old guy was snoring.

I walked as fast as I could toward my car. I passed Cappy's. (I'd live with my hunger and thirst.) I passed a small True Value hardware store and an empty barbershop. In ten minutes I was back at the abandoned gas station.

There was only one problem. My car was gone.

I looked to my right and to my left six or seven times, as if I might just have misplaced the damn car. Then I realized I couldn't do anything but use my feet. I could either walk or I could give myself up. I touched the flash drive, safe in my pocket, and I started walking.

That little plastic technobullet in my pocket worked like a good luck charm. I wasn't walking more than five minutes when a semi pulled up right alongside me and stopped.

CHAPTER 58

"TEN DOLLARS. Jump in if you got it. Jump back if you ain't."

This proposal was offered by a greasy-looking teenager who could have been the evil twin of the Greyhound ticket seller in Carolton. His bare feet just made it to the pedals of the truck. His hair was slicked back, and the black onyx (I'm guessing it was onyx) piercing on the side of his nose was almost as big as the nose itself. He was smoking weed.

I guess I didn't respond to his offer fast enough to suit him.

"You in or you out, man?" he asked.

I did what I had to do: I hopped in and handed him two fives.

"And you're going where?" I asked.

"More important, where are you going?" he said.

"Ultimately I need to be in New York."

"Well, you are extremely out of luck, 'cause this baby stops in Naperville, Illinois."

"Closer to New York than I am right now," I said. I was determined to sound like a casual wise guy instead of the scared, hungry, nervous, filthy mess that I actually was.

I looked at the clock on the dashboard.

"Holy shit," I said. "It's noon already."

"It's eleven o'clock," he said. "I always keep the clock an hour ahead of time. It gives me something to look forward to."

I didn't quite understand that sentence. And I wasn't really all that happy riding with a stoned driver who could pass for a thirteen-year-old.

We drove in silence for a few minutes.

"You got a name?" the driver said.

"Yeah. I'm George," I said.

George? Where the hell did that come from?

"Was you ever president of the country, George?" he asked, and then he laughed loudly, as if he had just told an incredibly funny joke.

"And your name?" I asked.

"Kenny. And no one named Kenny was ever president." He laughed at this joke even more loudly.

Then he said, "I think we both could use some food. Open the glove compartment."

I did. It was filled with five packages of Hostess cupcakes.

"Take as many as you want. Dinner is covered in the admission price. Gimme a pack. I want to hold off the munchies best I can."

As I was unwrapping the cellophane from the cupcakes the dashboard speaker blasted out a short siren and shot out the announcement about the *possibly dangerous* guy who was on the loose. The news was that the *middle-aged* white guy, *Jacob Brandeis by name,* was reported *possibly* in the areas of Iowa, Illinois, or Missouri. He had *not* been spotted in screenings at airports or hotels, and—in an unusual burst of Store honesty—*the suspect's tracking location is uncertain.*

I kept my eye on the young driver. Even when the

announcer mentioned those red-and-white shoes the kid didn't cast a glance at my feet. He seemed totally occupied licking crumbs and fake whipped cream from his lips.

"These cupcakes are good," I said.

He ignored me. He was way too busy flashing his brights at the "dumbass mother" car in front of us.

I slept.

CHAPTER 59

IT WAS dark night when I woke up.

The truck was parked somewhere on the side of the highway. I assumed it was still I-80. But I couldn't be sure, and I had no immediate way of finding out. The driver was not there.

I got out of the truck and left the door open so I could have a little light. I walked a few feet into the woods and urinated. As soon as I zipped up I heard my traveling companion's voice.

"Hey, we both had the same idea," he said. He was walking toward me from a spot deeper in the woods, and I thought that perhaps the friendliness in his voice came from the new big fat joint he was smoking. We both walked the short distance back to the truck.

He handed me a Thermos. "You thirsty?" he asked.

I was thirsty as hell, but I suddenly had a ridiculous, nauseating feeling: I didn't want to drink from a container where this punk's lips had been. The punk must have been a mind reader.

"Don't worry, man. I look like a scuz, but I don't have any disease."

I took a gulp and almost immediately choked.

"What the hell is that?" I asked.

"Tequila, OJ, and Amaretto. Wicked good."

"Plain wicked. You got anything else?"

"Whaddya think this is for ten bucks a night? The goddamn Hilton?"

He laughed, but I didn't think he was happy. We climbed back into the truck.

"Where are we?" I said as he drove us back on the highway.

He didn't answer, but he tossed me a cheap standalone GPS unit.

"See for yourself," he said. (I think he was still pissed that I didn't like his special cocktail.)

We were in Joliet, not very far from Naperville, the destination he had originally mentioned.

"What are you delivering to Naperville?" I asked.

He didn't answer, but he did laugh.

"Is that funny?" I asked.

"Sorta," he said.

"Something illegal?" I said, trying my best to sound like I was totally at peace with delivering drugs or guns or illegal immigrants.

"Yeah, something very illegal," he said.

"Like what?"

"Like you," he said, and he laughed again.

CHAPTER 60

"WHAT THE hell are you talking about?" I asked.

"You're one of those guys who think 'cause I *sound* stupid I actually *am* stupid. But you got it all wrong."

I had some idea where this little conversation was heading, and I wasn't happy to be participating in it. Especially when I heard the locks on both sides of the cab click shut.

"I know exactly who you are," Kenny said.

The truck driver's voice transformed from street-punk nasty into something just a little smoother.

"Here's how stupid I am. I'm stupid enough to listen to the radio and all the news announcements about the cops trying to catch you. I know a lot. I know that your name is something like Jacob Brady. And I know that you're the dude everybody's looking for. And I know that I could make myself a few pieces o' gold when I turn you in."

Options automatically began clicking through my head. If I tried to fight this guy, we'd end up in a sure-to-be-head-on highway collision, even if I had the smallest chance of taking the wheel from him and knocking him out. This was no road movie.

My next option was that I could try to bullshit my way out of the situation. I thought I'd give this option a shot.

"Man, I'm an out-of-work floor layer trying to get to see my girlfriend in New York. I sure am not any Jacob Brady."

He smiled at me.

"I know you're not Jacob Brady," he said. "Your name is Jacob Brandeis. I thought I'd screw with you a little."

I would be a jerk to keep playing possum with Kenny on this one. He was right. He may not have been particularly eloquent, but he certainly was not stupid.

"I'm curious, Mr. George-Jacob-Brady-Brandeis," he said. "What in hell did you do to get the folks at the Store so goddamn pissed off?"

I was silent for at least sixty seconds.

"Huh? What is it you did?" Kenny asked.

I was ready to answer. "I tried to tell the truth."

Now he was quiet.

"You're kind of a crazy mother, ain't you?" Kenny said.

"I don't mean to preach," I said. "But I just don't think that telling the truth is all that crazy."

"I guess I agree. But I'm still not buying you, man. The Store? They're gonna hang you when they get you."

"You're probably right," I said. "I'm going to get hanged for writing a book."

I slipped my hand into my jeans pocket. The little lump of a flash drive—my past, my present, my future—felt so stupid and unimportant next to my key chain, a box of Tic Tacs, and a few coins.

"You *wrote a book*? I just assumed you did something like kill some big shot at New Burg headquarters or that you messed with Tom Owens's wife."

"No. All's I did..." *Why was I starting to sound like Kenny?* "All's I did was write down the sneaky shit they do at the Store. How they weasel their way into people's lives. How they contol what you do, what you buy, maybe even what you think."

"A book," Kenny said. He shook his head. "That's amazing."

I thought, perhaps foolishly, that I heard a note of understanding in his voice, but I was wrong. He kept shaking his head in wonderment.

Then he added, "Amazing. It's goddamn amazing. Who the hell would want to read a book about that?" A pause. Then he said, "Shit. Who the hell would even want to read *a book?*"

CHAPTER 61

I PRETENDED to be asleep, as if pretending to be asleep were a plan in and of itself. I pretended to snore quietly, as if sleeping and snoring quietly were also part of the plan. But there was no plan. A not-so-dumbass teenager was my ultimate downfall. Who would have predicted that?

"I know you're not really sleeping, Jacob ol' buddy," Kenny said. "I got a girl who does the same thing. She pretends to be sleepin' and snorin' when she doesn't want to play around."

My response was simple: "Son of a bitch."

"There's a rest stop right up here," Kenny said. "I'm going to pull over before we haul in to Naperville. My bladder isn't what it used to be."

The rest stop was nothing but three unusable phone booths and a few weak streetlights. It was deserted and depressing.

"Now, here's how we've got to do this. I'm gonna lock the doors behind me, and then I'm gonna stand right next to your door and take a leak. Just in case you get rambunctious and decide that you can knock me over and take off. That would just be foolish."

So Kenny did what he said he would do. In fact

he leaned his back against my door while he relieved himself. Then he motioned for me to lower my window. I pantomimed back that I couldn't. I mouthed the words *electric window*. Kenny nodded. He scooted around to his side, unlocked the truck, and slid into the driver's seat.

"I was thinking," he said. "You got a name for it?"

"Of course. It's called *Twenty-Twenty*."

"I get it. You're a clever bastard, ain't you?"

"Not that clever," I said. "I'm going to Naperville with you."

"Twenty-Twenty," he repeated, as if he hadn't heard me speak. There was a long pause. Kenny looked ahead at the weeds and trees beyond the filthy phone booths and overflowing trash cans. Then he turned and looked at me.

"Get outta the truck," he said.

"No. I don't need..."

"Get outta the truck," he repeated.

He clicked open the locked doors.

"Go ahead," Kenny said as he started the truck engine.

I opened the door and slid down off my seat and onto the ground. Then I turned around and looked at Kenny.

"Twenty-Twenty," he said. "I think I may just read *that* book."

The truck took off.

CHAPTER 62

IN JOLIET, Illinois, I hopped a freight train.

That's right. I hopped a freight train. Suddenly I was living in a folk song.

In this Store-controlled techno-packed world, where the sky was covered with drones and supersonic planes, freight trains still existed. And when I saw a guy hoist himself from a ditch alongside the tracks onto a big red car marked NYC PENN STATION, I followed him on board.

After twelve hours of inhaling the overwhelming odor of pig feces, keeping an eye on two fellow travelers who, I knew, would gladly slit my throat to steal my wallet, and eating a Subway sandwich with shredded lettuce that had turned brown around three days ago, I was in New York City.

Twenty minutes later I was somewhere on West 24th Street and Tenth Avenue. Between a bodega and a Chinese restaurant was a FedEx store, and fifteen dollars later my cherished flash drive had been transformed into good old hard copy—a four-hundred-and-ten-page manuscript. I bought a cardboard box, slipped the pages inside, and asked the clerk to tie it with string.

I was nervous. I was exhausted. I was hungry as hell. I didn't even give a crap when the middle-aged woman behind the FedEx counter thought it was perfectly okay to say, "Hey, mister, have you considered taking a shower? You stink."

I was out of there and headed downtown to SoHo, to Anne Gutman's office. The drones were beginning to hover. The stress was making me light-headed. Although I had been to Anne Gutman's office around thirty times, I was having trouble remembering the precise address.

I wandered off course a bit, and I worried a lot. I would have been naive to believe that the Store had given up their search for me. In fact, their efforts had most likely intensified.

If I needed something to scare me even more, it was at that precise moment that I heard a woman on the sidewalk say, "That's gotta be him. That's the guy. Jacob Brandeis."

It was also the precise moment when I recognized that I was standing in front of the building that housed Anne's office.

Here goes everything.

CHAPTER 63

A FEW hours pass, and my life consists of waiting for Anne Gutman's opinion on my manuscript. I am waiting as a man accused of mass murder waits for a jury decision. I can think of nothing else—not the thousands of people searching for me, not the consequences of my possible capture. I think my book is really important. Now I need Anne Gutman to think so, too.

But she's not calling, and I realize that I'm living on nothing but luck—good luck and bad luck. There was Maggie Pine; that was good luck. There was Kenny at the start of my truck ride; that was very bad luck. Then there was Kenny at the end of my truck ride; that was unbelievably good luck.

Anne gave me two fifty-dollar bills when I left her office in my stinky state of anxiety and manic fear. If you want to know what kind of Manhattan hotel lodging you can get for less than a hundred bucks (with a little left over for a nine-dollar sandwich and two Heinekens), I can tell you this: I'm staying in a place on Twelfth Avenue called...get ready for this...HOTEL. That's it. That's the name. Not HOTEL WEST SIDE, not LARRY'S HOTEL, not ECONOMY LODGING.

No, just HOTEL, and it looks exactly what you think a place called HOTEL should look like: not just the flaking paint stained with fluids you don't want to think about, but also bedsheets and a dirty towel that clearly haven't been replaced in a few days, maybe a few weeks.

A shower helps. It helps as much as lukewarm water and a sliver of used soap can possibly help. It washes away the stink and the dirt and the grease and the sweat. But nothing can wash away the fear of something that could go wrong mixed with the hope that everything might turn out just fine.

Eleven dollars of Anne Gutman's money purchases a disposable phone. I bought it from an African guy who was displaying his merchandise on a sidewalk. But I knew the damn thing worked. As soon as I bought it I called Anne, left my temporary number on her machine, and told her to call me ("Please, please, please, call me, for Christ's sake. I'm living a horror story. I need to know what's happening").

By midnight—after I had spent way too much time with Jimmy Fallon and Seth Meyers and Charlie Rose—no Anne, no call.

I call her again and again, and all I ever hear is "You've reached Anne Gutman. I can't come to…"

I turn off the television. I lie on the filthy bed. I hold the disposable cell phone in my hand as if it were a religious object given to me by Jesus Christ.

Just before 4:00 a.m., my friend the phone and I take a walk to a liquor store, the kind of liquor store that has a bulletproof shield in front of all the bottles and a bulletproof booth where the owner takes your cash and completes your transaction.

Call me, Anne. Call me, Anne. Call me, Anne, for Christ's sake. This puts the march in my steps.

I buy a pint of Heaven Hill bourbon and a package of barbecue-flavored Pringles. I walk back to HOTEL.

Call me, Anne. Call me, Anne. Call me…

By 7:00 a.m., no phone call, no Anne, no bourbon, no Pringles…no hope.

CHAPTER 64

WHAT THE hell should I do now?

I'm afraid to walk the streets for fear of being spotted. I have definitely moved into crazyland. Even though I'm certain that they've got surveillance cameras in my rat hole, I can't actually find any. But looking for them—standing on the squeaky bed, kneeling on the broken dresser—kills some time.

I sneak down to Anne's office, in SoHo. Her assistants both say that Ms. Gutman is in Houston on business. ("We've given her your messages.") I am about to head to the elevator when one of the women says, "Oh, Ms. Gutman said to give you this." She hands me four fifty-dollar bills. Maybe I could make a nice living waiting for Anne Gutman.

I go back to HOTEL. Staying in that room makes me sadder than anyone deserves to be. Drinking cheap bourbon, eating cold burgers, and watching those bickering broads on *The View* is not the life I had planned for myself. Lonely? I think only dead people are lonelier than I am. I don't know for sure what it's like to be dead, but I sure as shit am standing mighty close.

I go into one of those chain drugstores near Times Square. Walgreens? Duane Reade? CVS? Who the hell knows? I buy a disposable razor, store-brand ibuprofen, store-brand shaving cream, and a Hershey's Special Dark chocolate bar (the giant size).

I go up to the cashier, a sweet-looking Latina no older than eighteen.

"How you doing today, sir?" she says. I'm thinking, *Is this New York, or have I clicked my heels and gone back to Nebraska?* (Yeah, I know it's supposed to be Kansas, but my life is in Nebraska.)

"I'm doing fine. How about you?"

She's ringing up the purchases with exceptional speed. Total, $11.47, and "Sure, I would like to make a one-dollar donation to the Children's Diabetes Fund."

She hands me back a few dollar bills and coins in change. Outside, I go to stuff it in my pocket and I realize that in among the paper money she handed me is a business card. It's blank except for four handwritten words: CHECK YOUR TEXT MESSAGES.

I run back into the store. The girl behind the counter is gone. I stand in front of an endcap display of skin moisturizer.

I punch into my messages as fast as I can. In those few seconds I think it might be Anne or even Megan or some thug from the store or…there's the text:

Hey, J, check out "The Store for Books" page. Very cool.

My sweaty fingers move faster than ever. I move to Google. Then Google moves me to the landing page of the Store. Just below the bullshit banners selling toaster ovens and Lego and plus-size bathing suits is this:

**The book the world's been waiting
for...**
Twenty-Twenty
**The blockbuster that's bound to bust
the Store wide open**

CHAPTER 65

BACK AT HOTEL, I click on the little line that says: "Read all about it. Now!" The screen fills with typography that's supposed to look like human handwriting. It says: "How can we make your life better today?"

I know Megan's username (Major345Meg) and her password (LindsAlex9#9). In a few seconds I'm on the "Books, E-Readers, Audio" page. My index finger is actually sweating. My hands are shaking. I feel as if I'm about to push the button that will start a nuclear war.

In a way I could be right about that. This is either the beginning or the end of my own personal crazy nuclear war.

Boom! There it is!

The gutsy exposé of the world's most
important and influential website
Behind the scenes at the Store
An anonymous author tells the truth
about the world's best-known
company
Twenty-Twenty
Enter the incredible world of the Store

My hands shake even more as I push the Download button. Within thirty seconds the words DOWNLOAD COMPLETED fill the screen. I move to chapter 1, page 7. It is a headache-making, eye-aching chore to try to read the small type on the crappy little disposable phone screen. I constantly need to enlarge the type and then reduce it in order to move on to the next paragraph.

But hey, who gives a good goddamn? This is *Twenty-Twenty*. This is incredible.

So what do I find?

This isn't my book at all.

These aren't my words.

My name isn't even on the cover.

Holy shit. It's not my book. And I'm no author.

This fraud is an epic windblast of praise to the genius of the Store.

This is a disgusting ode to the brilliance of Thomas P. Owens. The manuscript even keeps referring to him as "our beloved founder."

I rush pages and chapters ahead. No matter where my eyes land, it is a totally ridiculous piece of bullshit. I read how the Store has "made America a better place to live because it's given America a better place to shop."

According to this version, the Store is not interested in making a profit for at least another fifteen years (bullshit!). The Store underprices every item they sell—from prescription drugs to lawn mowers to disposable diapers to finely crafted Stickley furniture (bullshit!). The Store believes in full discretion and privacy for all their customers. "Without the trust of our consumer partners we have no business" (double bullshit!).

I begin scrolling with fierce speed. Perhaps every

fifteen pages I recognize a sentence from my original manuscript. Usually it's a harmless sentence like: "And this was just part of Thomas P. Owens's dream."

I leave the book itself and move to a page entitled "What Do Other Customers Think of This Book? Read the Ratings from A+ to F."

Here's a challenge for the Store. This must be the most hated book in America.

One customer writes: "In a few words: this book stinks. A boring valentine. *F* as in phony. *F* as in foolish. *F* as in freaking stupid."

Another customer says: "I guess the author was ashamed to put his name on this piece of garbage. I don't blame him or her."

I lie on the smelly HOTEL bed. I close my eyes. And then…then I sit up in bed as if the room is on fire.

I smile. The smile grows bigger. The smile turns into laughter. The laughter is unstoppable.

I'm tired and sleepy.

Yet I leap out of bed.

I stomp my legs and feet like a crazy little kid.

It worked! The Store published the stupid bogus version of my book.

CHAPTER 66

"HAVE WE heard anything?" the old man says.

"Nothing yet, sir," says the serious-looking young woman in brown canvas shorts and hiking boots. She carries a tan Osprey backpack. A single earphone is attached to her left ear. She is the old man's executive assistant, and she is seldom more than a few feet from his side.

The old man—perhaps he is nearing eighty—is in remarkably fine shape. Everyone in his entourage says so. He is tall and stands straight. His white beard is closely trimmed, and his gray hair is full and thick.

The old man flew by private jet last night to Flagstaff. This morning he is hiking the hills near Supai on the periphery of Grand Canyon National Park. He's not at all alone, however. His entourage includes the executive assistant, two mountain hiking guides, the old man's fifty-year-old son, and the old man's thirty-three-year-old wife. There is also a camp cook (well, a chef-nutritionist, actually), a tech support man, and the old man's personal physician.

"Call New Burg. I want to know what's happening," the old man says. His manner is strong but not unpleasant. He's so used to being rich and in charge that there's no need for him to be anything less than gracious. "Now!" he says sternly.

"Don't have to call, sir. New Burg is calling *us,*" the assistant says. As she pushes a few buttons to accept the message, he looks over the mountains above and below him. The red and brown and yellow and coral palette stuns him with its beauty. He thinks what he frequently thinks: *I'm a lucky man.* No one would argue with that.

"I'll take the message myself," he says to the executive assistant. She hands him the earphone, and he holds it close.

"What's the story?" he asks.

The caller says, "It's over. A big nothing. Done and done."

"Hah!" the old man says, then adds, "Not even a hiccup. Just a book. It's a stupid e-book.

"Can you imagine?" he says as he hands the earphone back to his assistant, "Just a book."

Thomas P. Owens begins to laugh. He looks out over the mountains. He owns thousands of acres of this land. A shiver of warmth rushes through him. The beloved founder's laugh grows louder. The colors of the mountains grow more intense.

His lovely wife touches his shoulder. His physician keeps a steady eye on him. His executive assistant replaces the earphone on her ear. The personal chef begins unpacking lunch.

He owns so much land in this area. Not merely the land he is standing on, but also so much land beyond that and then beyond that and…

His laughter winds down, and he speaks. His voice is firm and hearty and happy.

"Not even a hiccup. A book. The thing is just a book."

He takes a big gulp of water from the bottle that his beautiful young wife has handed him.

"I'd like to hike a bit more before we have lunch," the old man says.

Nobody dares disagree with him. A few of them wipe dirt and sweat from their faces. A few of them drink some water. They are about to begin.

"I'll have everything ready when you return, sir," the chef-nutritionist says.

"Perfect," says the old man. "Let's get going."

And then.

"Hold on just a minute, sir," his executive assistant says. "It looks like you're getting another message."

CHAPTER 67

"ARE YOU ready, Anne?"

"Completely. The question is, are *you* ready, Jacob?"

"I've only dreamed of a day like this day most of my life," I say.

We are standing in a small room in a large conference space on Wooster Street, in SoHo. Anne and I are about to—I can't believe I'm lucky enough to be saying this—hold a press conference.

Word is out: the Store has published a totally counterfeit version of *Twenty-Twenty*. The real version—a tough-minded, inflammatory, scandalous book—is going to be available starting tomorrow.

In the big space on Wooster Street, a noisy menagerie of bloggers and newspaper writers and e-zine journalists has gathered. People from the *Wall Street Journal* and Vulture.com and BuzzFeed and YouTube and *Salon* and *Slate* and virtually every website and cable channel in the country.

The only media source that's missing, of course, is the Store.

A PR guy holds open the door to our waiting room. *Ladies and gentlemen, please be prepared to have your heads blown off.*

We walk toward the cameras. The crowd moves closer to the dais, where we stand before a gigantic cluster of microphones.

After a few moments of the "press" settling down, I begin to speak. I am—to my own surprise—calm. My voice feels strong and sensible.

"Good morning. I'm Jacob Brandeis." I pause. There is no applause. I'm an idiot. This is the press, not the public. I start talking again.

"We know why we're here. You know why we're here…"

Why do I keep pausing? Of course they know why they're there.

"Beginning tomorrow, the authentic, unexpurgated, *real* version of *Twenty-Twenty* will be available. The people who want to know the truth about the Store can find it on a new site called WrittenTruth .com. It will be delivered within twenty-four hours. But if you just can't wait twenty-four hours, it will also be available at whatever independent bookstores throughout the country have not yet been devoured by the Store. And if I have to, I'll stand on the back of a truck in Times Square and sell copies to anyone who wants to read them."

Some laughter. Then mostly silence.

"I know that you all have plenty of questions…"

Suddenly an explosion of hands and shouts of "Mr. Brandeis"…"Jacob"…"Mr. Brandeis"…

I hold up my hands. I talk loudly into the mike. Reverb throughout the room.

"I will be very glad to tell you in detail how we pulled this off. We'll do that some other time. But I can give you the general answer right now: exceptional people—family and friends—were secretly in on the plan from the beginning. We all acted in a way that got the Store to believe we were writing one kind of book, but in fact we were writing the book that is *now* being released.

"My great kids, Lindsay and Alex, were continually making videos of my great wife, Megan, and me arguing venomously about my project. Then they'd send that video to the Store. The Store thought the kids were cooperating, but of course all they were doing was verifying that the Store was recording us on their own surveillance cameras. The one thing the Store didn't know was this: it was all a *huge act,* a delicately planned act—and, I might add, a very scary performance. The Store believed the story we handed them: a crazy father was writing a book, and the wife and kids were so loyal to the Store that…well, you get it.

"As to the others who helped us pull it off…they're all in the book. Suffice it to say that Megan and I had recruited certain of our neighbors—Marie and Bud and Bette—to become part of the plan. Even Megan's supposedly rotten boss, Sam Reed, had some secret scores to settle with the Store management. So Sam became part of the act.

"I'll be moving offstage in a minute. I'm a writer, not an actor. But I do want to talk about two of the most amazing people behind the scenes, two women who did as much as I did to make this book happen.

"Yes, I wrote the book, the real book, the true *Twenty-Twenty,* but nothing would have been possible without the unwavering encouragement and the wildly sneaky brain of the most important and honest book publisher in the world, Anne Gutman."

I swing my left arm backward, and Anne steps closer to the microphones. Her voice is sure and strong. As my mom used to say, "You can hear her brains in her voice."

"Jacob Brandeis wrote a brilliant investigative book under essentially wartime circumstances. I was a conduit, a fan, a citizen. I am proud to have been part of it."

Anne and I hug, and now—oh, shit, my eyes are filling up with tears—I replace Anne at the microphone.

"I...I...sometimes I was so arrogant...obnoxious to her, but she never gave up...I...nineteen years ago, I...I chose right. Here's Megan."

She walks out. She looks terrific. New York all the way: black slacks and black shirt and her hair tied back with a white scarf. As we kiss—I could honestly say the kiss was passionate—Alex and Lindsay walk over to us.

"I love you," I say again and again to the three of them. I hold them so tightly that I actually think I might squeeze them until they burst.

"Yay," shouts Alex. "Group hug!"

I don't think any of us wanted that hug to end. Megan tilts her head back and looks me squarely in the eyes. Then she says, "There's just one thing I've been wanting to tell you."

"What's that?" I ask.

Tears are streaming down her cheeks.

She looks at me. She speaks.

"Ugga-bugga."

FIFTEEN MONTHS LATER

CHAPTER 68

WHEN I began writing *Twenty-Twenty* I was so fueled by anger and self-righteousness that I had no idea what I wanted to accomplish beyond exposing the Store's policies and procedures.

Yes, at times when I was writing in my stifling attic in New Burg I had the occasional fantasy that the Store would come tumbling down. But of course I knew that would never happen, and I also knew (and worried about the fact) that thousands of people depended on the Store for their livelihood and even for their very lives.

So after the book appeared, the Store did not disappear from the face of the earth. It remained an enormous factor in the United States economy, but it did do a monumental job at self-reform. I don't doubt that this reform came about quickly to prevent state and federal governments from doing the reforming. But it came about.

Listening devices, surveillance devices, and video-recording devices were removed from streets and stores and restaurants and, most important, from private homes.

Were things perfect? Of course not. There would

always be people who would try to make a profit at all costs. (I'm talking to you, Thomas P. Owens.) But things were definitely better.

Bette and Bud were back in New Burg, and we e-mailed and texted back and forth quite a bit. Their observation: "The town looks the same, but it doesn't *feel* the same. It seems…better and calmer. Folks aren't looking over their shoulders all the time. We'll see what happens."

Yep. That's all we can do. We'll see.

As for the Brandeis family? Well, I can tell you this. The book did not make us rich. But it did make us—as my mother would say—comfortable enough not to worry ourselves half to death.

Megan and I were both tapped for a lot of juicy freelance assignments, and we worked hard at them. Investigative journalism was part of our mutual DNA. But so far, no subject has come along as important or provocative as the Store. I don't think anything will compare to that.

We moved back to New York City, away from our old neighborhood. We're now in SoHo. It's a lot more convenient than FiDi and close enough to Anne Gutman's office for she and I to have a standing Thursday lunch date at Balthazar (she pays).

Alex is a student at high school. He's doing very well…in tennis, soccer, and video club. The SAT tutors are lining up.

This past Thursday Megan and I drove Lindsay up to Connecticut. Alex came with us (reluctantly) to do the heavy lifting. Lindsay's starting at Wesleyan University. She'll be an English major with a minor in journalism. Surprise!

The car ride up to school was treacherous. Thunder, lightning, and lake-deep puddles on Route 66. By the time the four of us wrestled Lindsay's boxes and suitcases and that damn trunk into her dorm, we were so soaked that we didn't even bother opening umbrellas as we walked back to the car to say our good-byes.

"Hey, man, we've never been, like, so apart from each other before," Alex said to his sister. We hugged. Then we hugged some more.

"We're getting good at these group hugs," Megan said.

"That's *your* opinion," said Alex, but he did not pull away from the group.

"You know, this feels like we're four actors in a really dramatic ending of a French movie," I said.

Lindsay spoke: "There's so much rain that I can't even be sure if I'm actually crying."

There was no camouflaging the fact that both Megan and I were crying.

"In my humble opinion, I think this weather is absolutely beautiful," I said.

"You really are a crazy guy, Dad," said Alex.

"No. I'm right," I said. "Take a look. There's not a drone in the sky."

ABOUT THE AUTHORS

JAMES PATTERSON is the world's bestselling author. The creator of Alex Cross, he has produced more enduring fictional heroes than any other novelist alive. He lives in Florida with his family.

RICHARD DiLALLO is a former advertising executive. He lives in Manhattan with his wife.

OWEN TAYLOR IS ABOUT TO BE BETRAYED ON HIS FINAL COVERT MISSION. WILL HE MAKE IT HOME ALIVE?

PLEASE TURN THE PAGE FOR THE COMPLETE NOVEL BY JAMES PATTERSON WITH BRENDAN DUBOIS

THE END

CHAPTER 1

IN A REMOTE hangar at the Aviano NATO air base in northern Italy, I'm holding my government issue SIG Sauer P226 9mm pistol in my right hand, hammer pulled back, finger on the trigger, deciding when and how I should shoot the intelligence field officer standing before me.

Dunton is skinny, with thick brown hair, round wire-rimmed glasses, and a snippy attitude. He's wearing a BDU, a Kevlar vest, and heavy boots.

He says, "I'm telling you, Taylor, I don't care what the weather reports are saying for tonight, you and your buds are 'go' for this mission. The diplomats in Geneva are in a delicate position. Your successful op could tilt things to a satisfactory conclusion."

I keep quiet. I'm sure he thinks I'm pondering his warning, but what I'm really pondering is the best place to shoot him. Dead center in the chest would break a couple of ribs and knock him flat on his ass, but a round to the center of that shiny forehead would get the job done in a final and spectacular fashion.

But killing him would mean lots of paperwork and embarrassing questions, and I have no time for that.

I say, "Dunton, you may have operational control, but I have tactical command of this op. It's my job whether to say go, not yours. Or anybody in Geneva. Or Washington. Or Langley."

Dunton says, "Deputy Director Hunley has expressly—"

"You say he's a deputy," I point out. "Does he get a nice five-pointed star to go along with it?"

I sense the other four members of my team standing behind me, giving me quiet support, and Dunton glares at me before stomping toward one of the hangar's side doors. "I'm off to the weather office," he shouts back. "You better be ready when I come back!"

I try to be helpful. "Don't get lost."

The door slams and my teammates chuckle for a moment and wander away, their current mission achieved. It's still raining. I slowly draw the hammer down on my pistol and return it to my side holster, taking in the miserable weather. We'll wait for the final weather report, and that will tell us if we can go out on this rainy night to kill somebody in another country we've never been to before.

My teammates—Borozan, Sher, Garcia, and Clayton—now keep to their own routines, talking or smoking or reading from battered paperbacks. I just wait, looking out at the rain coming down and hitting the windswept runway, not wanting to think, just waiting for that one last weather report so I can complete my final mission.

We're all dressed nearly alike, with custom helmets, camouflaged BDUs, heavy boots, knee pads and elbow pads, body armor, MOLLE vests with flashlights, knives, survival packs, compass, encrypted handheld devices, and holstered pistols. Our assault packs and parachutes are carefully stored in the corner of the empty hangar. We each carry a modified Heckler & Koch HK416 rifle with a 10-inch barrel slung over our shoulders.

Occasionally air force personnel wander in and just as quickly wander out, knowing they shouldn't be here, not wanting to be in the same area with who we are: stone-cold killers ready to do a job.

I pace some more, feeling the wind hitting my face from the Southern Carnic Alps. On my BDU, my name tag, TAYLOR, is easily removable with one swift tear of Velcro, which I'll do once we illegally cross into Serbia. And that's it for any kind of identification in case I get wounded, killed, or captured.

Oh, and who are we, my four teammates and I? I'm sure you've heard of Rangers, SEAL Team 6, Special Forces, Marine Recon, Delta Force, and other elite secret units. Well, we're not any of them. For what use is an elite secret unit if its name is known to the outside world?

One of my crew comes up to me. It's Clayton, who looks like the cliché surfer dude from California, which is pretty much the truth.

"What do you think, Gramps?"

I wince at my nickname, knowing if I were to complain about it, my guys would use it more. My fault. Last time around with these special operators, I let slip that I was on active duty during the first Persian Gulf War, back in 1991.

"Gonna be tight," I say. "Dunton has his pressure, his boss Hunley has pressure, his boss's boss has pressure, and it all comes down to us. You know the drill—shit rolls downhill."

"Always nice to know we're here to catch it."

The door slams open and Dunton strides back in with a sheet of paper in one hand. Clayton says, "What do you think? I know he talks the talk, but is he really CIA? Or Defense Intelligence Agency? National Reconnaissance Office?"

"Probably NSA, son," I say to Clayton. "No Such Agency."

Dunton steps forward, thrusts the sheet into my hand. I glance at the map, seeing the weather report, the prediction for the next six hours. Iffy. It's up to me, the team leader. My last op, and I'd like to make it a successful one. But the bad weather could force us down over the Adriatic Sea or into the Carpathian Mountains. I could kill myself and these guys with one second's worth of decision.

Some last op. Even if I were to pull the plug, I'd be done, and these guys would be up to bat again at some later date. In other words, I'd finally be safe, and they wouldn't.

Dunton says, "Well? Well?"

I crumple up the sheet of paper, toss it at his chest. "We go."

Dunton smirks while I head over to our gear, and Clayton is behind me. He says quietly, "A question, Gramps?"

"Go ahead."

"I saw you draw on Dunton before he left to get the last weather report. Were you really going to shoot him?"

I pick up my assault pack and parachute. "We'll never know, will we?"

Clayton grins, which is a nice memory for me, because in three hours and eleven minutes, he'll be dead.

CHAPTER 2

TIME FOR ONE last briefing before we fly into harm's way and get dropped out of a perfectly good helicopter in the process. We've trained and briefed so much we don't need this final step, but them's the rules. The room is small, bare, and fits its purpose. A series of photographs of a bearded man is on one whiteboard, and next to the photos is a detailed topo map of where we're going to end up, if the army's 160th Special Operations Aviation Regiment—more commonly known as the Nightstalkers—doesn't screw up and drop us off in Monaco or on the Riviera.

Which wouldn't be that bad, all things considered.

I slap the center photo as my four guys settle into standard classroom chairs. "One last thought to bounce around in those thick skulls of yours. Our target for tonight. Darko Latos. Ever since the Balkan wars have heated up again, he's been one of the leaders stirring the hate. He made his name back during the first Balkan wars when he ran a paramilitary unit of snipers in the hills above Sarajevo, shooting kids in the head."

I touch the map next to the photo of Darko. "His house, more like a mansion, has two support buildings—here, and here—along with this adjacent warehouse. Just like the mock-ups we trained on back in North Carolina. Darko used to make his living the old-fashioned way, smuggling drugs and young Balkan sex slaves up to truck stops in Germany, France, and Belgium. Now he has the opportunity to go back to his first love, killing innocents, and we're going in tonight to stop him. After our insertion, at 0200 hours, we're to meet with an intelligence operative—code-named Alex—at this place, called Point Q. He'll lead us to Darko's compound. Any questions?"

My team is good, and they know better than to ask anything at this point, so I continue.

"The negotiations in Geneva are meant to halt this war before it gets worse, but the word is that those talks are in a delicate stage. First we zap Darko. That will disrupt operations in his region, give a little more momentum to the peace talks. If those negotiations fail, the Balkan wars will spread. Last time that happened there was a little misunderstanding called World War I that ended with seventeen million getting killed."

Sher says, "Hell of a thing, to have preventing World War III on our shoulders."

Garcia grins, kicks his leg. "Then that's why we're heading out, homie, 'cuz we're the best."

Borozan leans over, slaps Garcia on his thick shoulder. "Then how the hell did you end up here?"

A couple of laughs and insults, and Garcia says, "At least I passed the initial physical, *niñita*." More laughs but it's all in good fun, because *niñita* means *little girl* in Spanish, and there's nothing little about

Borozan. She's in great shape, passed every qualification without having it watered down, and she's had my back on a number of very bad occasions.

Oh, yeah, she's a woman. Pretty observant. Sure, most militaries in the world don't allow women on special ops missions like this, but we're not most militaries, and if the person can do the job, I don't care if that person goes to a restroom marked *M* or *W*.

I say, "Okay, saddle up." I strip down the photos and the map and find a metal wastebasket in a corner of the room. I pull free a hose from my water pack, cover the bottom of the wastebasket with some water, and drop the photos and paperwork in. In four seconds they become indecipherable sludge.

That's it. No record. Just like us, if we don't come back.

Outside the rain is coming down even heavier, but we don't run. What's the point if we're going to end up soaked anyway? Dunton, standing under a light-orange umbrella outside the door, gives us a thumbs-up and says something to Sher as we walk in a line across the airstrip. I move so I can talk to Sher. "What did the civvie say to you back there?"

"He said to make sure Darko's head came back on a stick," he says, gently scratching at his close-cropped brown beard.

"What did you tell him?"

Over the sound of the helicopter's engines winding up, Sher raises his voice. "I told him this was typical government op bullshit, 'cause none of us were issued a stick."

I slap him on his helmeted head as we get closer. The rotors of the highly classified and secret Stealth UH-80—the Invisible Hawk—start to turn, and as

I climb into the open side of the chopper, I recall a mission one of my navy buds did a few years back in Pakistan, killing the one and only Osama bin Laden. That was the official story. The unofficial and very dark story is that there were two missions that night: one to kill that son of a bitch OBL, and the other to have an "accident" in the compound so the Chinese and Russians would recover our helicopter wreckage, thinking they had secured the latest in Stealth technology.

Which they hadn't, but which gave them the excuse to waste years and billions of dollars in research, duplicating something we were never using. Still, as cool as it sounds, it complicated an already complicated op, which happens when people higher up the food chain want to get their fingers into all the supposed fun.

The rest of my crew gets into the helicopter, and Borozan holds onto my hand for about two seconds longer than she should, which is fine by me. I like the sensation. The last in is Garcia, and over the sound of the Stealth's chopper engines—they quiet right down once we get to cruising speed—Garcia leans into my ear and yells, "Got a problem, *abuelo!*"

"What's that?"

"Forgot my lucky rosary beads back at my bunk."

I shake my head. "No time for that."

"But it's my lucky rosary beads. I never leave without them!"

"Always a first time!" I yell back and push him in.

The Stealth chopper starts to move, and about a hundred meters down the runway, our backup helicopter's rotors are working as well, ready to follow us out of Italy and across the Adriatic in case we have mechanical difficulties and have to land somewhere.

One way or another, I think, this is my last op, and I'm gonna make it work.

The Stealth chopper starts to rise, and I find my spot on a canvas seat and pick up the headgear and microphone so I can talk to the lead pilot. The interior suddenly lights up, like someone is pointing a spotlight at us.

I quickly turn and see a yellow-red blossom of flame grow and then get smaller, down there back on the runway.

Our backup Stealth chopper, its four-man crew and everything else, is instantly being turned into cinders and ash.

Three of my guys say nothing and just look out the open door, but Garcia manages to get to me and yells, "Told you I should have gone back!"

CHAPTER 3

I SAY NOTHING, because what's there to say? We're all professionals—including the army guys who have just seen four of their friends turn into charred bones and flesh—and we get back to the job. The two crew chiefs help us get settled, and I take off my helmet, put on the headset, and switch it on. Up forward, the pilot and co-pilot look like gaunt insects with their oversized helmets. I say, "This is Wallaby One, Wallaby Strike."

Through the static I hear the calm and professional voice of the lead pilot. "Wallaby One, read you five by five."

There's a pause, and then he continues, "Tower tells us we lost the other Hawk to apparent mechanical malfunction. No word on survivors."

Any word won't be a good word, and I hate to say it, the Invisible Hawks are an ungainly beast to fly. Like the first couple years of the V-22 Ospreys, which had their share of accidents due to pilots getting used to the flying characteristics of something so new and complicated.

The pilot clears his throat. "Ah, so you know, Wallaby One, the only other available Hawk is at NAS Sigonella."

Sigonella. In Sicily, about as far away as possible, and where they speak Italian. Which means no second Stealth chopper is ready to help us out. Which means I now have to decide once more what we're going to do.

It's a quick decision. "Hawk, we're go."

"Roger that, Wallaby One, we're still go."

"All right, then." I keep quiet, letting this crew of Nightstalkers do what they're very good at doing, bringing people in and out of very dangerous places, and the troubled Balkans and the remote village we're going to in Serbia—southwest of Belgrade—certainly meets that definition.

My guys settle in and I leave them alone. We all have our own ways of getting in the zone, and I'm not for any of that "rah rah rah, band of brothers" pep talk. We don't need it, which is another reason why in picking our op name, I chose Wallaby Strike. Why not? Too many ops have been named Desert Storm, Desert Sabre, Neptune Spear, Desert Shield, rough-and-ready names like that.

I like Australia, and I like wallabies.

I start getting into my own zone, staring out in the darkness, thinking of our op plans, the procedures, the alternative plans if shit goes wrong—it always goes wrong—but other thoughts intrude, too, about this being my last op, and of a certain quiet lake in New Hampshire I want to find one of these days.

Someplace remote, someplace quiet, someplace where I would never be bothered.

So that's what's going on in my mind about two hours or so later, when the lead pilot breaks in. "Wallaby One, we are feet dry. Approximately forty minutes to drop zone."

"Roger that," I say, and in a practiced move, we all rip off our name badges and drop them to the floor, which is our routine. I gather them up, put them in a mesh bag, and secure it to the chopper's near bulkhead for later retrieval.

Then we get ready, like marionettes well trained in our motions, making sure all of our gear is in place, parachutes properly fastened, weapons securely attached. It would be very embarrassing to land in the middle of a free-fire zone with no weapons. My guys carry more than one firearm and are a giving crew, but they would probably draw the line at lending someone a weapon because the person was too stupid to secure his or her own.

In the crowded main cabin of the Invisible Hawk, I take an extra minute with Borozan, tugging a bit more than I should on her belts and straps, and that earns me a quick smile, which is highly unprofessional, but I decide to be a good sport and let it go.

"Wallaby One, ninety seconds."

"Roger that."

I remove my intercom system, retrieve my helmet, and lower and switch on my night vision goggles (or, as I call them, NVGs), mounted on my helmet. One of the crew chiefs moves to the main door, and we line up. We wait. The interior of the chopper—which had been lit by dim red lights to preserve our night vision—goes black, and in a very practiced motion, the crew chief slides open the door, the cold wind knocking us back.

We wait.

It's overcast with no moon but I can make out mountains, hills, and wooded forests below us. Fear leaps into me and I fight it back—*my God, you're going to jump out over this?*—and the crew chief makes a one-minute signal with a finger, and we shuffle forward, off to our dark drop.

Sher is the first one out and the rest of us don't waste time. In seconds we're all out in the Serbian night air, and as our chutes deploy, the slamming of the straps and rigging brings back all those muscle memories of previous successful jumps. We've jumped over and over again, training with HALO (high altitude, low opening) and HAHO (high altitude, high opening). However, we've heard that the Russian friends of the Serbs have new radar and search systems that can detect small objects like us high up in the air, so this is a low jump, and it only allows enough time for the parafoils to open up.

Since Sher is the lead jumper, he's guiding us in with compass and night vision gear, and the rest of us stack up above him, one after another. We turn like a corkscrew, descending, and way off to the eastern horizon, there's yellow-and-red tracer fire all around us. I ignore it. It's not aimed at us, and it's too far away to give a crap about.

But I can't ignore something else. Below us is our drop zone, a knobby, rock-strewn hilltop that stands out from the surrounding forest, and there should be four parafoil chutes below me, since I was the last one out.

Yet there are only three.

Damn mission is under way for twenty seconds and already it's gone to the shits.

One by one, we land on the outcropping, flaring out our black chutes, gathering them up, pulling them together, securing our site. The chutes are hidden and I count heads, and sure enough, one is missing.

It's Clayton.

I gather our group together, all of us alert with one knee down. We're talking but our night-vision gear is on, so everything around us is lit up in ghostly green.

"Anybody see what happened?" I ask.

No one answers.

"Anybody see a chute?"

Again, I'm met with silence.

I say, "Garcia, you were behind Clayton when we made the jump. What did you see?"

Garcia says, "Sorry, *jefe,* it went quick. You know how it is. Chute opened up and three corkscrews later, we're on the ground."

Borozan says, "I got him. He's alive." Besides everything else she's trained for, Borozan is our lead medic. She has an encrypted handheld device in her hand, and a small patch at the back of my neck itches. Attached there is a little sticky medical device with a low-range transmitter, allowing Borozan to track the medical status of me and everyone else in the group.

"Alive?" I ask.

"Yeah," she says. "He's about a hundred fifty meters to the northwest. Bearing 316 degrees."

All right, then, I think.

No question, no debate, no argument. There's the op, of course, but there are things greater than the op.

"Okay," I say. "Garcia, you take point. Let's go get our guy."

More gunfire, this time closer than before.

Sher whispers, "Welcome the fuck to Serbia."

CHAPTER 4

IT'S SLOW GOING because we're in enemy territory, aren't official combatants, and are outnumbered any way you look at it. But the other thing is that we're not headed to Point Q or the compound, where Darko Latos is sleeping in a drunken and cocaine-induced stupor. Nope, we're headed out in the wrong direction. I'm sure Dunton and his boss Hunley back in DC would be excreting the proverbial bricks if they knew.

I have a satellite phone hanging off the side that allows me to call anywhere in the world, at any time. I suppose I could have given them a ring, but why bother? So we keep on moving.

Garcia is on point and the rest of us spread out, me taking the rear, making sure no militias are out there, sneaking up on our six. The woods are a jumbled mess, but Garcia does a pretty good job of keeping us on track, until we run into a road.

A nice paved road.

I hate paved roads.

If you trot across, you're exposed, like a bug on a plate. If you trot across, an overhead asset—drone, aircraft, helicopter—can pick you right up. If you trot across, a fast-moving armored personnel carrier or squad vehicle can turn the corner and nail you with its headlights. Then follow that up with lots of incoming metal-jacketed rounds.

I hate paved roads.

We squat down, catch our breath. I hold up my right arm, make a quick circular motion with my right fist. My team gathers around me. I look up the road, Garcia looks across the road, Sher looks behind us, and Borozan looks down the road. We may be outnumbered and outgunned, but we're doing a lot of looking.

"Anything?" I whisper.

No reply. That's good. That means nobody sees anything of interest. I look up the road again. It's starting to snow. Why not? Still no sounds save those of the woods at night, no lights, no motion, nothing.

I make a quick chopping motion with my right hand, and we quickly scamper across the road and back into the woods. After checking our bearings, we move in a skirmish line, taking our time, knowing our guy is out there, but also knowing minutes are slipping away for us to get where we need to be to carry out our mission and get this op finished.

There's a slight pause as we take in a jumble of rocks. Borozan is next to me. She whispers, "About five meters away, if that. We're practically on top of him."

"Roger that."

She leans in so much that her lips nearly touch my right ear. "Hear this is your last op. That you're heading home. So where's home?"

I don't move my head. "How the hell did you learn that?"

"I'm the medic for this little Cub Scout pack, and word came down to forward your field medical records. Put two and two together. So where are you going when this is done?"

"A quiet lake in New Hampshire."

"Why?"

"Because it's not Massachusetts."

"Am I invited?"

"Only if you bring your bathing suit."

"Suppose I forget it?" she asks.

"Then you're definitely still invited."

She gives a sweet little chuckle and we move again, going up the rocks and brush and saplings, the forest still looking ghostly in green, and there's something up ahead, dangling from a group of birch trees. We move in a semicircle, swing around, and I freeze, seeing what's before us: Clayton's body, his undeployed parachute still on his back. Garcia moves ahead.

Borozan says in a low voice, "Telemetry says he's still alive."

Garcia comes back. "Really?"

Borozan says, "Yeah."

"Well, my personal telemetry—my two eyes in my goddamn head—says he's dead."

"You—"

"Go take a look, Borozan," Garcia says bitterly. "Or does your little computer say a guy can still live with his femurs driven up into his chest?"

CHAPTER 5

WHAT HAPPENS NEXT is something you never see on the History Channel or *Nova*. We gather up Clayton's faulty parachute, secure any gear that flew out when he hit the ground, and then do our best to conceal the gear and Clayton's body. We don't do a thorough job because we don't have the time, and because freshly dug dirt is one hell of a signpost that something has just happened. No, we do what we can, and I punch in the coordinates of where we left him, so at some point when this war ends—eventually they all do, even if they last a hundred years—we'll come back to take him home.

There's a deep sense of mission in what we do, in never leaving anyone behind in a battlefield, but in ops like this, you have to be realistic. I prefer to think it's temporary, that at some point, he'll be picked up and taken home to his beloved California.

I do one more thing, though, which takes a notebook, pencil, and red-lensed light. I write the coordinates down on paper, just in case my own handheld gets lost, shot up, or otherwise compromised.

Which, no surprise, is what is being urgently discussed when I rejoin my crew. Sher says to Borozan, "How the hell did that happen? What did you do? How come you kept on saying the poor bastard was alive?"

Borozan says, "It has to be a software problem, or some glitch in the system. Swear to friggin' Christ, do you think I wanted this to happen?"

Sher says, "The poor guy got killed when he hit the ground like a goddamn meteor. And your handheld kept on telling you he was alive?"

"That's right," she whispers back. "I've done a recheck, a diagnostics, and it still says—"

"Cut it out," I say. "Too much chatter, and it's not helping the situation. Enough."

Garcia whispers something in Spanish and I ignore him. I say, "Time to head back, time to hook up with Alex, time to visit Darko Latos and give him the best wishes of the United States. Got it?"

Garcia says, "Got it, *jefe,* but what pisses me off is because of Borozan's little piece of Japanese shit over there, we've lost an hour, looking for a—no disrespect—a dead man."

"It happens," I say. "Now, all of you, stow it. Back to work."

So we head out, moving quietly back down the stones and dirt and through the brush, leaving behind the remains of our comrade in a bit of soil that, for the time being, will be part of the United States.

I don't dare rush my team, because rushing leads to increased noise, increased visibility, and other chances of being discovered. But we do press on and then we're back to that same damn road, and we line up, and look up and down, back and forth, and I'm about to wave us all forward when I catch the tiniest little flicker out of the corner of my eye. I motion to everyone to flatten and freeze. There's just the slightest rustle as my team moves. I keep my head in a position that lets me see what's coming.

A glow at the end of the road expands and expands and then grows brighter.

Approaching headlights.

The sound of engines.

A four-vehicle convoy roars by, led by a tracked BVP M-80 infantry fighting vehicle, which can carry a load of six infantrymen—eight if you really squeeze it. It's armed with a 20mm cannon and a 7.62mm machine gun. Quickly following are two black Toyota pickup trucks—for some ungodly reason the vehicle of choice for insurgents around the world—with their rear beds packed with either regular Serb troops or one of the various paramilitary units that have sprung up like poison mushrooms in this fetid environment. Right behind the two pickup trucks is a four-wheeled armored personnel carrier—a BOV—with its own 7.62mm machine gun mounted on top. The falling snowflakes dance innocently in the harsh glow of the headlights.

The vehicles disappear down the road and I wait, and wait some more, and when my watch tells me it's been fifteen minutes, I get up and move my guys across and into the relative safety of the woods.

Didn't I say I hate paved roads?

Yeah.

CHAPTER 6

WE MOVE FORWARD, picking up a little time by skirting the outcropping of rocks and boulders that had been our drop zone. I refuse to think of Clayton, not because I'm a coldhearted bastard (which I've been accused of before) but because I need to be fully focused on the mission if we want to survive. Sometime down the road, I will mourn him both alone and with this group and others, and there will be lots of booze and jokes and stories, most of which will begin with this phrase: "So you won't believe what me and Clayton did next..." And then there'll be more drinking, and some glass-breaking and maybe a scuffle or two.

But not now. All thoughts of Clayton are put in a secure box and placed on a shelf somewhere in the back of my mind, a shelf that's awfully damn crowded.

About an hour after we left that damned road behind, I hole up for a quick rest and to double-check our coordinates. I don't let on, but I'm concerned about what happened to Borozan's device, the one that gave her faulty data. Stuff like that's not supposed to happen. So while we huddle in a quiet circle in the middle of the dark forest, I recheck our GPS coordinates, and I also insist on a backup check with topo maps of this hilly area and our compasses.

It all checks out. It's 0110 hours and we're on track. We're supposed to meet up with our guide Alex at 0200 hours at Point Q, and we have fifty minutes to cross terrain that should only take us thirty minutes to cover.

I whisper, "All right, saddle up," and that's when I hear the noise.

I freeze, and my team freezes with me.

The wind-driven snow shifts and the noise gets louder. Growling of engines. Lots of them.

Garcia says, "What do you think, *jefe?*"

"Might be an armored outfit, or just a transport unit," I say, shifting around so I can hear better.

"Yeah," Borozan says.

The noise gets louder and then dims a bit, like it's taking a pause.

I stand up. "We're going to check it out."

Sher says, "Boss, do we have the time?"

"We do," I say. "If there's an armored company over there getting ready to patrol this area, I want to know that now, not later. We move."

I sense their reluctance, but we spread out in our line, moving but taking care. I have an overly curious nature that's been criticized lots of times, but that curiosity has saved my ass and many others' over the years. There's something going on over there on our left flank, and I want to know what's what before proceeding.

The noises grow louder and then dim, and twice I hear yelling. At some point, we note bright lights have been switched on, so we go to ground, pure belly and elbow work, moving even slower. Now the lights are so bright I lift up my NVGs, and through the thin grass, some low bushes, and the snow that's fallen, I take in what's in front of us.

We're on a slight rise, above a small strip of bare field, and beyond that is a soccer pitch, with rows of wooden spectator seats on either side. There's a waist-high chain-link fence surrounding the soccer field, and its floodlights are on. At the near end is a cluster of soldiers and paramilitary, and the typical Toyota pickup trucks and two tracked transport vehicles.

At the far end, a yellow Volvo excavator is at rest. Deep trenches now scar the once pristine green soccer field.

Sher nudges me. At the right there's an access road to the soccer field, going past some low-slung buildings—locker rooms? refreshment stands?— and, trundling up the road like they're on a holiday, three municipal buses. They drive through an opening cut in the fencing and line up. They have LASTA inscribed on the side, and they're blue on the top and blue on the bottom, with a wide white stripe going across the middle.

The doors slide open.

Nobody comes out.

More yelling, shouting.

Some armed men go into the buses, and people are shoved out, mostly young men, with some older men sprinkled here and there. They're forced into a line, and then marched up to the trenches, their shaking hands held high. Shoving, pushing and it's a complicated mess for a few minutes. Two older men drop to their knees, holding up their hands, beseeching, and they're roughly pulled up and shoved back into line.

Two of the Toyota pickup trucks go out to the field and circle around.

The fire from the automatic weapons builds to a continuous roar. One row and then another of the men are chopped down like a thick line of wheat meeting an invisible scythe. The machine-gun fire stops.

Armed men go along the side of the trenches, AK-47s in hand. Occasionally, they stop.

Pop. Pop-pop. Pop.

The wounded are finished off.

The three buses amble off the field. As they go out the access road, two more municipal buses are heading toward the killing ground. The buses flash their headlights at each other and exchange cheery horn blasts.

Enough.

Not that we needed any reminder of the importance of our op tonight, but it's one thing to read the reports and look at the photos, and another thing to hear and smell the real deal.

I make a motion with my hands and we slither out of view. As we group up a few minutes later to check on our course and the time, there's another rattle of machine-gun fire, followed by the single shots.

Sher sidles up to me. "Hey, boss, remember what Dunton said to me back at Aviano, about bringing Darko's head back on a stick? And I said we didn't have a stick issued to us?"

"Yeah, I remember."

"Think I can pick up a stick between here and there?"

"Sure," I say. "And if you can't, I'll help you."

CHAPTER 7

I'M PRETTY DAMN proud of my guys as we approach Point Q—where we're supposed to meet our guide—because we're five minutes early. Civvies probably wouldn't understand my pride, but considering what we've gone through—sliding through hostile country, searching for Clayton, securing his body and effects, and witnessing the latest war crime in this bloody region—well, it's a pretty damn good achievement that we're early.

We wait. Lots of what we do is waiting. We're near another road, but this one is narrow, chopped up with potholes and chunks of missing asphalt. It's a crossroads, with another road bisecting it, and lots of woods. No farmhouses, no stores, and, best of all, no traffic.

Adjacent to the intersection is a monument, a dressed piece of stone with a wrought-iron fence around it. Point Q.

Borozan whispers, "What's the piece of stone?"

"Gravestone, maybe," I say. "Or a war monument.

Lots of war monuments in this part of the world. Lots of blood spilled, somebody always wants to mark it, so grudges can last forever."

Overhead there's a whisper of jet aircraft, not visible through the clouds and slowly descending through the snow, which has started up again. But even in the darkness and the cloud cover, we see flashes of light on the northern horizon, like giant flashbulbs are going off.

A thudding grumble of explosions reaches us, and I shift my weight, feeling that little worm of doubt at the base of my skull, the one that tells you just how isolated and alone you really are.

"How thoughtful," Borozan whispers. "Those pilots up there are guaranteeing work for stonecutters when this is all over."

"Somebody's got to look out for them."

"Hah," she says, gently nudging me with her shoulder. "See you at the lake, when you least expect it."

"Looking forward to it."

"Hard to picture you fitting in at a remote lake."

"I plan to be the perfect neighbor. Quiet and dull."

Another nudge. "I find that hard to believe."

She slips away. Garcia comes up to me. "Time, *jefe*. And nobody's there."

"I can see that."

"How long do we wait?"

I say, "Until I get bored. How does that sound?"

"Sounds fine, *jefe*." And then he's quiet. I know what he means. It's always preferable to go in alone, dependent on no one else, rather than relying on local talent to help you out. Maybe our guy Alex out there is legit, someone who wants to help us, or maybe he just likes the color of the gold or bitcoin that Dunton or his boss was offering. Fair enough. But sometimes guys like Alex get cold feet, or they encounter somebody with deeper pockets.

I check my watch. Five minutes late. No big deal. But I have Option B in my mind, which is that in another five minutes, we're gone. I'll take our chances finding our own way to Darko's place, and if that means roughing it, then we'll do it.

Watch check. Three minutes to go.

But having a local on your side, who knows where the paramilitaries are roaming, where the newly set up minefields or trip wires have been laid, well, that can be worth the extra risk.

Watch check. Two minutes to go.

The whisper of jets returns. Going back for another load of bombs? Why not?

One minute to go.

I shift my weight and Garcia says, "Movement, *jefe*. Going across the road."

I see what he sees, a shadow slipping across, and then someone hiding behind the stone monument. A little tightness in my chest eases up, but there's one more thing left.

My guys wait, just as I do.

More movement.

Then a light flashes at us, an infrared light that's only visible to us folks wearing our night vision gear.

One flash.

One flash.

Three.

One more.

The signal.

I take my infrared signal light out and send out three long flashes, pause.

He flashes back twice.

"Okay," I say, "we're good. Sher, take point, we'll be right with you."

From the darkness, Sher's quiet voice comes back. "Got it, boss."

"Let's go meet our Alex."

We slowly move out of our positions, Sher going out first, and there's a sudden *pop!* of light from the woods near the stone monument, and a noise like an orange crushed in your hand, and Sher falls flat on his back.

CHAPTER 8

NO HESITATION.

I duck, rush out, and with Borozan, we grab Sher's coat collar and start dragging him back to the woods. Garcia lays down suppressing fire, two-round or three-round bursts in the direction the shot came from, and we *move move move*.

Back into the woods, Garcia has our rear. I pant, holding onto Sher's collar with my left hand, my right hand holding my HK416, and Borozan is doing the same. We keep on dragging Sher and I know we need to stop and see how badly he's been hit, but we also need to find some cover.

The shooting back there has stopped, and I spare a two-second glance and see Garcia is moving through the woods right behind us, scanning and searching our six for any pursuers or ambushers. Without talking, I take the nine o'clock quadrant and I know Borozan has the three o'clock quadrant.

Move move move. I break left, just in case we were followed or there's an ambush ahead of us.

It seems clear.

Sher's breathing is ragged and gurgling, and I'm waiting for Borozan to make the call so we can stop and she can start working on him, and before I can say anything, she says, "Now!"

I stop, swing up and scan the area.

Trees, brush, blowdowns, and Garcia running up.

"You followed?" I call out.

"Nope. Nothing back there. How's Sher?"

"Borozan's working on him." I wave and say, "Keep your eyes over there. This area's mine."

"Got it, *jefe,* got it."

I get down on one knee, behind a fallen pine trunk, try to ease my breathing, listening to Borozan working back there, tearing open first aid packages, whispering to Sher, and as I scan the wooded area, my mind is racing.

Alex was compromised.

Or Alex wasn't Alex.

We were ambushed.

Check that: somebody out there had actionable intelligence of our location and intent.

I ease my breathing. Look back at Borozan. She's hunched over Sher, whose legs are extended and splayed out. I back up and Garcia sees what I'm doing and joins me, shuttling back as quiet as we can to where Borozan and Sher are set.

Borozan lifts up her head.

"Well?" I ask.

"Dead," she says. "Single shot, right through his throat, out the back of his neck. Professional and to the point. Didn't have a goddamn chance."

She crumples up a bandage wrapper. "Not a goddamn chance."

CHAPTER 9

WE DO WHAT we have to do with Sher's body, which is to quickly hide it. We find a place where two pine trunks have fallen near each other, and Garcia, Borozan, and I work together nearly silently. In my mind, that imp of the perverse speaks up— you know, that tiny voice inside your head that tells you to "jump" when you're standing at the edge of a cliff.

My little voice at about 0230 hours is saying, *Well done, old boy. When this op is done and you reenter The World, you can go back to government service as a high-priced consultant and give seminars and demonstrations on the best way to stash a teammate's body in the field after getting hit by a goddamn ambush you should have seen coming.*

Then we're done, and we move out, none of us saying a word.

After about forty minutes of rugged travel, I hold up my arm and call in Garcia and Borozan. Snow is coming down heavier, and we're holed up inside a tangle of brush and brambles.

If starting out on an op means no "rah rah" or "band of brothers" talk, then this definitely isn't time for such allegedly inspiring language.

I say, "Any of you guys remember the Kosovo bombing, back in 1999?"

I'm hoping for a smart-ass reply—like, "No, I was too busy growing pubic hair"—but instead I just get grunts. Not a good sign. I go on.

"Most of the NATO bombing raids started from the same place we did—Aviano. The Serbs and others had civilians outside the gates, with binoculars, cell phones, and compasses. They could see aircraft take off, plot their direction, and then call in the info to their buddies across the Adriatic."

Borozan speaks up, voice tired. "Given known flight time, they could figure out when the bombing would start."

"Right," I say. "Based on an eyeball sighting of our chopper taking off and noting the time, and also noting our warlord friend Darko has been in the news lately, well, wouldn't be too hard to set up a welcoming committee."

Garcia spits into the snow. "What now, *jefe*?"

"Good question. Our guy Alex was either turned or killed, meaning we don't have friends around here. This was supposed to be a five-guy op. We're three. We're being hunted and the whole countryside is probably on alert. That's where we're at."

The snow is coming down at a steady pace, and I'm surprised at how warm and comfortable I feel. It must be all of the adrenaline and other chemicals racing through my aging bloodstream.

Some last op.

"All right, just in case smart-ass hackers in Belgrade have tapped into our systems, we're going nineteenth century. Cell phones, handhelds"—I tug at the telemetry patch on the back of my neck—"and this get dumped. Now."

In a minute, there's a tidy little pile of electronic devices, and then I rip something off my MOLLE vest and dump it there as well.

Garcia says, "Holy shit, *jefe,* that's our sat phone."

"Very observant," I say. "I'll make sure you get high marks for that on your next eval."

Borozan says, "How are we gonna call for extraction without a sat phone?"

"Simple," I say. "We find an empty house with a phone, get a hold of long-distance, and we call ops at Aviano, tell 'em where to pick us up. It worked in Grenada."

"What worked in Grenada?" Garcia asks.

"Okay, now you're weak on operational history, so forget the kind words about your eval," I say. "Invasion of Grenada, back in 1983. Some SEALs were caught in the governor-general's mansion. The batteries for their radio gear ran out of juice. They used the landline in the mansion to call Special Ops Command in Florida, and with that, they were able to get a handful of AC-130s in to give them air support."

"Hell, yeah," Borozan says.

"So what do you think, *jefe?*" Garcia asks.

I say, "We go on. I'm not buying the crap that if we zap Darko, a wave of love, peace, and understanding is going to roll through the Balkans. But he's a bad guy, and sometimes all you can do is find the right bad guy and put a round in his forehead. Tends to discourage other bad guys."

Borozan says, "We're only three now. That makes

it harder for us to get spotted. And we're pretty pissed off, so that's working for us, too. I don't like the idea of losing Clayton and Sher and then running back home. I want some payback, and I want it tonight."

"Me, too," pipes in Garcia.

I check my watch. With the foul-up at Point Q and all of our running around, we've now lost an hour.

"Okay. Ten-minute rest break, and then we're on the move."

Garcia says, "Screw that, *jefe,* I'm ready to roll now."

"Affirm on that," Borozan says.

I can't speak for a moment. I'm near Borozan, so in the darkness and falling snow, I gently touch the small of her back.

"All right, we go," I say. "But Garcia, you see a stick about a meter long, with a sharp point on the end, let me know."

"What for?"

"Somebody's head is going on it before sunrise."

CHAPTER 10

EVERY FIFTEEN MINUTES or so, I stop so we can consult our topo map, which is extremely detailed and helpful. Without the electronic gizmos, it's the only thing keeping our minds clear and showing us what's ahead. There are areas of rocky cliffs, gorges, and rugged terrain, and we're going to pass through all of it. It's cold, it's the middle of the night, and snow is still coming down.

I know how our enemies, paramilitary or otherwise, will be operating on their home turf. In the first hour or so, they will be filled with piss and vinegar, determined to find the evil Americans out there in the darkness and capture or kill them in triumph.

That'll work for a while, but then the cold will start to get to them, and the wind, and the melting snow down the backs of their necks, and they'll get lost, stumble around. They'll get to a rocky gorge, look at it, say the Serbian equivalent of "the hell with it," and go find a warm barn or farmhouse to hole up for the night.

I don't blame them, but I intend to use that to our advantage.

So it's rough going, and that's when all the training pays off. Our friends and co-combatants in the SEALs have a saying: "The only easy day was yesterday." Despite being swabbies, they're pretty much on the mark.

At an exposed knob of rock, with the wind really whipping up, I check our map once again. "We drop down from these rocks, go about two klicks, and we run up against this stream. We find a place to ford the stream, and that puts us only a klick away from Darko's compound."

Garcia says, "Asshole creep's probably deep in a warm, dry bed, dreaming about shooting kids and humping women."

"Well, we're going to give him special room service," I say. "We've still got time to do the job in the dark and get the hell out."

"You really think so, boss?" Borozan says.

I slide the map into a side pocket. "What are you getting at?"

"We trained for a five-member assault. What are we going to do when we get there?"

"What we always do," I say. "Improvise, adapt, and overcome. Didn't you get the memo?"

"I try not to read memos," she says. "They usually waste my time, talking about briefings on recycling and sensitivity training."

Garcia laughs. "Oh, that explains your bitchiness, not going to sensitivity training."

Borozan responds with an extraordinarily vulgar suggestion involving Garcia, a goat, and three testicles, and in the dark and falling snow, I smile. It's good to see them bicker.

We get a move on, descending from the exposed

rock. Without the driving wind, it feels good to be out of the snow, but that good feeling lasts only until we finally meet up with the stream.

Which is not a stream but a raging river.

We squat down. I check the map and glance up and down the jagged rocks and dirt of the riverbanks. Across the river is the same expanse of tall pine trees, exposed rocks, and some roots.

I'm beginning to hate trees.

I say, "On the map it looks like a teeny-tiny stream."

"Things change," Borozan says.

"Yeah," I say. "Borozan, you go downstream about a hundred meters, see if there's a way across. Garcia, you do the same upstream. Maybe there's a place where it slows down and widens, so we can wade across. Get back as quick as you can."

Borozan says, "And you'll be doing what…?"

"Pondering the burdens of command," I say. "Go."

My guys—only two!—slip away and go into the darkness. I take out the topo map and in the ghost-green light of my NVGs give it a once-over, seeing if I might have been wrong in getting here. Wouldn't be the first time.

And I wasn't really joking when I mentioned "burdens of command." This is what it all boils down to, your crew relying on your experience, skills, and judgment, and it was my decision to dump all of our electronics back there.

Including our GPS system, which is about five times more exact than what the civvies use in their gas guzzlers. It would have told us where we were within a half-meter-range of error.

But now I was relying on the old-fashioned methods, and though I wouldn't admit it to Borozan and Garcia, I didn't like it.

Movement to the left and right. Nice to see my guys working in tandem, and, like the competitive sorts they are, both move faster to see who gets to me first.

And it's Borozan, and she says, "Sorry, boss. It even gets worse down there. Another stream feeds in and it gets deeper and rougher."

Garcia is in a good mood. "And it's Garcia for the win, *jefe*."

"What do you got?"

"Wooden footbridge, up about fifty meters. Perfect."

I put my topo map away. "Let's go check it out."

Garcia takes point, Borozan is in the middle, and I bring up the rear, and in the falling snow, something else is tickling at the back of my neck. I don't know why, but something is bothering me, though I'm not seeing anything out of place. When you're in deep woods, that something can be anything that doesn't match, or a straight line—like a weapon. Nature doesn't work in straight lines.

The riverbank drops down, and as Garcia promised, there it is. A wooden footbridge, spanning the river. Perfect. I catch a scent of fresh wood and move up some, to look upstream.

All clear.

I look across the river.

All clear.

Garcia and Borozan look at me with expectation. "Well?" he asks.

"No," I say. "We're not going across."

CHAPTER 11

GARCIA SWEARS AND Borozan says, "Why not, boss?"

The bridge is empty, long, and oh-so-inviting.

"I don't know, but I don't like it," I say. "You know how good our maps are. There's no bridge marked on it."

"Maybe the map's wrong," Borozan says. "It happens."

"Or...no offense, *jefe,* maybe we got turned around somewhere."

If I was younger I'd be pissed at that last answer, but since I'm not, I let it slide. "Maybe we do have the wrong map, and maybe we are lost, but for now, we're not using that bridge. I don't like it."

Garcia says something but I hear something else. A little tinkling sound, like a bell. I hold up my hand and my crew looks to me.

The little tinkling sound returns. I move a hand and we're going up the river, slowly, and we're all scanning, and then I hear a familiar bleating sound, and I feel a bit better. The land to the left rises up and it's been cut and trimmed, and I smell wood smoke and the rich scent of manure. We get low and slow and come up along a wire pen, and in the pen are scores of sheep. Beyond the pen is a cluster of farm buildings, and a chimney, softly lifting out smoke into the snow.

Garcia whispers, "Feel like roast mutton later?"

"No," I whisper back, looking over the wire fencing, and back to where we were. "Not at the moment."

Borozan chimes in. "Then what are you thinking, boss?"

I rub at my chin. "Freedom. I'm thinking of freedom."

I spend a few minutes discussing what I want, and my crew does act like I've bumped my head one too many times, but they don't give me any lip.

I go back down to the bridge and wait. Back at the farm, Garcia and Borozan are at work, and I check my watch, ignoring the minutes slipping away. I breathe in the cold, sharp air, admire the snowflakes drifting down, and in those brief seconds, I manage not to think of Clayton and Sher.

Lots of movement, lots of tinkling, lots of bleating.

Seven or eight sheep are scrambling down the side of the riverbank, and Garcia and Borozan are moving them right along—I don't think herding sheep was in their job description but they're definitely rising to the occasion—and then I widen my arms, holding my HK416 in my right hand, and I whistle, whistle, and I block the sheep from going any farther.

There's brush and rocks to their right, and an open bridge to their left. The lead sheep moves left, and the rest follow, their little hooves trotting across the wood. Garcia and Borozan catch up to me, and Borozan says, "Hey."

Garcia says, "Shit, they stink."

I'm not sure what I was going to say, because when the sheep get halfway across, the middle of the bridge explodes with a bright light and a sharp booming *crack!* that thumps my chest.

CHAPTER 12

IT WAS A long slog, racing down the riverbank, away from the sheep farm, away from the mined bridge. Going upstream would have meant passing that farmhouse, and probably a farmer or three racing out to find out a) who stole their sheep and b) who just turned them into bloody, airborne lamb stew.

Not to mention a little footbridge down below was blown to splinters.

The race down the river had been a fast one, as quiet as possible, and even though we don't hear anything, I'm sure the chase is now on. Villagers around here have definitely been told to report anything suspicious, and while I like to think I'm an easygoing guy, I'm sure if I lived where exploding sheep parts were dropping into my backyard, it would stir me to call the local militia.

We go on and on, until the raging waters calm some and then widen, and rocks appear, and we wade across knee-deep—finally!—and locate a hidey-hole in a mess of rock splits and fissures. The frozen water in my boots sears when we stop moving.

There's the *rumble-grumble* of artillery in the distance, but we're so covered up that I can't make out any flashes of light in the heavy overcast night sky.

Above us a few more jets fly by, and I admire their professionalism, flying low and slow in the mountain-filled terrain. Everybody save our State Department knows the Russians have been secretly arming and aiding one side of this conflict, and I'm sure those professional jet jockeys up there hail from Moscow or St. Petersburg.

And I have a quick memory of that briefing back when we were all warm and dry, and when we were five instead of three: what we do tonight might just stave off World War III.

Just might.

The three of us sit there, breathing, looking at the ground and each other, and Borozan says, "You knew. You knew something was wrong. What was it?"

"It was the bridge."

"I know that, boss, but what about the bridge?" she asks.

"I smelled freshly cut wood," I say. "That means it was recently built. And it was in the wrong place for any farmers and villagers. It wasn't near any open trails, or a road, or anything else. It was a trap, built just for us."

"Assholes," Borozan says.

Garcia speaks up. "Why you talking trash all of a sudden?"

"The hell you mean?" she says.

Garcia says, "You heard me. I said, why you talking trash? I think you'd be impressed by your relatives being able to pull off something so slick."

Borozan shifts her weight and says, "You better explain yourself, Garcia, or I'm gonna put you in a world of hurt, right here, right now."

He laughs. "No big secret, is it? Borozan, your last name. It's a Serb name, am I right? This whole part of Europe is goin' back to clans, families, tribes and shit, cuttin' off each other's heads 'cause some family talked trash to another family five centuries ago. So why not you, huh? You got family members back here, family members you wanna help out?"

Low and slow, she says, "Knock that off right now, Garcia. It's been decades since my family immigrated."

"But you still got family here, right? Family who you might want to support, help out in the troubles? You know what they say, right? Blood is thicker than water."

She says, "I'll show you some blood, jerk."

And just because she's closer, I punch her on the side of her head when she makes her move.

She gasps and falls back against a boulder.

Then I quickly whip my left hand around and slap Garcia across his face.

Just to show I'm a fair kind of guy.

CHAPTER 13

MY TWO GUYS sit there in this rock cleft, quiet, shocked.

Good.

Mission accomplished.

I've certainly gotten their attention.

"This is how it's going to be, and when I'm done, it's either yes or no. No discussion," I say. "I'm heading out of here in ninety seconds. If you two want to fight over whose immigrant story is more pure and clean, then you can stay right here and go on as long as you want. Or you can take a nice swallow of shut-the-fuck-up and come with me and get this job done. First and last time you two are going to have a choice on this op. With me, yes or no?"

"Yes, *jefe*."

"Yes, boss."

"Outstanding," I say. "Check your gear and get a move on."

But when it comes to eighty-five seconds having passed, Garcia says, "*Jefe,* if I can?"

"Make it snappy."

"No excuse, all on me," he says. "I...I lost it, just for a second. Won't happen again. I mean, all the shit that's happened since we got here and—"

I interrupt. "The shit began way before we got here."

Borozan says, "Boss?"

I readjust a helmet strap, look at the ghostly faces of my two surviving team members in this cold and wet. "It started back in Italy. Our backup chopper got croaked. You know how the Nightstalkers sometimes decide which chopper is primary and which one is secondary? Toss of the coin, that's it. That wasn't mechanical failure or pilot error. It was sabotage. So whoever screwed with one of the choppers had a fifty-fifty chance of killing this op before it even started."

Garcia whispers something in Spanish. Borozan says, "That means Clayton's parachute was rigged to fail. They would have tampered with ours as well, except it would have been too suspicious to have all of the chutes fail."

"Exactly," I say. "And once we reached ground, we were harassed, whittled, and chased, with lots of nice traps set along the way. Because they were waiting for us."

My two crewmates keep quiet. I say, "But now we have an advantage."

Borozan says, "What's that?"

"Even though we know we've been screwed, we're still going to finish the op. Let's move."

I try not to pay too much attention to the time—it's slipping away, like a melting ice cube in your hand in the desert. At one break point, I quietly say to Borozan, "How's your face?"

"Won't know until we get back," she says. "But that's not the kind of love tap I've come to expect from you."

"Had to do it for the good of the group," I say.

She suggests that something foul and probably illegal in most states should happen to the group, and we move on. I suppose I should check in with Garcia, but in the excitement of the next several minutes, it slips my mind.

It begins when, thankfully, the woods end and a field so big I can't see how far it goes from one end to another appears. We pause at the edge of the thin woods, where hedges butt up against the field, and take a much-needed break.

With my eyes-of-a-nighttime-God around my head, I scan up and down the field, and so do my two teammates. The sleet continues, but the snow has started to accumulate. There are three big haystacks before us, a tractor, a wagon, and something with circular disks attached that looks like a hay mower. No lights, no sounds, no buildings.

The map comes out and I find this large farmer's field well enough. Huddled together, Garcia and Borozan are looking, too. If we can scamper across it, we'll be in a good position to reach our target before day breaks.

I put the map away.

"If we go across this field, we can make up some time," I say.

Sleet pitter-patters against our helmets. For once my team is quiet. Borozan says, "I don't like it."

Garcia says, "I don't like it, either."

"Good," I say. "It's unanimous."

"Boss?" Borozan asks. "Care to share?"

310 · JAMES PATTERSON

"The haystacks," I say. "Too late in the season. And with winter coming, farmers wouldn't let their equipment stay out exposed like that. Maybe these farmers got caught up in the fighting...who knows. But we're not running across the field."

I point up to our left. "We're going up this side. There's a small village up there, but don't ask me to pronounce the name. Maybe we can steal a car or truck, get on the road, make up some of our time."

"Grand theft auto," Garcia says. "Thought I gave that shit up when I left East LA and joined up."

As we start to move Borozan says, "We all got family history, right?"

I'm about to check in with Garcia about the slap I gave to his face when it happens, a small, metallic *click*.

We freeze in place.

"Garcia?"

"Not me, *jefe*."

Borozan swears. "That was me, boss. I stepped on something. Feels metallic. Like I closed a switch."

Garcia swears, too. "Land mine?"

"Gee, I don't know," she snaps back. "You want I should step off it, see what happens?"

"Quiet," I say, and I duck down to check out what's what when this part of the world suddenly lights up.

Along the treeline and hedges, a row of flares light off, and it's clear Borozan hasn't stepped on a land mine but something almost as bad: a set of flares to il-luminate the field and us.

We all drop as machine-gun fire erupts from in-side one of the near haystacks, tracer fire skittering overhead.

As one, we return fire as well, quickly going

through one magazine and then another. We call out "Reloading!" where necessary, and the noise of our suppressed fire is overwhelmed by what's coming at us. But we're giving as good as we're getting, and I feel happy that we're firing back at a visible enemy, not one that tampers with parachutes and mines a wooden bridge.

The three of us have tracer rounds in our magazines, and maybe luck is on our side, or the rain hasn't penetrated the hay that far, but soon enough, flames are flickering and it's getting pretty damn smoky over there. It's not fair and not nice of me, but when somebody over there starts screaming, I really enjoy the sound.

I slap Garcia on the head and he starts falling back, and I join him, and Borozan does the same, and we send out a couple more "see ya!" rounds downrange as we slip back into the woods, and damn, wouldn't you know it, I seem to hit my lower right leg against something sharp because there's a harsh, biting pain down there, and I ignore it as we haul ass away from the latest kill zone.

When we catch our breath a little while later, I check my lower leg and see it's wet with blood.

My blood.

I've been shot.

CHAPTER 14

WE IGNORE THE target village and maneuver to the west, going across smaller, emptier fields and clambering over stone walls. I fight to keep up, fight to ignore the throbbing pain in my lower right leg, fight to ignore the sopping-wet feeling of my pants leg. In all three fights, I'm losing.

At some point we come across a collapsed shed alongside a dirt path, and Borozan checks it out, whispers, "Clear," and we few, we exhausted few, take cover. Freezing rain is pelting on the tarpaper and wooden roof, and the place smells of old grain and dirt.

I sit down, grimace and take off my battle pack, retrieve a med kit, and get to work on my leg. Borozan says, "You okay, boss?"

"I've been better, but I'll pull through."

"Need a hand?"

"If I do, you'll be the first to know."

I wash away the blood the best I can and am thrilled to see the bullet hole's smaller than it first appeared. It looks like a round fragment tore through the flesh in my right calf and messed things up. I wipe it down, wince as I smear some antibiotic cream on it, and then slap on two gauze bandages, wrapping them nice and tight. All the while, Borozan and Garcia are keeping view of the outside through cracks and gaps in the shed's wall.

Good crew, ignoring me, focusing on keeping watch.

As I put stuff away Borozan says, "Well?"

"Good to go," I say. "You?"

She settles down. "When I was a kid, there was this antique store down the street from our apartment building in Indianapolis. Guy who ran the store loved those old-fashioned pinball machines—you know, the ones with the flippers and the metal ball wandering around, getting slammed and hammered? After school me and a couple of friends, we'd hang out there, go through quarter after quarter, seeing the lights flash and those numbers clunk into view as we ran up the score."

Garcia says, "Where we grew up, if we had a cardboard box to play with, we was lucky."

I laugh at that and so does Borozan, and she goes on. "Yeah, that was something, but Christ, never thought I'd grow up to be somebody's pinball, boss. Somebody's really gone to a lot of trouble to square away this piece of countryside, laying out traps and surprises and shit."

"Yeah."

"Makes you wonder just how powerful this Darko is…what kind of friends he has."

"Powerful ones, with lots of money and resources," I say. "That's for damn sure. Not to raise old wounds and arguments, but the clans and families in this neck of the woods, they really look out for each other."

I stretch out my wounded leg, wince at the pain now making its sharp and hot presence known, and Garcia is examining his own map, and so we sit for a few more minutes, checking weapons, reloading where necessary, and then Garcia says, "*Jefe,* there's a road up ahead."

"I don't like roads."

"Who does," he says. "Thing is, I like what you said earlier, about stealing a car from that village. Too dangerous to head back there, but here"—he leans over, points a gloved finger at his topo map—"there's a road here, maybe just a couple of hundred meters. We go up there, set up a nice little reception committee, and we wait."

Borozan says, "Wait for somebody to drive by and offer us their car?"

"Nope, we wait and I'll show you how we do things in East LA."

I think about that for a long, long ten seconds or so. "Risky."

"Yeah, that's why I like it," he says. "This whole countryside is all screwed up, with the airstrikes and fighting and shooting. One speeding vehicle might not get noticed. We hijack a car, we can make up some serious time, haul ass to just outside of Darko's compound and get there in time to get the job done."

Borozan says, "Sounds crazy to me, too, boss, but I like it."

"Yeah, well, that's three of us," I say, clumsily getting to my feet. "Garcia, it's your idea, so lead on."

He grins. "You got it, *jefe.*"

*   *   *

We do move on, though it's hard to breathe through gritted teeth, working through the pain in my lower right leg. There's assorted pain meds in my med kit, but I sure as hell won't be dipping into them until the job is done and we're someplace relatively safe and secure. We're trooping through small muddy fields, separated by low hedges and stonework. Off in the distance are small farmhouses. Once, a dog barks and we freeze, and when nothing happens, we move on.

I hear a truck going by and Garcia turns to me, waves in triumph, and I wave him on. I'm suddenly so very tired, thirsty, and aching. I can take care of one of those things, so I drink some lukewarm water from a tube leading to the water pack on my back, and have a quick memory of being back at Aviano, destroying the evidence of our mission, and I realize no official records will ever exist of what is happening on this cold night in rural Serbia.

Only apologetic letters would go out to our various relatives, saying we had perished in a remote training accident. And that would be that.

The water helps and I shake off some of my fatigue, and by God, we get to the road.

Some days, I love roads.

We huddle up and I say, "Borozan, trot up the road about fifty meters, take cover. Garcia, you stay here. I'll go over to the other side, move up about twenty-five meters. I'll take down any car or small truck that comes our way."

Garcia touches my shoulder. "*Jefe,* it can't go that way."

"The hell it can't."

He says, "With all due respect, sir"—my God, the first time he's called me sir, ever—"you're wounded.

We need to be one hundred percent to hijack what comes by. Not limping, hurting, and bleeding."

Borozan says, "Boss, he's talking sense."

He *is* talking sense, which I hate. I take a breath. "All right. Change of plans. I'll stay here. Garcia, you take the lead. Borozan and I have your back."

"Glad to hear it," he says. "Oh, and *jefe?* Next time, let me go back to get my lucky rosary, all right?"

My last op.

Next time.

"You got it, Garcia," I say. "Now go out there and make us and East LA proud."

That earns me a quick smile, and Garcia crosses the road, leaving me alone with Borozan. Even in the ghostly-green glow of my NVGs, I can see the concern on her face.

"How are you feeling?" she asks.

"Like shit," I say. "But I'll feel better if you take your position."

She says, "I know several positions, but this one will have to do for now," and she touches my cheek then moves up the side of the road.

We wait.

And then the lights appear.

CHAPTER 15

THE ENGINE IS high-pitched, whining, which makes me feel good, because it means it's not a military vehicle or a heavy truck. It rounds a curve and brightens it up, and in my NVGs—which automatically adjust to the glare—I see it's a small car, an old four-door Fiat.

It rolls past Borozan and then comes down the road. Garcia steps out, bulky in his armor and gear, holding up his HK416. He yells something and fires off a shot, and then another.

The muzzle flash in the darkness is sudden and quite bright, and the Fiat brakes to a halt, sliding so it's blocking both narrow lanes. Garcia advances and I stand up, and the driver's side window lowers and an older woman starts yelling, and Garcia yells back, and the door opens and the woman steps out, now crying, holding her hands up.

Garcia moves forward some more, and out of the corner of my eye, I spot Borozan coming down the road toward us, and as I'm processing what we can do to this older woman and how to secure her, the rear two doors of the Fiat slam open and two men tumble out, AK-47s in hand, and they start shooting.

You know those movies where gunfights go on and on and on?

Pure and total bullshit.

It's over in less than a minute.

The two men open fire on Garcia and he returns fire, and I open up and so does Borozan, and there's a crossfire that takes down one of the shooters. The odds are in our favor right until the moment the second shooter gets nailed. As he falls he tosses a grenade, which rattles and rolls under Garcia's legs.

The bright and sharp explosion knocks him right into a ditch at the side of the road.

Damn it all to hell.

I move forward and the woman driver is tugging underneath her coat, comes out with a pistol, and I put one in her head and two in her chest, and she slams back against the Fiat's fender and drops to the ground.

Borozan is on the far shooter and says, "Clear," and puts a round into him just to make sure, and I do the same to the second shooter, the one who tossed the grenade, and Borozan runs to the side of the road, and I go to the Fiat, and it's stalled out, but it looks okay. Side windows shattered and windshield with a round through it, but the tires are still inflated, and it doesn't look like the engine's been hit.

But Garcia...

I turn and Borozan comes off from the side of the road and says, "Boss, let's go."

"Garcia?"

"Both legs gone. Bled out in seconds."

I hammer down my mind and get back to the Fiat, and I drag the body of the woman away to the side of the road, and Borozan does the same to the other shooter. I'm ice-cold now, moving right on autopilot. I'm on the passenger's side of the Fiat, and clumsily, with all her gear and her HK416, Borozan gets into the driver's seat.

The keys are in the ignition.

I get in, squeezing myself tight, knowing that we'd move as slowly as fat beetles if we were stopped or challenged, and Borozan slams the steering wheel with her gloved hands, starts weeping, and says, "Shit, shit, shit."

I say, "Stow it for later. Go!"

"I can't."

"Why the hell not?"

She turns to me. "It's a standard. I can't friggin' drive a standard!"

At any other time I would have burst out laughing, but this isn't that time, so I say, "Move!"

We climb out, switch seats, and I push down the clutch and turn on the ignition. I ease down on the accelerator with my right foot while I release the clutch and then we're off before Borozan can even get her door shut.

The interior smells of tobacco, sweat, and some sort of booze. I speed down the road and glance up at the rearview mirror.

Lights.

"We got traffic back there," I say.

She turns, glances back. "Of course we do, the shitty night we're having."

I say, "Haul out your map, give me an idea of what's ahead of us."

"Got it, boss."

She fumbles for a second as I drive as fast as I dare, along the narrow and twisty road, slippery with snow and ice, the wheels sometimes losing grip. I stay tunnel-focused straight ahead as I speed through the night. Two more glances and it looks like the head-lights behind us are keeping pace.

"Borozan?"

She's looking down at her own topo map and says, "This is good. We're coming up to a bridge and right after that bridge, we're less than a half-klick from Darko's home."

"Outstanding," I say. "What does the bridge cross over? Ravine? Gulch?"

"River, it looks like," she says.

"Outstanding again."

The engine roars right along and Borozan works on reloading her weapon, and I should do the same but I can't drive and do that at the same time.

Another look in the rearview mirror.

No lights.

Then lights appear.

Two more swerves through curves and she says, "Bridge up ahead!"

To the left is a mess of trees and brush, and to the right is low ground. I brake hard, swerve to the right, stop.

"Out!"

I switch off the engine and the lights, peer ahead.

Great.

The ground here slopes down sharply, right to a fast-moving river.

"Give me a hand," I say. "We're dumping our wheels."

We dig in and with hands on the door frames and the shift in neutral, we push the Fiat a few meters and let gravity do the rest.

"Down!"

Borozan joins me in flattening out. Two Mercedes-Benz four-wheel-drive military vehicles painted in Serbian camouflage pattern speed by on the bridge.

We lie there for another minute.

Check my watch.

Slap Borozan on the helmet. "Come on, let's finish this job."

"You got it, boss."

CHAPTER 16

AFTER TEN MINUTES of traveling along the side of the river, my shot leg decides to make itself known and starts throbbing and screaming at me. No matter how much I try, I can't hide the limp, and at a five-minute rest break, sitting in the brush along the river, Borozan says, "Let's see your leg."

I lift both up and wiggle them, even though I have to bite my lower lip to keep from crying out. Borozan kneels next to me and says, "Knock it off. We don't have enough time."

"So says you."

"You want to lose that leg?"

"You want to get to the target area before dawn breaks?" I check my watch. "Break time is over. We go."

We follow the riverbank for another half hour, and then at a minor stream feeding into the river, I check my compass reading, see we need to bear 45 degrees due east to get away from the river. I show the compass and map to Borozan and say, "Damn close we are. We got this hill to climb, then go down and up a slope, and right below us, beyond this road, is Darko's house."

I check my watch. "An hour before daybreak. Not bad...considering."

"Yeah," she says. "Considering."

The rain and snow have stopped, but it's still over-cast, meaning we both see the illumination to the south when artillery rounds are fired off. "Hell of a thing," she says. "All this fighting, all this dying. And for what? So one village prays differently from an-other?"

I slip the topo map into a pants pocket and mis-quote a bit of poetry: "Ours is not to reason why..."

"Ours is to do and die? For real?"

"No, not for real," I say. "Ours is to get the job done. Let's move."

We get out, splash through the stream. Behind us, there are more flashes of lightning, more grumbling of artillery.

As we move up the first hill, the first thing I note is that there are a lot of tall evergreens, but the under-brush has been cleared out, like this spare hill is a park or farmland. The second thing I notice are the smells: feces and dead bodies.

I motion for Borozan to hold up, and she does so. I scan around us, see two lumps about the size of large potato sacks. I slowly walk over, Borozan at my side.

Two bodies, torn and bloody and swollen. An AK-47 with a broken stock is nearby.

I wave us forward, and we climb higher, seeing and smelling more signs of a battle, maybe a day or so earlier. The land is chewed up. More bodies, some foxholes, broken equipment, lots and lots of brass shell casings.

I don't like it, not at all. Not that I think there are any scared survivors out here, ready to open fire at any second, but there's always the chance of tripping over a land mine, or a shell or munition that goes from un-exploded to exploded in under a second, maiming or killing anyone nearby.

I lean over to Borozan, whisper, "Watch your step. Christ knows what got left behind here."

"Got it, boss."

So even though we're so close to Darko's home, we climb carefully, safely, watching where we place our booted feet.

Jets scream overhead.

Neither of us looks up.

A low mound is before us, stretching left to right, and I slow even more.

A trench line, mostly empty, save for more swollen bodies, some broken machine-gun emplacements.

I scan up and down the line.

Nothing's alive, nothing moving.

I catch Borozan's eye and we climb down into the trench, and just as quickly, climb out. Before us are evergreen trees, a few more bodies, and an overturned pickup truck that's so burnt and blackened I can't tell if it's a Toyota, a Chevy, or a Ford.

There's a hill before us.

Close.

When we get to the top, we quickly scan the land below us. Then we scramble up one more slope. We're in Darko's neighborhood.

Finally.

Then that little voice inside says, *Then what? This last op was designed with you being part of a five-member team. Now it's down to Borozan and you, and you're limp-ing like an old black bear with its foot caught in a trap.*

Good question.

What will we do when we get there?

We get closer.

Then, I think, *I'll figure it out when I get there*.

Borozan whispers, "Boss!" and then I hear it, too.

The whistling sound of incoming fire.

"Down!" I yell, and we flatten ourselves out.

Damn them, damn them all. The incoming fire sounds like 120mm mortar rounds. Whoever's shooting knows exactly what they're doing. They're not fuzing their rounds to explode at ground level. No, they're fuzing them to explode at the treetops, so survivors from the previous day's battle will be showered with metal shrapnel and razor-sharp wood fragments.

Not sure what might be surviving on this hill, but right now it's me and Borozan, and I slap an arm around her as we try to melt ourselves into the ground. There's that trench line to our rear, and maybe we can scuttle back there like crabs on the run from certain death, but the sharp explosions and the whistling sound of the incoming mortar rounds shove that idea away. Better to be lying flat than moving.

Something peppers my lower legs and I grunt, and then the firing stops.

Borozan whispers, "Oh, shit. I think I'm hit."

"Me too," I say, lifting up my head. "My legs feel like they got hit by really sharp toothpicks. What about you?"

She rolls, a hand firm against the side of her neck, blood sliding through her fingers. "They got my throat, boss."

CHAPTER 17

I MANAGE TO get the job done, listening to Borozan's steady and easy whispers. Wipe. Clean. Put in clotting powder. Fasten bandage. Not too tight. There. Good enough.

I take three deep breaths. "You okay?"

"Hanging in there."

"Can you move?"

Through my NVGs, I can see that Borozan's eyes are clear and steady, even with the bulky bandage on the side of her neck. "Did you say your legs were hit?"

"No."

She picks up her weapon. "Then let's move and get this job done...and be grateful for one thing."

"What's that?"

"No matter the scar, I can still wear a bikini."

My chest eases some. "Then I'm grateful."

So there it is, I think, we're finally on the other side of the slope after a half hour of moving through the spruces, looking down with NVGs, checking out our target. The slope falls down with nice spots to hide along the way—fallen tree trunks, brush and boulders—and then comes up against a narrow paved road.

A guarded gate lies straight ahead, with a paved driveway that goes up and makes a circular approach to a mansion that wouldn't look out of place on Long Island's Gold Coast. Three floors tall, with lots of bay windows, arches, and steep roofs. There's a waist-high wrought iron fence along the road that's decorated along the top with coils of razor wire. How cheerful.

To the left of the mansion is a metal warehouse with two roll-up doors that stand open. Pickup trucks and military trucks are backed into it. Even at this distance, I can make out metal and black hard-plastic crates filled with weapons—automatic rifles, RPGs, and heavier anti-tank weapons. Three armed men walk around the warehouse entrances, sipping cups of coffee or tea.

Between the house and the warehouse is a muddy expanse of what was probably a lawn. Things look quiet at the mansion, but there are high-powered lights on poles illuminating the joint.

Behind the house and the warehouse is a thick expanse of woods.

I lower my binoculars.

My right leg is aching like the proverbial son of a bitch, and both my lower legs are hurting and itching where dozens of wood splinters nastily peppered them.

The original plan called for us to split in a three/two approach, with two—Clayton and Sher—responsible for killing the lights and backup generators and setting up a diversionary attack at the rear of the warehouse, making the guard force think the weapons store was being threatened.

That would have allowed me, Borozan, and Garcia to break into a side entrance of the mansion—

where the kitchen was located and where we figured nobody would be hanging out in the early hours of the morning—and then trot up a set of rear stairs that led to Darko's master bedroom.

In and out, and wire cutters to the fence, into the woods behind.

Exfil point another bare rocktop about three klicks away.

Tough but doable.

Now?

Now it was time to check on Borozan.

I crawl back up the slope.

She is sitting up against an oak tree, with her HK416 across her lap and her right hand firmly held against the side of her throat.

I kneel down. "Hey."

"Hey."

I look closer. "What's up with your hand being there? I thought we had everything bandaged up tight."

"I did, boss," she whispers. "But my body had other plans."

"Borozan…"

She manages a weak smile. "I got hit worse than I thought. I put in more clotting powder, compress after compress, but everything's soaking through. I'm out of bandages, boss."

No more talking.

I shuffle closer.

More grumbling of artillery fire.

I say, "Talk to me, Borozan. What's going on?"

She sighs. "My carotid artery. I think it got nicked."

"Meaning?"

"Meaning I'm bleeding out, boss," she whispers. "I'm going to die in the next few minutes."

CHAPTER 18

I DROP MY weapon. "Not going to happen."

"Can't see how it won't."

I start fumbling with my assault pack. "I'll slap a fresh compress on, and then we'll get up that hill...and we'll surrender. Get you some medical care."

"We will, huh? Don't I get a vote in this matter?"

"Look..."

Borozan coughs. "No, you look. We've got a mission to finish."

"Screw the mission."

She says, "You know what these paramilitaries do to female prisoners. Even dying ones. Especially dying ones who are American. Not happening."

"But..."

Her free hand grabs mine.

"Finish the damn op."

"I just can't leave you here, damn it."

She squeezes my hand. "Boss...I won't be alone...you know it. Pretty soon I'll be hooking up with the rest of Wallaby Strike, and we'll be watching to make sure you don't screw up."

Words fail me. All I can do is look at her calm face, her bloody fingers, and the blood on the snow.

Dark snow.

She says, "You know I didn't betray this op."

"Never thought you did."

"Maybe you didn't say it aloud, but I know how your mind works. Me having a Serb back-ground…nope, didn't happen. But…"

My NVGs seem to be fogging up, because my sight isn't as sharp. "We sure got screwed over, didn't we?"

"Yes."

Another squeeze of the hand, not as strong as be-fore. "You get this op done, okay? And I mean god-damn complete. Got it?"

"Yeah."

"And…Owen?"

A shock to the system indeed, for we made a pledge some time ago never to use first names on duty, or drop any other clues about what we've been up to, violating about a half dozen regulations along the way.

"This…is my last op…too…" Her hand slips away from my hand. "You get to that lake…think of me, will you?"

I kiss her cold, dry lips.

"Always, Emily. Always."

"Go…get it done…now."

I reach gloved fingers under my NVGs, wipe my eyes, gather up my gear, and limp away as fast as I can.

CHAPTER 19

BACK UP TO the top of the slope again. I temporarily place my Emily in a box and add her to the crowded shelf back there in my mind. All I'm focused on now is what's in front of me, and I'm not liking it.

This was an op designed for five.

Now it's only me.

And I'm bleeding, aching, and white-hot with fury.

No longer cold. No longer wet. No longer tired.

The NVGs come back up. Nothing much has changed, except the three gunmen by the large warehouse have been reduced to two.

Goodie.

The lights are still on, and dawn is less than a half hour away.

No time to think, mourn, or plan.

Time to act.

I start down the slope, heading to the target...no, *my* target.

* * *

It's slow going, because I'm concerned that somewhere over there might be guards hidden away with binoculars and their own night vision gear. I'm on my belly, moving through slush and ice, using boulders and fallen tree trunks as cover. The closer I get to the house, the more focused I get. I can smell cigarette smoke wafting over from the compound, and the conversation of the guards—even though I can't understand their language—is so loud that it seems to be coming from right next to me.

I move, and move, and move again.

A roar of engines as a convoy—two Mercedes-Benz trucks, a command car, and three BOV M-86 armored personnel carriers—race by the compound, and I use this opportunity to cover more distance, and then I flop down.

Close.

But now what?

I peer around and smell diesel mixed with the cigarette smoke.

That impertinent busy little voice inside my head says, *all right, buddy, what next? Stroll across the road and ask the guards if I can share a quick takeout breakfast with Darko Latos, saying takeout is two 9mm rounds to his forehead?*

Doubtful, but at least it's a plan.

Right now I don't have another one.

I move closer, going past one more snow-covered boulder, and I scan the raised roadway, left to right, and—

Hold on.

Something oval is off to the right. I squirm closer.

A culvert, by God, going underneath the road, and

looking like it ends up on the other side of the compound.

Nothing that had been noted in the overhead surveillance and ground intelligence reports in prep for this op, but I sure as hell ain't complaining.

I move closer.

A trickling stream runs out of the culvert.

Closer still.

Well, shit.

There's a metal grille covering the entire outlet, and twigs and brush and other debris cover about a third of the bottom, where the outgoing stream has clogged the grille.

Another truck races by, the headlights flashing quickly.

Light's coming.

Dawn.

Maybe Darko is not an early riser, but I'm going to lose all cover and concealment if I don't haul my aching ass.

I eyeball the width of the culvert and make a command decision, leaving my HK416 behind, because there's a good chance it will snag on the way through the culvert.

If I get through, of course.

I slither through the stream and the mud, get up to the metal grille.

Just for the hell of it, I give it a tug.

No joy.

All right, worth the five seconds wasted.

From a near side pocket of my assault pack, I take out a customized roll of detonation cord—also known as detcord—and wrap small lengths around the bottom and top of the grille. I snap off the end, attach a pull-fuse, and give it a tug and turn around.

Thump, thump, thump, thump.

Usually detcords make loud noises and give off bright flashes of light.

But this isn't the usual detcord.

I slowly slosh back, tug at one side of the grille.

And it makes an ungodly loud squeak, like the Gates of Heaven suddenly needed a good dose of WD-40 lubricant.

I freeze.

And much worse, a voice from overhead.

Šta je ovo?

I don't know Serbian, but I know the questioning tone. Somebody up there wants to know what's going on. Maybe that squealing noise carried across to the other side of the road.

I wait, knife now in hand. I've come too close to start firing left and right with my SIG Sauer 9mm pistol.

Wait.

Something starts trickling from up on the roadway, raining down in a narrow stream to where I'm located, a strong ammonia smell, the liquid nearly splashing me.

Another voice pipes up.

Ah, ništa.

Again, I don't recognize the words, but I recognize the dismissive tone.

No more voices.

I wait.

Another vehicle seems to be approaching, and with the roar of the engine overhead, I tug open the grate and crawl into the culvert.

I'm in.

CHAPTER 20

A RANDOM BIT of luck comes my way. There's no grate on the other end, just a collection of rocks and weeds. I slowly make my way out of the mud and cold and take in the scenery. I'm on the other side of the warehouse and the mansion, and the dark woods are about a hundred meters behind me. There's a high chain-link fence with razor wire curled around the top, with spotlights set every ten meters.

I'm covered with mud and twigs and other crap, which is fine. And the cold water of the stream has helped dull the pain in my legs.

My 9mm is in my right hand. I take in the surroundings. The warehouse is still dimly lit and I don't like what I see over at Darko's house. There are more lights on than when I began crawling into the culvert. Off to the west there's more gunfire, more rumbling of artillery.

Almost there, but I take a moment.

Take a moment.

Too many ops have crumbled at the very end because there was a get-it-done rush, overlooking last-minute changes, last-minute developments.

Not this early morning.

A light comes on over at the mansion.

Okay, then.

I recall all the planning, replanning, and training that went into this op.

All tossed out the window.

Just me and...well, just me.

No coordinated assault, no elimination of the lighting, no diversionary attack on the warehouse, no three-person hard assault through the house.

Just me.

There's the side entrance to the kitchen. That was the basis of the assault, go right through, up the stairs, and into Darko's bedroom.

Well, why not?

I move slowly through the slush and the grass. A Toyota pickup truck drives by on the road. It's not speeding, and the armed men clustered in the rear break out singing, like they're paying tribute to their warlord.

The two guards at the front of the warehouse wander out, wave and shout greetings at the Toyota. The driver honks the horn and then drives away.

Another light comes on at the house.

It's the kitchen.

Damn it all to hell.

There are two or three guys in there, in camo gear, and it looks like they're...

Making breakfast.

How damn domestic.

They're laughing, too, bustling around in the large kitchen.

I retreat some.

Check my watch.

Dawn and the rising sun ain't gonna wait for me.

You get this op done, comes a challenging voice in my memory. *You get this op done.*

The two guards who had been in front of the warehouse and waved at the pickup truck are now coming my way, chatting with each other, both smoking a cigarette.

I freeze.

Anything that moves within eyesight of these two guards could be enough to set them off, and then I'd die in the mud and slush here, the history of Operation Wallaby never being reported or known, except in a highly classified memo slipped into a burn bag somewhere, never to be seen again.

The two guards saunter over to the kitchen door. One yells out, and then the door opens, spilling light out onto the yard. For all I know he's placing a breakfast order.

The light from the door misses me by a meter or so.

Jesus Christ.

Someone in the kitchen yells down to the guard, and someone else calls out, *"Hej, umukni, hocçeš da se probudiš Darko?"*

Again, I don't know the words, but I get the intent. *Don't wake up the boss, idiot.*

Some low laughs.

The two guards outside walk away from the kitchen, the door closes, and the men are coming right at me.

You get this op done, says the whisper.

Which is what I do.

CHAPTER 21

DURING THE FINAL task, I'm amazed at how quickly and efficiently I dispatch two perimeter guards, who were probably bored and tired after a long night of work. I can tell that they aren't used to working together as a team, because when I take the first one down, the second one seems surprised and doesn't react instantly by coming to his partner's aid.

No matter.

In less than a minute, they're on their sides, duct tape across their mouths, wrists and ankles zip-tied, weapons stripped away and tossed into the darkness. I waste a few seconds to make sure both are alive and breathing, and with 9mm in hand, I move to the house.

And don't go through the kitchen entrance.

I have another plan, one made on the run, which is sometimes the best kind.

The foundation of this huge home has windows set in the granite. I carefully examine one at the rear, looking for an alarm system, and find one that's pretty simple. It sounds off only when an open window breaks the circuit.

I bypass the circuit, work in a shim, and slide the window open. I slip inside to the cellar, wincing at the pain in my legs.

The cellar is dark and well organized. I find the stairs, move slowly but efficiently up to the first floor, open the door.

No squeaking. No noise. Nothing.

On the first floor, keeping to the walls, my NVGs lighting the way, I pass through a large and comfortable living room. Bookshelves with leather-bound volumes. Big couches. Comfortable heavy chairs. The room is about the size of my own quarters.

There.

Wide stairs ahead of me, with a banister.

I avoid the banister and the center of the stairs.

Too much of a chance of an errant creak to wake up the man slumbering up on the second floor, so I keep to the wall.

Second floor now.

Keep the focus.

I know the upstairs layout of this place, so nothing surprises me as I advance to the large bedroom. A quick check of my watch. I still have enough time, though barely.

I'm at the bedroom door.

It's closed.

I take out a small container of lubricant, spray the three hinges. No noises allowed, thank you very much.

I put the lubricant away. I'm still cold and damp and hurting.

I turn the doorknob, open the door.

The room comes into view.

Large four-poster bed in the center. Two big windows overlooking the equally large rear yard.

I move forward, across the carpeted floor.

A man is sleeping in the bed.

Alone.

He's curled up on the left side of the bed and I slide around and move forward. Now I can hear his regular breathing. Deep in sleep, probably having happy dreams, sleeping the sleep of the innocent.

Or the innocence of the sociopath, whose only motive is to do what he wants, with no doubt or recriminations.

I'm so close I can smell his cologne. His face is exactly what I was expecting, after seeing photo after photo after photo.

I bring my SIG Sauer closer to him.

You get this op done. The whole thing.

Two quick squeezes of the trigger, two rounds into that peaceful forehead, and then I'm done.

I tighten my finger.

So very, very close.

I let my finger loose.

Not yet.

I move the pistol down, right to his lips, and push the muzzle in.

He instantly wakes up, eyes wide, hands reaching up, and I push the muzzle in deeper so he chokes and coughs.

I speak to him. "Hello, Henry Hunley, Deputy Director for Directorate Operations, Central Intelligence Agency. So nice to finally meet you."

CHAPTER 22

I GIVE HIM props—he doesn't raise a fuss, doesn't yell, doesn't protest his innocence. He's wearing a light-blue pajama top and his gray hair is still in good shape. I pull the gun out a few inches, but keep it trained on his face. Then with my left hand, I lift up my NVGs and turn on a lampside light. Books and folders are piled high on the nightstand next to the lamp.

He blinks, rubs his eyes.

"My security force?"

"Taking a break."

He looks around, blinks again. I say, "Hands right there."

"All right. Can I have my glasses?"

I pick them up from the nightstand, pass them over. He slips them on and with awe in his voice, he says, "You…you're Taylor."

"Good recall."

"What the hell are you doing here?"

I say, "You know the phrase 'tying up loose ends'?

Let's just say one way or another, I'm tying you up very tight tonight."

"But…why?"

"What? You think I was through with the op once Darko got smoked? Nope. That was just Phase One. This is Phase Two. And I came up with it all by myself."

"You…" he stalls, then repeats himself. "But why are you here?"

I'm not impressed.

There's a chair over to the side, up against a vanity. His wife and young boys are out in Oregon, visiting relatives. We have the place to ourselves. I back up, grab the chair, and drag it over to the bed. I sit down, shrug off my assault pack.

"You're not playing nice," I say. "Obviously you don't keep up with popular culture. I'm the one with the firearm. I'm the one that asks the questions."

"You…you were supposed to quietly take out Darko Latos," he manages to stammer out. "Quietly!"

"He's dead, isn't he?"

"Dead? Yeah, he's dead, along with a half dozen of his men, plus the top part of his mansion. It goddamn made CNN worldwide. What the hell did you use? An anti-tank weapon?"

"Close," I say. "I used a Russian-made RPG-7 with a TBG-7V thermobaric warhead. Used for urban warfare. You should have been there. It was as impressive as all get-out."

"Why the hell did you use that?"

"It was handy."

"It was supposed to be quiet!" Hunley repeats himself again. Makes me wonder how he made it so high up in government. "What you did…it was like using a cannon to ring a doorbell!"

"Still got the door open, didn't it," I deadpan.

"The job was done. You…you shouldn't be here. Why?"

"To wrap up my op, to conclude Operation Wallaby," I say. "No op ends out in the field. It ends some safe distance away, when there's a debrief, a review, a list of lessons learned, mistakes made."

Hunley wipes at his eyes again. I say, "Dunton at Aviano said he was working for you. True?"

"Yes."

"So he was the conduit for the planning, the operational orders, all that information."

"That was his job."

"He was pretty thorough," I say. "Right up to making sure we were betrayed from the very beginning."

Hunley slowly blinks.

Doesn't say a word.

I go on. "Fascinating op on your end, Deputy Director," I say. "Betraying my four teammates and me, and for what? Dunton wasn't sure, but I would guess that it was a larger geopolitical issue. One of our Stealth helicopters was sabotaged, Clayton's parachute was disabled, paramilitary forces on the ground in that district knew we were coming. Why?"

"Way above your pay grade," he says with confidence.

"No doubt," I say. "But I still want to know."

"Why?"

"To settle up accounts, to make things right."

He makes a point of yawning. "Well, that's fascinating…I tell you what, let's talk about it some, okay? I'll even overlook the fact that you broke into my house and did…something to my perimeter security. I'll make us some coffee."

"Best offer I've had today, but I'll have to decline, Deputy Director." I glance at my watch. "We both know that if your perimeter guards don't check in every fifteen minutes, a quick reaction force is dispatched to ride to the rescue. It's been eight minutes. We have maybe twelve or so minutes left of fruitful discussion."

"Not interested."

I make a point of sighing. "Dunton told me you'd be a hard case."

"Glad to hear it."

"Dunton also asked us to do something after our op was done. Was that your order or his?"

"Don't know," Hunley says. "What did Dunton ask you to do?"

"To come back with Darko's head on a stick."

I pick up my assault pack, unzip it, toss it on the bed next to Hunley.

And then I add, "Sorry, I don't have a stick."

Hunley won't move, but I do.

I get up, turn the pack over, and a plastic-wrapped object rolls out.

He swears, pushes back, and sits up against the polished dark wood headboard.

I say, "Darko's in little bits of bone and burnt flesh, so I did the next best thing. Brought back your boy Dunton."

CHAPTER 23

TO ADD A bit of clarification, I pull back the hammer of my SIG Sauer, a nice loud *click* in the pleasant bedroom. "Let's have a frank and open exchange of views, Deputy Director. I've made my statement. Let's hear yours."

I glance at my watch again. He licks his lips, quickly, not daring to look at the bloody package in his lap. "Above your pay grade...so above your pay grade..."

"You're repeating yourself again. Not impressed. Go on."

"Negotiations were under way...very sensitive negotiations."

"They always are sensitive, aren't they? We were told that eliminating Darko Latos would be a good thing, to quiet his district, tilt the balance in favor of a peaceful outcome. Maybe it'd stop World War III. What else was going on?"

"With you?"

I say, "Me personally? Or my team and I?"

"Does it make a difference?"

"Probably not," I say. "I bet you can't even remember their names. Can you?"

"It...well, no. I can't."

I stand up and dig out something from a battle-pack pocket.

Four name tags, stripped and deposited some weeks ago on the floor of that Stealth helicopter.

I drop each name tag on his pajama-clad lap.

CLAYTON.

SHER.

GARCIA.

And lastly, BOROZAN.

He looks down and looks back up. "You...you know how it is. Do I really have to explain it to you, Taylor?"

"No, but I want to hear the facts from your mouth. I'm funny like that."

He wipes at his lips. "The negotiations...the Russians were backing the different Serb factions, and they were willing to end this conflict, but we had to show how serious we were in getting the agreement settled."

"They knew we were going in."

"Yes."

"They didn't care about Darko."

"No."

"The Russians didn't like well-armed Americans traipsing around in their backyard, what they think is their sphere of influence."

"Correct," he says.

"The Russians only cared if we were offered up to the Serbs, as a gift, to show how committed the diplomats were to concluding the deal. By sacrificing my teammates and me, you were showing the Russians just how serious our side was."

"That's how it was," Hunley says. He glances over at the small digital clock on the nightstand, and I know he's counting down the minutes. "You're an experienced man. You know how it is. Soldiers, professionals, sometimes they're sacrificed for the greater good. No offense, you and your team were pawns in a very high-stakes and important chess game."

"Always thought of myself more like a bishop," I say. "Liked their fancy hats."

He takes a breath. "The quick reaction force will be here shortly, Taylor. I don't think you came here to get captured. What do you want?"

"I want it made right," I say.

"Define right."

"The families of my teammates are compensated above and beyond the standard government insurance. Also, they receive official letters acknowledging their relatives' service, and if they have direct relations who are children aged under eighteen, those kids get their education paid for."

Hunley's face tightens and I don't think he's taking this well, but I go on. "Oh, and a letter of apology. From the secretary of state would be nice. From what I've seen in the newspapers, he's calling this latest Balkans deal his signature accomplishment. It would be nice for him to acknowledge those sacrificed to make it happen."

Hunley makes his quick decision. "Not going to happen."

"It better."

He says, "It can't. Your unit…so dark in the shadows that we can never, ever allow even a hint of its existence. It can't be done."

"Make it happen."

"I can't."

"Then I guess we're through here, and I'll have to go work up the command structure until I find someone more agreeable."

"Ah…what, you thinking of doing me like you did Dunton?"

"Yes."

Hunley shakes his head. "And then what? Go after my boss? The secretary of state? Everyone who had a hand in this decision?"

"It's a thought."

"Go to hell," Hunley says.

"After you," I say, and then I shoot him.

Only once.

No need to overdo it.

CHAPTER 24

AFTER ALL THOSE years of dreaming and planning, the lake is just as I had imagined it. It's in a remote part of New Hampshire, near the small town of Nansen, and I'm told that there aren't too many tourists who pass through here. The water is clear and dark blue, with lots of freshwater fish and nesting loons that come in the summer. Even though there are over 1,300 acres of land around the lake, it is sparsely populated.

I'm sitting at the end of a dock, warming myself in the sun. It feels good. It's been some months since my trip to Virginia, long enough to get things settled after negotiating with folks more amenable than Hunley. There's a thick light-brown envelope in my lap, and so far, I'm ignoring it. I'm just taking in the view and trying to relax.

Trying.

I turn in the old lawn chair, glance up at the house that I'll make into my new home. It's about fifty or so years old, with an enclosed porch that overlooks some rocks and the lake. It's a solid house but needs work, as does the yard. It's overgrown with brush and saplings, and mounds of dead leaves.

Lots of work ahead, but I don't mind.

I'm actually looking forward to it.

After a long time wandering and a short time threatening and negotiating, I got here to Nansen and purchased a house right along the shoreline of Lake Marie with the assistance of your somewhat friendly federal government. I didn't waste much time and I didn't haggle or bargain. I found a place I wanted and made an offer that was about a thousand dollars less than the asking price, and in less than a month it belonged to me.

I had never had a residence that was actually mine. Everything else had been apartments, hotel rooms, or temporary officers' quarters. The first few nights I couldn't sleep inside, and I would go outside to the long dock that extends into the deep blue waters of the lake. I bundled myself up in a sleeping bag and rested on a thin foam mattress, and lay back and stared up at the stars, listening to the cries and howls of the loons getting ready for their long winter trip. The loons don't necessarily fly south; the ones here go out to the cold Atlantic and float with the waves and currents, not once touching land for the entire winter.

I snuggled in my bag and thought that was a good analogy for what I'd been doing. I had drifted for too long. It was time to come back to dry land.

But at night the memories would come, of that last op, of their names and what we had gone through, and always Emily, always Emily.

Out on Lake Marie there's a shout. A young couple is going by in a dark-blue fiberglass canoe. They both wave.

I wave back.

That feels good, being welcomed.

I pick up the thick envelope, shake out the papers.

Pretty impressive collection. The title to the house, in my name. A nice fat account at the local Citizens Bank, with paperwork indicating how much will be deposited every month for the rest of my life.

Copies of the correspondence and documentation sent to the families of Clayton, Sher, Garcia, and Borozan.

Very thorough and complete. I made phone calls yesterday to each family to make sure they had received the same package, so I knew I wasn't being spoofed by fakes.

Two thick pieces of correspondence are revealed as I flip through. The first is a nice, thorough, apologetic letter from the secretary of state. I hold up the letter to the light, check out the signature. It looks like the real deal, not an autopen.

A little tingle of satisfaction.

That little tingle grows some more as I look at the second piece of correspondence. At the top are two simple lines:

THE WHITE HOUSE
WASHINGTON

And underneath that is a sentence that begins *Granting pardon* and goes on with my name and then a carefully crafted and thorough paragraph, with another scrawled signature.

Definitely not an autopen.

There's another envelope in there, one with a doctor's name on the front, but that envelope's not for today.

I put all of the papers back into the envelope.

You get this op done.

I whisper, "You got it, Emily."

At the bottom of the envelope is a piece of Velcro-backed cloth. I take that out as well, rub old and callused fingers across the raised letters: TAYLOR.

A bass boat floats by, one of those boats with huge twin engines in the rear with enough power to cross the Atlantic in a day, and a small electric outboard thruster at the bow for close-in maneuvering.

Two burly fishermen are at work. They have beards and thick, hairy, tattooed arms, and they're wearing shorts and tank tops. They get pretty close to my new home, and I give them both a pleasant wave, thinking of the canoe couple from before.

The two fishermen look at me through their dark sunglasses, camo-style baseball caps turned around.

They don't wave back.

And a thought comes to me, so quick it almost makes me gasp: that I wish I had my old SIG Sauer with me under these papers.

Just in case.

I wave again.

No wave back.

One hell of a way to spend my long-awaited first day on the lake.

I take a long, deep breath, hoping it calms me down, and it doesn't.

Not at all.

I look down once more at the piece of cloth.

TAYLOR.

CHAPTER 25

AFTER I GOT the power and other utilities up and running, and moved in the few boxes of my belongings, I check the bulky envelope that accompanied my unusual retirement situation and pull out an envelope with a doctor's name.

Inside the envelope are official papers that direct me to talk to him, and I shrug and decide it's better than sitting here in an empty house, getting drunk, and so I phone him and get an appointment for the next evening.

His name is Ron Longley and he works in Manchester, the state's largest city and about an hour's drive south from Lake Marie. His office is in one of those refurbished brick buildings along the banks of the rushing Merrimack River, and I imagine I can still smell the sweat and toil of the French Canadians who worked here for so many years in the shoe, textile, and leather mills, until their distant cousins in Georgia and Alabama took their jobs away.

I'm not too sure what to make of Ron during our

first session. He shows me documents that prove he's a Department of Defense contractor and give his current classification level, and then after signing the usual insurance nonsense, we get right down to it. He's about ten years younger than me, with a mustache and a merry grin, and not much hair on top. He wears jeans and a light-blue shirt and a tie that looks like about six tubes of paint had been squirted onto it, and he says, "Well, here we are."

"That we are," I say. "And would you believe that I've already forgotten if you're a psychologist or a psychiatrist?"

That makes for a good laugh and a casual wave of the hands. "Makes no difference. What would you like to talk about?"

"What should I talk about?"

A shrug, one of many I would eventually see. "Whatever's on your mind."

"Really?" I say, not bothering to hide the challenge in my voice. "Try this one on, then, doc. I'm wondering what I'm doing here. On the surface, I know it's because of the agreement I signed when I left, and because of the circumstances leading up to that agreement. And if there are no doctor's visits with you, there's no monthly check, and maybe that pardon gets revoked."

He says, "Pretty direct, but pretty true."

I go on. "But is there more than that? And another thing I'm wondering about is all that nice paperwork you have. Are you going to be making a report down south on how I do? You working under some deadline, some pressure?"

His hands are on his belly, and still, he has that smile. "Nope."

"Not at all?"

"Not at all," he says. "If you want to come in here and talk baseball for fifty minutes, then that's fine with me."

I look him in the eye, and maybe it's my change of view since retirement, but there is something about him that makes me trust him, something that I've long ago learned to pick up. This time it's my turn to shrug. "You know what's really on my mind?"

"No, but I'd like to know."

"My new house," I say. "It's great. It's on a big lake and there aren't any close neighbors, and I can just sit on the dock at night and see stars I haven't seen in a long time. But I've been having problems sleeping at night."

"Why's that?" he asks, and I'm glad he isn't one of those stereotypical head docs, the ones who have to take a lot of notes.

"Weapons."

"Weapons?"

I nod. "Yeah, I miss my weapons." A deep breath. "Look, you've seen my files, you know the places I've been sent and the jobs Uncle Sam told me to do. You know the recent...events that brought me here. All those years, I've kept pistols or rifles or heavy weapons, always at my side, under my bed, or in a closet. They help me sleep. But when I started living in that house, well, I don't have them anymore. According to the agreement I reached with the government, I had to start fresh. So there aren't any weapons."

"How does that make you feel?" Even though the question is friendly, I know it's a real doc question, and not a friendly end-of-the-barstool-type question.

I rub my hands. "I feel glad that they're not there. I really feel like I'm changing my ways. But damn it..."

"Yes?"

I smile. "I sure could use a good night's sleep."

CHAPTER 26

WELL, AS I drive back home, I recall what I said and think, hell, it's only a little white lie.

The fact is, I do have weapons.

It's just that they are locked up in the little basement, in strongboxes with heavy combination locks. I can't get to them quickly, but I certainly haven't tossed them away.

It's a bit of progress, and it has to be considered as such. And I wasn't fibbing when I told Ron that I couldn't sleep. That part is entirely true.

But there's another fib that gnaws at me a bit as I drive up the dirt road to my house and scare a possum, scuttling along the side of the dirt and gravel. There's another problem about living at my new home, and one that's so slight I'm embarrassed to bring it up.

It's the noise.

You see, I'm living in a rural paradise, with clean air, clean water, and views of the woods and the lake and mountains that almost break my heart each time I climb out of bed, stiff with old dreams and old scars, the whispers of *Emily* calling to me. The long days are filled with work and activities that I'd never had the time for. Cutting old brush and trimming off dead branches. Planting annual bulbs for the next spring. Clearing my tiny beach of dead leaves and other debris. Filling up bird feeders. And long evenings on the front porch or on the dock, reading thick history books that I can really sink my teeth into.

But one night after a dinner of roast pork and red potatoes—I've surprised myself by enjoying cooking—I'm out on the dock, sitting in one of those 1950s-era web lawn chairs, a glass of red wine in my hand and a history of the Apollo space program in my lap. It's dusk, and out along the shoreline of Lake Marie are the dim lights of cottages and other homes. Every night there are fewer and fewer lights, as more of the summer people close up their places and head back to suburbia and whatever the hell kind of life they have that they think is better than being on this lake.

So I'm enjoying my wine and the book and the slight breeze, but there's also a distraction: three high-powered speedboats, racing around on the lake and tossing up great spumes of spray and noise. They're dragging people along the rear in inner tubes, and I guess they're having fun, but it's hard to concentrate on my book. After a while the engines slow down and I'm hoping they're heading back to their docks, but the boats drift together and ropes are exchanged, and soon they form a large raft. A couple of grills are set up. I hear more hoots and yells, and then a sound system kicks in, with rock music and a heavy bass that echoes through the hills.

It's then too dark to read and I've lost interest in

the wine and I'm still sitting there, arms folded tight against my chest, trying hard to breathe. The noise gets louder and I give up and retreat into my new house, where the heavy *thump-thump* of the bass follows me. If I had a boat—a purchase for next year, I suppose—I could have gone out and asked them politely to turn it down, but that would have meant talking to people, and I don't want to do that.

Instead, I retreat upstairs to my bedroom and shut the door and windows, and still, that *thump-thump* shakes through the very wood and beams of the house. I lie down, staring up, pillow around my head, and try not to think of what's in the basement.

CHAPTER 27

LATER THAT NIGHT, I get up for a drink of water, and the noise and music are still there. I walk out to the rear porch and see movement out on the lake and hear laughter. On a tree near the dock is a spotlight the previous owners had installed. I've rarely used it, but at this hour in the morning, I go over and flip the switch mounted in the porch. Some shouts and there's a shriek or two. Two powerboats, tied together, have drifted close to my shore. The light catches a young and muscular man, with a fierce black mustache, standing on the stern of his powerboat and urinating into the lake. His half dozen companions, male and female, yell and curse in my direction. The boats start up and two men and a young woman stumble to one side of a boat and drop their bathing suits, exposing their buttocks. A couple of others give me a one-fingered salute, and there's a shower of beer bottles and cans tossed over the side as they speed away.

I spend the next hour on the porch, sitting on my hands, just looking out into the darkness.

* * *

The next day, I make two phone calls, to the town hall and the police department of Nansen. I make gentle and polite inquiries and get the same answer from each office. There's no local or state law about coming to within a certain distance of shore with a boat. There's also no law about mooring together. With Nansen being such a small town, there's also no noise ordinance.

Home sweet home.

CHAPTER 28

THIS VISIT RON is wearing a bow tie, and we ramble on about necktie fashions before getting to the business at hand. Sometimes we never get to the business at hand—last session we talked for fifty minutes about an ongoing political scandal involving the governor—but this time, he says, "Still having sleeping problems?"

I was proud to be smiling. "No, not at all."

"Really?"

"Honest," I say.

"And why's that?"

"It's fall," I say. "The tourists have gone home, most of the cottages along the lake have been closed up, and nobody takes out boats anymore. It's so quiet at night I can hear the house creak and settle."

"That's good, that's really good," Ron says, and I smile and change the subject, and a half hour later, I'm heading back to my new home in Nansen, thinking about the other white lie I'd just told. Well, not really a lie. More of an oversight.

I hadn't told Ron about the hang-up phone calls. Or how every few days, trash is dumped in my dirt driveway. Or how a week ago, when I was shopping, someone drilled a bullet hole through one of the side windows of my house. Maybe a hunting accident. Even though hunting season hasn't started yet, I know that for some of the workingmen in this town, it doesn't really matter when the state allows them to do their shooting.

I just cleaned up the driveway, tried to shrug off the hang-up phone calls, and cut away brush and saplings around the house to eliminate any potential hiding spots for, um, hunters.

Still, I'm beginning to love it here. I can sit out on the dock, a blanket around my legs and a mug of tea in my hand, watching the sun set in the distance, the reddish-pink highlighting the strong yellows, oranges, and reds of the foliage. The water is slate-gray, and though I miss the loons, the smell of the leaves and the distant tang of wood smoke from my house seem to settle in just fine.

In the years and months and weeks leading up to my retirement, this is what I've dreamed of, this is what I've desired.

At moments like that, it's easy not to think of what's in the basement.

CHAPTER 29

AS IT GROWS colder, I begin going to downtown Nansen for breakfast every few days. The center of Nansen could be Exhibit A in a presentation on typical New Hampshire small towns. Around the small green common—with a Civil War statue in the center—is a bank, a real estate office, a hardware store, two service stations, a general store, and Gretchen's Kitchen.

I stop by Gretchen's for lunch and occasionally dinner, but I also enjoy going for breakfast so I can read a handful of papers while letting the morning drift by. I listen to the old-timers sit at the counter and pontificate on the ills of the state, nation, and world, and I also enjoy seeing the harried workers fly in, trying to grab a meal before their eight hours of misery. I usually take a corner booth by myself, and a waitress named Sandy has taken some interest in me.

She's about twenty years younger than I am, with a pleasing body that fills out her regulation-pink uniform, and raven-dark hair and a wide smile. After a couple of weeks of serious flirting on her part and generous tips on my part, I actually ask her out, and when she says yes, I go out to my pickup truck and burst out laughing. A real date. The laughter stops when I think of Emily, dear, sweet Emily, and then I start my truck.

She would understand. If anyone would, it would be Emily.

And she would warn me to be careful, and, being who I am, I ignore her.

CHAPTER 30

THE FIRST DATE is dinner a couple of towns over in Montcalm, the second is dinner and a movie outside of Manchester, and the third is a homemade dinner at my house that's supposed to end with an on-demand movie in the living room but manages to become a stumble into the bedroom. Along the way I learn that Sandy has always lived in Nansen, is divorced with two young boys, and is saving up her money so she can go back to school and become a legal aide. "If you think I'm going to keep on slinging hash and waiting for Billy to remember to send his support check every week, then you're a damn fool," she says.

After a bedroom interlude that surprises me with its intensity—well, at least on my part—we end up back in the enclosed porch. I open a window for Sandy since she needs a smoke, and I won't allow cigarette smoke in my home. The house is warm and I have on a pair of shorts, while she's wrapped a towel around her torso. I sprawl out in an easy chair while she sits on a nearby couch, feet in my lap.

Both of us have glasses of red wine and I feel warm, comfortable, and tingling, and Sandy glances at me as she works on her cigarette. I've left the lights off and lit up a couple of candles, and in the hazy yellow light, I make out a small tattoo of a unicorn on her right shoulder.

Sandy looks at me and asks, "What did you do when you was in the government?"

"Traveled a lot and ate bad food."

"No, really," she says. "I want a straight answer."

Well, I think, *as straight as I can be without violating certain agreements.* I say, "Sometimes I was a consultant to foreign armies. Sometimes they needed help in using certain weapons or training techniques. That was my job. Other times I worked straight up for the Department of Defense, doing what I was asked to do."

"Were you good?"

Too good. "I did all right."

"You've got a few scars there."

"That I do."

"Your legs look pretty messed up."

That long and seemingly endless night in Serbia. "That they are."

She shrugs, takes a lazy puff of her cigarette. "I've seen worse."

I'm not sure where this is going, and I'm even more unsure when she says, "When are you going to be leaving?"

Confused, I say, "You mean, tonight?"

"No," she says. "I mean, when are you leaving Nansen and going back home?" I look around the warm enclosed porch and I say, "This is my home."

She gives me a slight smile like a teacher correcting a fumbling but eager student. "No, it's not. This place was built by the Gerrish family. It'll always be the Gerrish place, doesn't matter that you live here. You're from away, and this ain't your home."

I try to smile, though my mood is slipping. "Well, I beg to disagree, Sandy."

She says nothing for a moment, just studying the trail of smoke from her cigarette, and then she says, "Some people in town don't like you. They think you're uppity, a guy who should be someplace else, a guy that don't belong here."

I begin to find it quite cool on the porch. "What kind of people?"

"The Garr brothers. Jerry Tompkins. Kit Broderick. A few others. Guys in town. They don't particularly like you."

"I don't particularly care," I shoot back.

A small shrug as she stubs out her cigarette. "You will."

CHAPTER 31

THE NIGHT CRUMBLES some more after that, and the next morning, when I sit in the corner at Gretchen's, I'm ignored by Sandy. One of the older waitresses serves me, and my coffee arrives in a cup stained with lipstick, the bacon is charred black, and the eggs are cold. I get the message and start making my own breakfast at home, where I sit alone on the porch, watching the leaves fall and the days grow shorter.

I spend a lot of time alone on the porch, wondering if Sandy had been here on her own, or if she had been scouting out enemy territory on someone's behalf.

If. Dumb word.

Civilian life seems to be softening me.

At another visit, this one in December, I surprise myself by telling Ron about something that's been bothering me.

"It's the snow," I say, leaning forward, hands clasped between my legs. "I know it's going to start snowing soon. And I've always hated the snow, especially since…"

"Since when?"

"Since something I did once," I say, remembering so much in such a small amount of time.

Emily.

"In Serbia," I say.

"Go on," he says, fingers making a tent in front of his face.

"I'm not sure if I can."

Ron tilts his head quizzically. "You know I have the clearances."

I clear my throat, my eyes burning and tearing a bit. "I know. It's just that it's…it's the snow, Ron."

"Excuse me?"

"The snow," I say. "Ever see blood on snow, at night?"

I think I have his attention. "No," he says, "no, I haven't."

"It steams at first, since it's so warm," I say. "And then it gets real dark, almost black. Dark snow, if you can believe it. It's something that stays with you, always."

He looks steadily at me for a moment and says, "What happened over there?"

"It didn't go well," I say. "I went in with four other folks. I was the only one who came out."

"Do you want to talk about it some more?"

Emily.

"No."

CHAPTER 32

I'M SHORT WITH Ron when he asks me about the dreams. I say of course I have dreams, but they don't bother me. He raises his left eyebrow in a way that tells me he thinks I'm lying, but for once I'm not. Dreams don't bother me, not at all.

There's an entire collection, beginning from dank and noisy nights in Laos, through places on every continent in this world—including Antarctica, believe it or not, and God help a certain senator if that story ever gets out—ending with Central Europe and Serbia. The dreams vary but they have a common theme: of bloodletting, of being trapped, of being cut off with the enemy approaching, and me sitting there, bumbling and out of ammo.

For the first few seconds after waking up, I'm always disconcerted and maybe a little upset, but with the bed firm beneath me and the smell of the forest, I calm down in seconds. The dreams don't bother me, not a bit. They are merely reminding me that I am alive, that I can fear, that I can be scared. Some of my old comrades told me that they never dreamed, never knew fear, and I never could understand them.

I usually get back to sleep after one of those nightmares with a smile on my face. Once again, I've proven that I'm human.

It's gray outside late one afternoon, and I'm in the little cubbyhole off the bedroom that I've turned into an office, trying to get a new computer up and running. I'm intrigued by the idea of connecting myself to the world of cyberspace after spending so much time on the move. I'm no longer in the mood for traveling, but my innate curiosity and temperament tells me that I still want to find things out, even if it's only over a computer and a fiber-optic cable.

When everything is humming along, I go downstairs for a quick drink and I look outside and there it is, snowflakes—big and fat and white, lazily drifting to the ground in a fierce torrent.

Forgetting about the drink, I go out to the porch and look at the pure whiteness of everything, of the snow covering the bare limbs, the shrubbery and the frozen waters of the lake. I can't see much out to the lake because of the snow, but what I do see is beautiful. I stand there and hug myself and see the softly accumulating blanket of white, and not in a single place do I see the dark snow.

For now.

CHAPTER 33

TWO DAYS AFTER the snowstorm, I'm out on the frozen waters of Lake Marie, breathing hard, sweating, and enjoying every second of it. The day before, I drove into Manchester, went to a sporting goods store and came out with a pair of cross-country skis. Early in my training, I had learned how to use the thin skis, and I'm surprised by how quickly it comes back. The air is crisp and still, and the sky is a blue so deep I half-expect to see brushstrokes. I go out a ways and look back. For the very first time, I see my home from out on the lake, and I like what I see. The house is fairly well hidden among a stand of white birches, and looking at its white paint and plain construction makes me smile for no particular reason.

I turn to continue skiing, getting into the particular rhythm of breaking a trail through the snow. I don't hear a single sound, except for the faint drone of a distant airplane. I stop again after a few more minutes, resting on my ski poles. Before me, someone has placed signs in the snow and orange-colored ropes, covering an oval area near the center of the lake.

Each sign says the same thing: DANGER! THIN ICE! I rest and recall hearing the old-timers at Gretchen's Kitchen, back when I still ate there. Some story about a hidden spring coming up through the lake bottom, or some damn thing, that always causes the ice at the center of the lake to be thin, even in the coldest weather. I rest for a while, hearing some creaking noises from the ice, and then I get cold and it's time to go home.

About halfway back to the house is when it happens.

At first it's a quiet drone, and I think that it's another airplane. Then the noise gets louder and louder, becoming distinct and separate.

Engines.

Several of them. I turn and they come out of the woods, speeding out into the snow, tossing up great rooster tails of snow and ice. Snowmobiles, an even half dozen, and they're heading straight for me.

I crave my weapons so much that it makes a bitter taste in my mouth.

I turn away and keep on my steady pace, trying to shut out the growing sound of the approaching engines. There's an itchy feeling crawling up my spine to the base of my skull, and the loud noise explodes in pitch as they race by me.

Even with the roar of engines, I can make out the yells as the snowmobiles roar by, tossing snow in my direction. There are two people to each machine and they don't look human. Each one is dressed in a bulky zippered jumpsuit, heavy boots, and padded motorcycle crash helmet. They race by and sure enough, they circle around and come back at me. This time I flinch as they race by—and sure, I'm not proud of myself—but the engines are quite loud and each machine has its headlight on. This time, too, a couple of empty beer cans are thrown at me.

After the third pass I'm getting closer to my house and the roaring in my ears is competing with the roaring of the snow machines. I'm thinking that it's almost over when one of the snowmobiles breaks free from the pack and races across in front of me, about fifty feet away.

The driver turns so the machine is facing me lengthwise, and he sits there, looking at me, racing the throttle, his companion at the rear. Then he uses both hands to pull off his helmet, showing an angry face and thick mustache.

I recognize him from a few months ago, the one who had the powerboat in my cove. He hands his helmet to his woman friend and steps off the snowmobile and pulls down the front zipper. It only takes a moment, as he marks the snow in a long, steaming stream of urine, and then there is more laughter from the other snowmobilers as he pulls his clothing back on, gets back on the machine, and speeds away.

I ski over the soiled snow and force myself to take my time climbing up the snow-covered lakeshore and enter my home, carrying my skis and poles like weapons over my shoulders, feeling like a soldier defeated in the field.

I hate that feeling.

CHAPTER 34

THAT NIGHT AND every night afterward they come back, breaking the winter stillness with the throbbing sounds of engines, laughter, drunken shouts, and music from portable sound systems. Each morning I get up and clean up their trash and scuff fresh snow over the stains, and in the quiet of my house, I find myself constantly on edge, always listening, always waiting for the noises of the engines to suddenly return and break up the day.

A couple of more phone calls to the police department and the town hall reconfirm what I already knew: except for maybe littering, no ordinances or laws are being broken.

One particularly loud night, I break a promise to myself and go to the tiny, damp cellar to undo a combination lock on a green metal case. I take out a pistol, go back upstairs to the enclosed porch, and with all of the lights off, I switch on the night vision scope and gaze at the scene below me.

Six snowmobiles are parked in a circle on the

snow-covered ice, and in the center, a fire has been set. People stumble around in the snow, talking and laughing, and throwing beer cans in all directions. Portable stereos have been set up on the seats of two of the snowmobiles, and the loud music with its bass *thump-thump-thump* echoes and re-echoes across the ice. Lake Marie is one of the largest bodies of water in this part of the county, but they always set up camp right below my windows.

I watch for a while as they party on, and it seems to fall into a dreary routine, even when two of the black-suited figures start wrestling in the snow. More shouts and laughter, and then the fight breaks up and someone turns the stereos up even louder. *Thump-thump-thump.*

I switch off the night vision scope and return it to its case in the cellar, and then go to bed. Even with yellow foam rubber earplugs in my ears, the bass noise reverberates inside my skull. I put the pillow across my face and try to ignore the whispers inside of me, the ones that tell me to get used to it, that this will continue all winter, the noise and the littering and the aggravation, and when spring comes, they'll just turn in their snowmobiles for boats, and they'll be back out here all summer long.

And in addition to trying to ignore those whispers, I'm also trying to ignore the other whispers that tell me to return to the cellar, to unlock the other metal boxes.

Thump-thump-thump.

CHAPTER 35

AT ONE SESSION with Ron, we talk about the weather for a few minutes before our conversation drifts off into painful silence, and he pierces me with his gaze and says, "Tell me what's wrong."

In my mind I go through a half dozen versions of a nonsense story I can say, and then I skate to the edge of the truth. "I'm having a hard time adjusting, that's all."

"Adjusting to what?"

"Adjusting to my home," I say, my hands clasped before me. "I never thought I would say this, but I'm really beginning to get settled, for the first time in my life. You ever been in the military, Ron?"

"No, but I know—"

I hold up my hand. "Yes, I know what you're going to say. You've worked as a consultant and you've traveled with us and lectured to us, but you've never been one of us, Ron. Never. You'll never know what it's like, being ordered around, being told to go here and live in a place for a year and then uproot yourself and go halfway across the world to a place with a different language, customs, and weather, all within a week. You never really settle in, never really get into a place you call home."

He swivels a bit in his black leather chair. "But that's different now."

"It sure is," I say. "For once in my life there's a place that I can call my own."

There's a pause as we look at each other, and Ron says, "But something is going on."

"Something certainly is."

"Tell me."

And then I know I won't, not everything, at least. A firewall has been set up between my sessions with Ron and the exact details of what is going on back at my home. If I let him know what's really happening, I know that he'd make a certain report, and within the week, I'd be told to go somewhere else. If I was younger and not so dependent on a monthly check, I would put up a fight.

But now, no more fighting. I turn away for a moment and say, "An adjustment problem, I guess."

"Adjusting to civilian life?"

"More than that," I say. "Adjusting to living in Nansen. It's a great little town, but…I still feel like an outsider."

"That's to be expected."

"Sure, but I still don't like it. I know it will take some time, but…well, I wish I was fitting in more, that's all. I get the odd looks, the quiet little comments, the cold shoulders."

Ron seems to choose his words carefully. "Is that proving to be a serious problem?"

Not even a moment of hesitation as I lie: "No, not at all."

"And what do you plan on doing?"

An innocent shrug. "Not much. Just try to fit in, try to be a good neighbor."

"That's all?"

I firmly nod. "That's all."

CHAPTER 36

IT TAKES A bit of research, but eventually I manage to put a name to the face of the man with the mustache who's been dribbling his scent on my territory. Jerry Tompkins. A floor supervisor for a computer firm outside of Manchester, married with three kids, and an avid boater, snowmobiler, hunter, and general all-around regular guy. His family has been in Nansen for generations and his dad is one of the three selectmen who govern the town.

I use a couple of old skills and track him down, and pull my truck next to his in the snowy parking lot of a tavern on the outskirts of Nansen on a dark afternoon. The tavern is called Peter's Pub and the windows are barred and blacked out.

I step out of my truck and call out to him as he walks to the entrance of the pub. He turns and glares at me. "What?"

"You're Jerry Tompkins, aren't you?"

"Sure am," he says, hands in the pockets of his dark green parka. "And you're the fella that's living at the old Gerrish place."

"Yes, and I'd like to talk to you for a second."

His face is a bit rough, like he has spent a lot of time outdoors, in the wind and rain, and an equal amount indoors, with cigarette smoke and loud country music. He rocks back on his heels with a little smile and says, "Go ahead. You got your second."

"Thanks," I say. "Tell you what, Jerry, I'm looking for something."

"And what's that?"

"I'm looking for a peace treaty."

He nods, squints. "What kind of treaty?"

"A peace treaty. Let's cut out the snowmobile parties on the lake by my place and the trash dumped in the driveway and the hang-up phone calls. Let's start fresh and just stay out of each other's way. What do you say? Then, this summer, you can all come over to my place for a cookout. I'll even supply the beer."

He rubs at the bristles along his chin. "Seems like a one-sided deal. Not too sure what I get out of it."

"What's the point of what you're doing now?"

A furtive smile. "It suits me, that's why."

I feel like I'm beginning to lose it. "You agree with the peace treaty, we all win."

"Still don't see what I get out of it," he says.

"That's the purpose of a peace treaty," I say. "You get peace."

"Feels pretty peaceful right now."

"That might change," I say, instantly regretting the words.

His eyes darken. "You threatening me?"

A retreat, recalling my promise to myself when I came here. "No, not a threat, Jerry. What do you say?"

He turns and walks away, moving his head to keep me in view. "Your second got used up a long time ago, pal. And you better be out of this lot in another minute, or I'm going inside and coming out with a bunch of my friends. You won't like that."

No, I won't, and it won't be for the reason you believe.

If they did come out I'd be forced into old habits and old actions, and I had promised myself I wouldn't do that. I can't.

"You got it," I say, backing away. "But remember this, Jerry. Always."

"What's that?"

"The peace treaty," I say, going to the door of my pickup truck. "I offered."

CHAPTER 37

ANOTHER VISIT TO Ron's, on a snowy day. The conversation sort of meanders along and I don't know what gets into me, but I turn to the old mill windows and look outside and say, "What do people expect, anyway?"

"What do you mean?" he asks.

"You take a tough teenager from a small Ohio town, and you train him and train him and train him to do horrible and nasty things in the service of his country. Each year he gets older, each year he gets better, as you turn him into a very efficient hunter, a very efficient meat eater."

I take a breath, everything pouring out. "Then, he's betrayed. He makes a rough-and-ready deal. Apologies and arrangements are extended, they say thank you very much and send him back to the world of quiet vegetarians and expect him to start eating cabbages and carrots with no fuss or muss. Every year, hundreds of hunters like me get discharged and are sent back to the world of civilians. A hell of a thing, thinking you can send a hunter home without any problems, expect him to put away his tools and skills. Especially...especially after a betrayal."

"Maybe that's why we're here," he suggests.

"Oh, please," I say. "Do you think this makes a difference?"

"Does it make a difference to you?"

I keep on looking out the window. "We've been seeing each other for about four months. Too soon to tell, I'd say. And I can't speak for everybody else. Truth is, I wonder if this is meant to work, or if it's meant to make some people feel less guilty. The people who did the hiring, training, betraying."

"What do you think?"

I turn to him. "I think that for the amount of money you charge Uncle Sam, you ask too many damn questions."

CHAPTER 38

AT 2:00 A.M. I'm outside on the porch, again with the night vision scope in my hands. They've returned, and if anything, the music and the engines blare even louder. A fire burns merrily in the snow among the snowmobiles, and as they prance and holler, I wonder if some base parts of their brains are remembering thousand-year-old rituals, rituals as old as the ice fields or the savannas.

As I look at the dancing and drinking figures, that damnable whisper comes back. *Go back down to the cellar. The long case at the other end of the cellar. Nice Remington Model 700 rifle with the same night vision scope, except this one has crosshairs. How can it hurt? Might make you feel better. Scan and track those characters down there. Put a crosshair across each one of their chests. Feel the weight of a 7.62mm NATO cartridge in your hand. Know that with a sound suppressor on the end of the rifle, you can take out that crew in a fistful of seconds, before anyone knows what happens.*

Practice. Get your mind back into the realm of possi-

*bilities, of cartridges and windage and grains and veloc-
ities. Figure out what it would take. How long could it
take, between the time you say "go" and the time you say
"mission accomplished."*

*Might make you feel better. Might make you sleep
tonight.*

"No," I whisper back, switching off the scope.
"Can't do it. Can't go back."

I stay in the porch for another hour, and as my eyes
adjust, I see more movements. I pick up the scope. A
couple of snow machines move in, each with shapes on
the seats, behind the driver. They pull up to the snowy
bank and the people move quickly, intent on their
work. Trash bags are tossed up on my land, about
eight or nine, and to add a bit more fun, each bag is
slit several times with a knife beforehand, so it can
burst open and spew its contents when it hits. A few
more hoots and hollers and the snowmobiles growl
away, leaving trash and the still-flickering fire behind.
I watch the lights as the snowmobiles roar across the
lake, zigzag around the warning signs in the center,
and finally disappear.

The night vision scope is in my lap. The whisper
returns: *You could have stopped it right there, with a
couple of rounds through the snowmobile engines. Highly
illegal but it would get their attention, right?*

Right.

CHAPTER 39

IN MY NEXT session with Ron, I get to the point. "What kind of reports are you sending south?"

I think I have surprised him. "Reports?"

"Sure. Stories about my progress, how I'm adjusting, that sort of thing."

He pauses for a moment, and I know there must be a lot of figuring going on behind those smiling eyes. "Just the usual things, that's all. That you're doing fine."

"Am I?"

"Seems so to me."

"Good." I wait for a moment, letting my thoughts bounce around my head for a moment. "Then you can send them this message. I haven't been a hundred percent with you during these sessions, Ron, not by a long shot. Guess it's not in my nature to be so open. But you can count on this. I won't lose it. I won't go into a gun shop and come out and take down a bunch of civilians. I'm not going to start hanging around 1600 Pennsylvania Avenue. I'm going to be all right."

He smiles. "I've never had any doubt."

"Sure you've had doubts," I say, smiling back. "But that's awfully polite of you to say, anyway."

CHAPTER 40

ON A BRIGHT Saturday, I track down the police chief of Nansen at one of the two service stations in town, Glen's Gas & Repair. His cruiser, a dark blue, is parked near the pumps and is now a ghostly shade of white from the road salt used to keep the roads clear. I park at the side of the garage and in walking by the three service bays, I sense I'm being watched.

I look in to see people working on three cars that have their hoods up, and I also see a familiar uniform: black snowmobile jumpsuits. The chief is having a cup of coffee and he joins me outside to talk for a while. He's overweight and wearing a heavy blue uniform jacket with a black Navy watchcap, but his face is open and friendly, and he nods in all the right places as I tell him my story.

"Not much I can do, I'm afraid," he says, leaning against the door of his cruiser, one of two in the entire town. "I'd have to catch 'em in the act of trashing your place, and that means a surveillance, and that means overtime hours, which I don't have."

"Let's be straight, chief," I reply. "Any surveillance would be a waste of time. These guys, they aren't thugs, right? For lack of a better phrase, they're good ol' boys, and they know everything that's going on in Nansen, and they'd know if you were setting up a surveillance. And then they wouldn't show up at my place."

"You might think you're insulting me, but you're not," he gently says. "That's just the way things are done here. It's a good town and most of us get along, and I'm not kept that busy, not at all."

"I appreciate that, but also appreciate my problem," I say. "I live here and I pay property taxes, and a group of men are harassing me. I'm looking for some assistance, that's all, and a suggestion of what I can do."

"You could move," the chief says, lifting up his coffee cup.

"Hell of a suggestion."

"Best one I could come up with. Look, friend, you're new here, you've got no family, no ties. You're asking me to take on some prominent families here just because you don't get along with them. So why don't you move on? Find someplace even smaller, hell, even find someplace bigger, where you don't stand out that much. But face it. You don't belong in Nansen, and it's not going to get any easier."

"Real nice folks," I say, letting an edge of bitterness into my voice.

That doesn't seem to bother the chief. "That they are. They work hard and play hard and pay taxes, and they look out for each other. I know those snowmobilers look like hell-raisers to you, but they're more than that. They're part of the community. Why, just next week, a bunch of them are going on a midnight snow run across the lake and into the mountains, raising money for the crippled children's camp up at Lake Montcalm. People who don't care about each other wouldn't do that."

"I just wish they didn't care so much about me."

He shrugs and says, "Look, I'll see what I can do...." But the tone of his voice and my little answering nod are only used to give each other the appropriate signals. He isn't going to do a damn thing, and I understand that.

The chief clambers into his cruiser and drives off, and I walk past the open bays of the service station, hearing some snickers. I go around to my pickup truck and see the source of the merriment.

My truck, resting heavily on four flat tires.

CHAPTER 41

AT NIGHT I wake up from another cold and bloody dream and lie there, letting my thoughts drift into wonderful fantasies. By now I know who all of them are, where all of them live. I can go to their houses and take them out, every single one of them, and bring them back and bind them in the basement of my home, and rail at them.

I could tell them who I am and what I've done and what I can do, and all I would ask is that they leave me alone. That's it. Just give me peace and solitude and everything will be all right. Just like I told Emily back in Serbia. Peace and quiet. That's all I want.

It's a wonderful fantasy. They would hear me out and nod and do what I said, but I know that I would have to do more to convince them. So I would go to Jerry Tompkins, the mustached one who enjoys marking his territory, and, to make my point, break a couple of his fingers, the popping noise echoing in the dark confines of my tiny basement.

Nice fantasy.

But it could never happen. I had made a promise.

I turn over and try to sleep, and wait for a long time for those engines to come back.

Such a happy retirement.

At Ron's, our conversation drifts to this and that, and then I stare at him and say, "What's the point?"

He's resting comfortably in his chair, hands clasped over a little potbelly. "I'm sorry?"

"The point of our little sessions."

His eyes meet mine unflinchingly from behind his glasses. "To help you adjust."

"Adjust to what?"

"To civilian life."

I shift some on the couch. "Let me get this straight. I work my entire life for this country, doing service for its people. I operate in an environment bounded by duty and loyalty, where there are clear goals and leaders, where things count. I travel far and wide, exposing myself to death and injury every week, making about a third of what I could in the private sector. At the very end, I'm betrayed. Four others…dead. All of this, and when I'm through, I'm told that I have to adjust, that I have to make allowances for civilians. But civilians, they don't have to do a damn thing. Is that right?"

"I'm afraid so."

"Hell of a deal."

He continues his steady gaze. "Only one you've got."

CHAPTER 42

WHEN I GET to the steps of my lakeside house, the door is open. I slowly walk in, my hand reaching for the phantom weapon at my side, everything about me extending and tingling as I enter the strange place that used to be my home. I step through the small kitchen, my boots crunching the broken glassware and dishes on the tile floor. Inside the living room with its cathedral ceiling the furniture has been upended, as if an earthquake had suddenly struck.

I pause for a second in the living room, looking out the large windows and past the enclosed porch and down to the frozen waters of Lake Marie and, off in the far distance, the snow-covered peaks of the White Mountains. I wait, trembling, my hand still curving for that elusive weapon. They are gone. My house is empty.

But their handiwork remains. The living room is a jumble of furniture, torn books and magazines, shattered pictures and frames. On one clear white plaster wall, right next to the fireplace, two words have been written in what looks to be ketchup:

GO HOME.

This is my home. I turn over a chair and drag it to the windows. I sit and look out at the crisp winter landscape, legs stretched out, holding both hands quite still in my lap, which is quite a feat.

My hands, at that moment, want to be wrapped around someone's throat.

Old feelings and emotions are coursing through me, taking control. I take a few deep breaths and then I'm in the cellar, switching on the single lightbulb that hangs down from the rafters by a frayed black cord. As I work among the packing cases and undo the combination locks, my shoulders strike the lightbulb, causing it to swing back and forth, casting crazy shadows on the stone walls.

The night air is cool and crisp, and I shuffle through the snow around the house as I go out to the pickup truck, making three trips in all. I drive under the speed limit and brake completely at all stop signs as I go through the center of town, wasting minutes and hours and listening to the radio. Since Nansen is so far north, a lot of the stations I pick up are from Quebec, and there's a joyous nature to the French Canadian music that makes something inside of me ache with longing.

When it's almost a new day, I drive down Mast Road. Most towns around here have a Mast Road, where colonial surveyors would mark tall pines that would eventually become masts for the Royal Navy. Tonight there are no surveyors, just the night air and darkness, and a skinny rabbit, racing across the cracked asphalt.

When I'm near the target, I switch off the lights and engine and let the truck glide the last hundred feet or so. I pull up across from a darkened house. A pickup truck and Subaru station wagon are in the driveway. Gray smoke is wafting up from the chimney.

I roll down the window, the cold air washing over me, almost like a wave of water. I pause, remembering what has gone on these past weeks, and then I get to work.

CHAPTER 43

THE NIGHT VISION scope comes up and clicks into action, and the name on the mailbox is clear enough in the sharp green light. TOMPKINS, in silver and black stick-on letters from the hardware store. I scan the two-story Cape, checking the surroundings. There's an attached garage to the right and a sunroom off to the left. There's a main door in front and another door for the breezeway that runs from the garage to the house. There are no rear doors.

I let the night scope rest in my lap and reach my hand over to the side, to my weapons. The first is an old-fashioned M79 grenade launcher, with a handful of 40mm white phosphorus rounds clustered next to it on the seat, like a gathering of metal eggs. Next to the grenade launcher is a reminder of my past life, a Heckler & Koch HK416. Another night vision scope with crosshairs is attached to the rifle.

Another series of deep breaths. Easy enough plan. Pop a white phosphorus round into the breezeway and another into the sunroom. In a minute or two, both ends of the house will be on fire. Our snowmobiler friend and his family will wake up, and, groggy from sleep, and in the terror of the fire and the noise, they'll stumble out the front door onto the snow-covered lawn.

And the HK416 will be in my hands, and the crosshairs on a certain face, a face with a mustache, and then I'll take care of business and drive on to the next house, and then the next one after that.

Sure.

I pick up the grenade launcher and rest the barrel on the open window. It's cold. I rub my legs together and look outside, up at the stars. The wind comes up and some snow blows across the road. I hear the low *hoo-hoo-hoo* of an owl.

I bring the grenade launcher up, resting the stock against my cheek. I aim. I wait.

It's very cold.

I begin trembling, so I let the weapon drop to the front seat. "Fool," I whisper to myself. "Damn rookie."

I sit on my hands, trying to warm them up, and the breeze continues to blow. *Idiot. Do this, and how long before we're in jail, and how long after that are we on trial, before a jury full of friends and relatives of those fine citizens you gun down tonight?*

You call that planning? You call that thinking ahead?

I start up the truck and let the heater sigh itself on, and then I roll up the window and slowly drive away, lights still off.

Damn rookie. Trying so hard to do the right thing, trying so hard to ignore your background and training and experience. Your old comrades would be laughing at the amateur-hour stunt you've almost pulled.

Especially Emily.

Emily.

"Fool," I say again, and with the truck's lights now softly on, I drive home.

CHAPTER 44

ANOTHER SESSION WITH Ron, and the only thing worth mentioning only takes a few minutes.

"I've decided to give it another go," I say.

"How's that?"

"I'm not going to let some of the people in town bother me," I say. "Whatever it takes, I'm going to make the adjustment, I'm going to fit in. I've worked too hard and survived too much to toss it all out and try to start over again. I want to stay in Nansen and keep on with my new life."

A little nod, maybe even a triumphant little nod. "I'm glad to hear that."

"I know you are."

CHAPTER 45

A HANDFUL OF days later, I'm in my house. There's a fresh smell to the air—I've done a lot of cleaning and painting, trying not only to bring everything back to where it was but also to spruce up the place. The only real problem was in the main room, where it took me three coats of paint to cover up the words GO HOME. I ended up doing the entire room. The funny price of homeownership.

The house is dark and it's late and I'm waiting, a glass of red wine in my hand, standing on the enclosed porch, looking out to the frozen waters of Lake Marie, seeing the light snow fall. Just waiting. Every light in the house is off, and the only illumination comes from the fireplace, which is slowly dying and needs some more wood.

But I'm content to wait. I'm at peace, finally at peace after these weeks and months in Nansen. Finally, I'm beginning to fit in, and I'm remembering who I really am.

I sip my wine, waiting, and then comes the sound

of the snowmobiles, and I see their little wavering dots of light, racing across the lake, doing their bit for charity. How wonderful. I raise my glass in salute, the noise of the snowmobiles getting a bit louder as they head across the lake in a straight line.

I put the wineglass down and then walk into the living room and toss the last few pieces of wood onto the fire, the sudden heat warming my face in a pleasant glow. The wood I toss in isn't firewood, though. It's been shaped and painted by man, and as the flames leap up and devour the lumber, I see the letters begin to fade: DANGER! THIN ICE!

I stroll back to the porch, pick up the wineglass, and wait. I think that wherever Emily and the rest of Task Force Wallaby are, they would approve.

Below me, on the peaceful and quiet shores of Lake Marie, my new home for the rest of my new life, the lights go by.

And then, one by one, they blink out, and the silence is just wonderful.

ABOUT THE AUTHORS

JAMES PATTERSON is the world's bestselling author. The creator of Alex Cross, he has produced more enduring fictional heroes than any other novelist alive. He lives in Florida with his family.

BRENDAN DUBOIS is the award-winning author of twenty-one novels and more than 160 short stories, garnering him three Shamus Awards from the Private Eye Writers of America. He is also a *Jeopardy!* game show champion.

JAMES
PATTERSON
RECOMMENDS

THE WORLD'S #1 BESTSELLING WRITER
JAMES PATTERSON
"No one gets this big without amazing natural storytelling talent—which is what James Patterson has, in spades." —LEE CHILD
HUMANS, BOW DOWN
AND EMILY RAYMOND

HUMANS, BOW DOWN

Nothing is more thrilling than a story where the stakes are high. And in HUMANS, BOW DOWN, I made sure what's at stake is nothing less than the fate of humanity itself. Imagine that people must submit to vicious rulers or be banished to a desolate place where it's a crime just to be human. But there is one hope. Her name is Six, a determined fighter whose parents were killed in the initial attacks and whose siblings lie rotting in prison. She is a rebel with a cause: the overthrow of her relentless oppressor. Her partner is Dubs, the one person who respects authority even less than she does. On the run for their lives after an attempted massacre, pushed to the brink of survival, Dubs and Six discover a powerful secret that can help set humanity free. But they'll have to trust the unlikeliest of allies…or they'll be forced to bow down, once and for all.

JAMES BOND AND JASON BOURNE
HAVE JUST BEEN TOPPED!

JAMES PATTERSON

TOYS

& NEIL McMAHON

TOYS

I've always been intrigued by the promising—and potentially terrifying—ways that science and technology shape society. After doing some research about bioengineering, I started to wonder: What would happen to human civilization if we actually were able to engineer a race of superhumans? Hence, Agent Hays Baker and the world of the Elites were born. Elites rule the New World, and with their superhuman speed, extraordinary intelligence, and incredible strength, it's no wonder humans have been relegated to the outskirts of society. Hays, who's the very best of the Elites, finds himself caught in the middle of these two groups and thrown into a life he never thought possible: fighting to save humans. If you know anything about me, you'd probably guess that the story doesn't turn out the way you'd expect. I call Hays the "James Bond for the future"—he's unstoppable, effortlessly stylish, and most of all, deadly.

"This book series is worthy of being as famous as the TWILIGHT SAGA or the HUNGER GAMES."
—*Guardian* (London)
THE BEST OF MAXIMUM RIDE
JAMES PATTERSON
THE ANGEL EXPERIMENT

THE ANGEL EXPERIMENT:
A MAXIMUM RIDE NOVEL

If you could have a superpower, what would it be? Most people would choose being able to fly. And why not? After all, it would be such great fun. Now, this is where my devious mind asks, "What if being able to fly turns out to be the worst thing that could happen to you?" And so Maximum Ride was born. She and her closest friends are products of an experiment. The result? They can fly. But after escaping the "School" in which they were glorified lab rats, they discover that they were designed for a very dark purpose. And the people who created them will stop at nothing to get them back. No one is safe, and no one knows what to expect. My favorite kind of story. Trust me, you'll fly through the pages of this one.

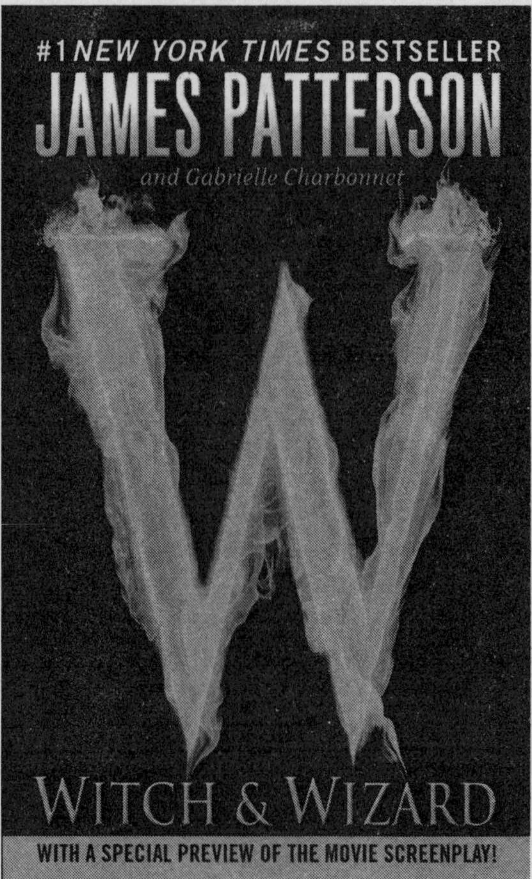
#1 NEW YORK TIMES BESTSELLER
JAMES PATTERSON
and Gabrielle Charbonnet
WITCH & WIZARD
WITH A SPECIAL PREVIEW OF THE MOVIE SCREENPLAY!

WITCH & WIZARD

One of the best things in life is realizing you have a special gift or ability. But what if your gift is special enough that you become the target of very dangerous, very powerful enemies intent on destroying you? That's exactly what happens to Wisty and Whit. The very people who are supposed to protect them are the ones hunting them down, and they won't stop until Wisty and Whit are dead. WITCH & WIZARD has everything: magic, prophecy, a dystopian society, and a brother and sister who will risk everything to save themselves and their family. If you're looking to go on an adventure, look no further—your quest is complete.

For a complete list of books by

JAMES PATTERSON

VISIT
JamesPatterson.com

 Follow James Patterson on Facebook
@JamesPatterson

 Follow James Patterson on Twitter
@JP_Books

 Follow James Patterson on Instagram
@jamespattersonbooks